THE YES FACTOR

ERIN SPENCER
EMMA SABLE

D1367039

One
Night
Stand
Studios

Cover design/illustrator: Farjana Yasmin

Copy editor: Marla Esposito at Proofing With Style

Format: Jayne Frost

THE YES FACTOR

ERIN SPENCER & EMMA SABLE

CONTENTS

PROLOGUE

BEX

MY PALMS ARE SWEATING AS I GRIP THE STEERING WHEEL AND pull into a parking spot. I've finally found the courage to park after two drive-by's of the café where Sean and I are supposed to have our first...let's call it *meeting*. Picking up my phone, I scroll through photos he's texted me. My face blushes as I come across his latest dick pic, one of many that I scroll past, trying to find a clear photo of his face. His dick pics are impressive, but now's not the time for a lengthy perusal. Near the beginning of our text thread is a photo that looks like a realtor's headshot—did I ever even ask what he does for a living? Looking from my phone to the café patio, I search for a man who resembles the photo. The man I've been texting/sexting for nearly two months, but haven't met in person. Yet.

It started like it usually does.

A swipe. A match. A message.

The typical back and forth that turns into late-night banter. Loneliness masked in lust. The desire for love downplayed to not seem desperate.

That must be him. At least he looks somewhat similar to the photo. He's sitting alone in the café waiting for me, just as we'd planned, but my mind begins to whirl with doubts. Why would

1

this go anywhere? He knows nothing about me, really—only made-up sexual fantasies and embellished truths. Not that I downright lied. But let's just say I omitted a few mundane facts of my reality. Now, about to meet him in real life for an actual, in-person meeting, what will we even talk about? Trying to find love on an app, in Los Angeles, as a single mom, inching toward forty. Who do I think I am? How can sexting a few times a week translate into a real relationship? It was doomed from the first dick pic.

Feeling utterly defeated, I reach for my phone and start typing a text.

Sorry for the last-minute cancelation, but I can't make it.

I quickly delete it. Too cold and impersonal after all the late-night NC-17 details we've shared with each other over the past few weeks.

What about, *I hate to cancel on you last-minute, but I've realized that after all this sexting, maybe we're better off letting the fantasy just be a fantasy. I wish you all the best.*

I re-read the text and it just seems kind of cruel. Maybe honesty isn't the best policy, after all. Fuck it.

Sorry for the last-minute cancelation, but I have a family emergency. Rain check?

And send. The text bounces into the ether. Too late for second thoughts. I slouch in the driver's seat, taking a moment to wallow in my self-inflicted defeat, as I watch Sean check his phone then gather his things to leave. Simple as that. No harm. No foul. Regret starts to weigh on me. Maybe I should have met him after all.

Annoyed, I flip down the car visor and look at myself in the mirror. *What are you doing, Bex?* I answer my own question with a shake of my head. Another failed attempt at a connection, over before it even begins.

Liv

"ETHAN?" Emma says.

My husband is staring out the window, the rush of a busy London street below, with a bored look on his face as Emma calls out his name.

"Ethan?" she says again. "How does it make you feel when you hear what Liv just said?"

Waiting for Ethan to answer, I stare at Emma's long, curly hair, the kind that looks like it takes a lot of discipline and hard work to control. I wonder if she washes it every day. I wonder if she fights with her partner.

"Sorry, what?" Ethan snaps out of it as if he realizes he's in this room, on this sofa, looking out that window for the first time in his life. Instead of the fourth time, at a cost of £100 an hour. "Oh, um." He clears his throat and shakes his arm so that his Patek Philippe watch moves around his wrist so he can see the watch face. I know this move and what it means.

"I was just thinking," he says.

"Yes?" Emma nods encouragingly from her throne-like chair opposite the sofa, urging him on with an open look.

"I was just thinking. I need to leave early. I'm sorry. I completely forgot I had a deposition today," Ethan says, not at all sorry. He gets up and slowly makes his way to the door, stopping to turn to us before he leaves. "Thank you, Emma. Lovely to see you again. Bye, Liv. I'll see you tonight at the gala."

And just like that, he's gone.

I turn to Emma and throw my hands in the air. "Do you see? I mean, seriously. I don't know how much longer I can take this."

Emma just nods at me, silently.

"Can we talk? Since I'm here?" I hate the pleading note in my voice.

"Liv, you know the rules."

"But, we're not even halfway through the session." My stomach is churning with a mix of exasperation and desperation.

"Liv, I can't do sessions with either of you separately. It'd be a breach of my ethics and a breach of our trust—you, me, and Ethan. You remember the patient covenant you each signed."

"Ha!" I laugh out loud. "Trust..."

I grab my bag and throw my scarf around my neck as I try to get up from the sofa, which is like quicksand pulling me in. How many sad, angry, depressed, anxious butts have sat on this sofa? It must be my new heels that are throwing me off balance. After a good rocking motion, I finally rise to my feet but lose my balance and almost fall into Emma's lap, catching a scent of her crisp, grassy perfume. She's so perfectly put together and composed it irritates me during our sessions.

"Are you okay, Liv? I think it's best if you leave now and we can regroup next week."

"No, I'm not okay. You need a new sofa. And I am leaving." I huff out of the room.

This isn't me. I hate being angry. I'm not supposed to be like this—bitchy to other people, like a child throwing a tantrum. Ethan makes me like this. I had to practically kidnap him, brainwash him, and bodily drag him to therapy. The first session was fairly easy—who we are, what we do, our history as a timeline of places and events. Ethan loves beginnings. He's always charming in beginnings, and with a run of his hand through his thick, salt and pepper, wavy hair, he ingratiates himself to everyone. And everyone seems to fall under his spell. By now, I know all of his moves, but I was just as dazzled by him during our beginning, too. That's why he's a good lawyer, I suppose. But this particular session with Emma, when things are starting to get real, when we're finally scratching below the surface of who we are together as a couple, whether there's even a *together* for us, he bails. Considering everything that's happened over the years, I shouldn't be surprised, but it still hurts.

I stumble out into the crowded hustle and bustle of Tottenham Court Road on a blustery London day. It's always such a jarring juxtaposition—the quiet, soft hues, and minimalist decor of Emma's office, her well-watered plants, and just interesting enough paintings on the wall, then hitting the frenetic pace of the pavement outside. The car horns, the jostling with other pedestrians. London still manages to overwhelm me all these years later.

How did it come to this? I think to myself for the millionth time.

I reach into my bag to get my phone and see there's a text from Ethan. In spite of myself, my heart leaps for a nanosecond. Maybe it's an apology.

Don't forget it's black tie tonight.

Nope, I should have known better. I almost let out a scream in the middle of the street when I think about the boredom and small talk that awaits me tonight.

Bex

"Mom! Is that you? What are you doing home? I thought you weren't gonna be back until three?" Maddie yells from her bedroom.

"Yeah, it's me. I decided not to go to Zumba after all. You ready to go?" My dating life is such a disaster that I can't bring myself to tell Maddie anything about it. So my date with Sean was a Zumba class to Maddie. I look at it as protecting her from becoming jaded about love before she even has her first kiss. At least I don't think she's had her first kiss yet. In any case, thirteen is way too young to know about the black hole of dating apps.

"We don't have to be at the drop off until four. Mom, chill," I hear her whine.

"No harm in getting there early. You never know about traffic. If we have time to spare, we can just stop along the way for a milkshake." Here's hoping the lure of a treat will bend her to my will like it did when she was little.

She huffs from the bedroom, followed by a series of bangs

and groans as she descends the stairs, her luggage dinging the walls which are in need of a fresh coat of paint.

"Jeez, Mom. What's the rush? You got a date later on or something?" She scoffs.

I hesitate a moment too long, which pings Maddie's radar. Oops.

"Oh God. You do have a date, don't you?"

"No, of course not," I say quickly. "Now, let's get going. You got everything?"

Maddie gives me a suspicious look, then begrudgingly turns and heads out the front door, hauling her bags to the car in the driveway.

It's tragic that my own daughter thinks it's an impossibility that I would have an actual date. But, sadly, she's not off base. It's been years since I've had a real date. At least, not with anyone that I'd ever bring home. I'm glad to have bailed on Sean, even if it was rude to do so at the last second, because I know what would've happened anyway. After all the weeks of texting, we'd realize there is absolutely no chemistry between us in person, and after a stilted conversation about which shows we're currently bingeing, we'd give each other an awkward but friendly hug and go our separate ways. The digital buildup leading to a lackluster IRL encounter. This has happened to me so many times before, I don't know why I'd even agreed to meet him.

Heading out the door, I pause in the entryway and turn to take a look at myself in the mirror and see nothing. No matter how long it's been since the divorce, I still look at that spot on the wall, forgetting that the mirror is gone. It was Patrick's family heirloom and I fell in love with it the first time I went to his house to meet his parents. His mother gave it to us as a wedding present and I've never found another mirror that I like well enough to replace it, at least not one that I can afford.

"Mom! Waiting on you!" Maddie calls out as she slams the trunk shut.

I have to laugh a little. She sounds just like me when I was her age. My best friend, Liv, and I would be waiting in the car while Mom finished her tenth Salem Light 100 for the day. "Only an addict rushes through their cigarette," she used to say. I don't know what she thought she was, but smoking a pack a day, no matter how elegantly and leisurely done, sure seemed like an addict to me.

I do a fast walk-run out to the car and hop in.

"All right, let's do this. Here we go! Camp's gonna be great, I just know it." I squeeze Maddie's knee.

"When are you gonna get the AC fixed? It's like a sauna in here." Maddie fiddles with the air-conditioning vents.

"Summer is more than half over, hun. We don't need it." I roll down the windows as we back out of the driveway then turn on the vents, a futile effort to get more air circulating, even if it is the smoggy, summer heat of LA. My dad offered to pay for the AC to be fixed but I'd said no out of pride. I'm too old to still be a daddy's girl but I'm seriously having second thoughts.

Neither Maddie nor I are being talkative. I tell myself it's the heat as she taps away on her phone. She probably won't even want to go to camp next summer. Most of her school friends are staying home and we had more than a few arguments about her not wanting to go this year.

We pull up to the meeting point and find a shady place to park. The usual circle of Botox'd and boob jobbed alpha moms has already congregated to say goodbye to their daughters. Maddie's been going to the same camp since she was eight years old and I see these moms year after year. They seem to be getting younger, or at least more frozen, while I'm looking more and more haggard. I can't keep up with their diamond rings, laser peels, and balayage. And frankly, even if I had the money or time, I wouldn't want to.

"Bex, long time no see! After the bus leaves, we're all going for cocktails. Want to join us?" Samantha says in a way that I know is just her being fake nice.

"My mom has a date!" Maddie blurts to my mortification.

"I don't have a date," I protest, but I'm quickly drowned out.

"Oh, really? Do tell!" Samantha says, more loudly than she needs to.

I wave Samantha off like it's nothing. Because it is. Unless a date with Ben & Jerry's counts.

"You're going like that?" Samantha looks me up and down. "I just went shopping and got the cutest bracelets. They're in my car, you can borrow them. Just to add a pop of color, you know?" She scrutinizes my jeans and black one pocket tee. "Do you want me to go get 'em?"

"Oh, no, really, but thanks. I don't have a date tonight, or any night. I'm solidly single." The note of depression in my tone is undeniable. I try to recover with a little too much enthusiasm. "I'm focusing on my career!"

With a look of dramatic sympathy, Samantha says, "Oh, Bex, you should really be getting out there!" She pulls her phone out of her purse and begins scrolling quickly. "I have just the man for you. He's Hal's new financial adviser, recently divorced, a little pudgy but great hair, and he..."

And so it begins. I zone out as she rambles on, detailing Hal's stats and specs.

This is perhaps the worst thing about being single—married people who always try to set me up with some recently divorced guy. As if just by virtue of being divorced, we'll automatically be the right fit for each other. My married friends are always so insistent that I have to meet "so and so" and then when I do finally meet him, it's apparent we have nothing in common other than our mutual friends.

"That's nice of you, Samantha, thank you so much, but honestly, I'm just doing me right now. Maybe down the road, okay?"

"Okay, sweetie. If you say so." She smiles at me with a look of pity and gives me a little pat on the shoulder. Then she saunters over toward the bus to help her daughter load her suitcase.

Maddie seems to have woken up from her sulky mood of the

car ride and bounds over to a few friends who are waving to her from the bus. I grab her bags that she's left beside me and do a waddling walk over to the bus, weighed down by whatever it is she's packed.

"Maddie, honey, here, your bags." I stand a few feet away from the giggling circle of Maddie and her friends.

"Mom," she walks over to me, "don't call me honey, please."

I lean over to give her a quick kiss and a hug.

"Ew, Mom, stop. I'm just going away for two weeks." She wriggles out of my arms.

Teenagers.

"Now listen, Maddie. I put a little, blue cosmetic bag in your duffel with some supplies, in case you need them," I whisper in her ear, knowing she's been worried about starting her period while away from home.

"Thanks, Mom." Maddie gives me a quick worried look, then hugs me. I relish it. My little girl is growing up.

As she scampers into the bus, I cross my arms, subconsciously giving myself a hug and thinking about how quiet the house will be when I get home.

Liv

"You look fabulous, my love!" Clarissa says, air kissing me on both cheeks.

"Hello, Liv. You do look ravishing. That dress fits you like a glove." Alan reaches for my hand and kisses it.

Ugh, when is #metoo going to hit the senior ranks of these centuries-old law firms.

"Oh, this, thanks." I gesture to my dress. "I got lucky on an eBay auction and the purse is a long ago hand-me-down from my best friend Bex."

God, I miss Bex at times like this. We'd have a field day making fun of these fussy one-percenters. Even though I've been accompanying Ethan to events like this for years, I still feel out of my depth. Before Ethan, the closest I got to a black-tie event with waiters circulating canapes on silver trays was crashing wedding receptions at the Four Seasons in Atlanta—which I'm not ashamed to say Bex and I did a few times. It was definitely the best way for a broke college student to get a free drink. In hindsight, we weren't being as rebellious as I thought we were. Black tie and fancy hotels were such a novelty for me then; I might as well have been on Mars. But Bex grew up going to cotillions at the country club and five-star hotel ballroom wedding receptions of her dad's business associates. Even at college, she knew how to act and blend in like she was an invited guest. We got away with it every time.

Ethan gives me a curt look as he leans in to give me a peck on the cheek.

Clarissa laughs a little too loudly. She's probably already tipsy.

"Darling," she says to me, "don't you know one of the perks of being a Treadwell & Sloan wife is that you never buy second-hand. Why on earth would you buy something on eBay? And don't even get me started on hand-me-downs."

She turns to Ethan. "Did you know about this?" Then she playfully gives him a little push and champagne sloshes out of her glass. A worried look flashes across Alan's face as he reaches for Clarissa's arm to steady her. "Ethan, what *are* we going to do with our dear little Liv. She is just so...quaint," Clarissa says with a peal of laughter.

I look around the room nervously. God, I hate these things. Ethan barely even talks to me and we just do the rounds of the room, stopping for banter and superficial exchanges. No one asks me anything about myself, beyond a "How are you?" if even that. But they all have time for Ethan. Questions about a case, what does he think of so and so's judgment on the such and such case. I tune it all out.

As we make our way to the bar, Ethan whispers in my ear, "Don't say things like that, please. Really, Liv. I'm a partner. People are going to think we're having money problems."

"Why did you leave the session today?" I stop and look at him.

"I told you. The deposition," he says, miming a hello with a fake smile on his face to someone across the room, then ushers me toward the bar. I know he's petrified I'll make a scene.

"You're coming next week, aren't you? We wasted £100 on today's session."

"I can't. I've got to be in Dubai."

"What? For how long?"

"I don't know. I thought I told you already." He pauses, looking around the room briefly, then continues. "Liv darling, I know you Americans like to talk about feelings and emotions, but I really don't think we need to be going to those sessions with Emma anymore. We're fine—just a few bumps along the road, that's all. Happens to everyone."

"But what about our trip? Did you forget?" I say, wanting to believe what Ethan's just told me.

Ethan orders two glasses of champagne from the fresh-faced young man behind the bar. He forgot. Of course, he forgot. He turns to hand me one of the champagne glasses.

"Of course, I didn't forget about the trip. I'll be back in time, don't worry. Let's do another round of the room. I need to see if David is here from Lewison's."

"You go ahead," I say to Ethan who's already walking away. "I need to get something in my stomach. Shouldn't they be circulating canapes by now?"

Ethan melts back into the hubbub of the room. His broad shoulders seem to part the crowd, like some kind of egotistical Moses in a custom-made Savile Row suit. When Ethan finally made partner at Treadwell & Sloane, we had one perfect week of vacation at a luxury resort in Capri. After that, I hardly ever saw him. He disappeared for weeks at a time when late dinners with clients after long days of meetings blurred into each other. I knew he'd come and gone because I'd stumble on a tie discarded on the stairs, or find myself alone at the kitchen table in the morning, drinking coffee surrounded by stacks of his work papers and books that had risen overnight like a paper skyline. One morning, I'd come downstairs and found a pizza box on the sofa with a cold half-eaten pizza still inside. Traces of Ethan, but never Ethan. It seemed as the years went by I spent more and more time alone. Just like I am now. I sigh in resignation and reach for a tray of mini quiches that's floating by on the outstretched arm of a caterer.

After a few more canapes, I make my way toward the exit to get my coat from the coat check.

"Leaving so soon?"

Shit, it's Clarissa.

"Oh, um, yeah, I have an early day tomorrow."

"Let me guess. An eBay auction to wake up for?" She gives me a look up and down, her fake lashes fanning dramatically. "I swear you're such a riot, Liv."

"Thanks, Clarissa." I hope she doesn't pick up on the sarcastic tone in my voice.

The clerk hands me my coat. Not a moment too soon.

"Call me," she says in between air kisses. "Let's go shopping. And I mean Harvey Nicks, not eBay. Believe me, Ethan will thank you."

"I have to run, Clarissa."

"Remember, we're Treadwell & Sloane wives. It's part of our job to look good for our partners. And by partner, I don't just mean husbands." She winks.

The walk from the party to the tube is blustery for a summer evening. Despite the crowded sidewalk, I feel completely alone. Before descending the concrete steps into the station, I drop a text to Ethan.

Have a good time. Need to get an early night.

He probably won't even realize I've left the party. It's times like this that I miss Bex so much it hurts. I wish I could call her up out of the blue, that I could magically transport myself to her, or better yet go back to the easy days of our childhood before things got so confusing and complicated.

Bex and I endured every emotional hardship together, from the hormonal roller coaster of first crushes to Bex moving to Chattanooga when her dad got a promotion. We spent four crazy years together at college that blurred into the excitement of our first place together in Atlanta. We took our friendship and the freedom of youth for granted, as if neither could ever end. Parties, one-night stands, boyfriends, serious boyfriends then, somehow, marriage.

Bex tied the knot at twenty-five. It took me a little longer to do the same. Ethan and I met in LA and married just as I was turning thirty-one, which for a girl from the South meant I was practically an old spinster. As my grandmother Jackie said at the time, "Better late than never."

Bex loved Patrick, but her dad definitely didn't. Considering how close Bex and her dad are, it always bothered her that Patrick didn't have his approval. Bex's dad probably always imagined his princess with a "good ole country boy." A Sundance Kid era Robert Redford with a dash of the Marlboro Man, someone who could chop wood while hog-tying a calf. Even though Patrick was from rural Georgia, he was more at home in spreadsheets and boardrooms than the great outdoors. Maybe her dad just saw all along that Patrick couldn't give Bex the attention she needed.

Ultimately, the bickering and squabbling of two people who loved each other but had grown apart finally reached nuclear levels. My heart actually hurt when I thought about how nasty things had gotten between Bex and Patrick in the end. She got full custody of Maddie and kept the house, thank God. After the divorce, her dad never said "I told you so." He didn't need to. Unspoken words can be the loudest of all.

Could I handle a divorce? I'm starting to ask myself that question more and more. Thinking about the routine of the next few days, weeks, and months, just more of the same, makes me so anxious and unsettled. There are times when it seems impossible to even get out of bed each morning.

At the entrance to the tube, I look at my phone one last time to see if Ethan has replied to my text, or indeed if anyone might have texted me. Nothing. I make my way toward the long escalator down to the platform and wait for the train back to an empty flat.

Chapter One

LEFT OR RIGHT

BEX

IT'S 10:30 P.M. AND I'VE BEEN LYING IN BED FOR ALMOST AN hour now, aimlessly swiping left and right on my old iPhone. Back at it again. You'd think I'd have taken a break from all this since my failed attempt with Sean a few days ago, but the house has been so quiet with Maddie gone, I've fallen back into the black hole of online dating. Does insurance cover Tinder induced carpal tunnel syndrome? If this was the first night I'd been doing this, I'd be excited. But it's not the first night. And I'm definitely not excited. I'm frustrated, and frankly, if I weren't tipsy on cheap rosé from Trader Joe's, I'd be crying.

I pick up my long-stemmed wineglass, the only one left from the wedding set that my ex-cousin-in-law Chuck gave to Patrick and me, to polish off the last remaining room temperature gulp, when I spy "Devon." He has brown hair, dark walnut skin, and a hot bod in Levi's with a dark green tee that's just tight enough. He looks mid-forties with a smile that says trouble, and basically, one hundred percent my type. I take a moment to swipe through a few of his photos—sitting on the bed of a pickup truck, with a girl who looks to be his daughter at Café du Monde with the obligatory beignet photo, powdered sugar all over their shirts. So cute. Intrigued, I take a look at his bio, feeling the beginnings of what could actually be excitement brewing in my belly. *Finally! Someone with potential!* I read that "he's a woodworker who likes..." In my eagerness, I sit up too fast, splash that last cherished gulp of wine down my nightgown and swipe left. Yes, left. Even though I've done this hundreds of times, I can't ever remember which direction I'm supposed to swipe when I'm interested or not interested, and in my current state of wine spillage, and let's be honest, desperation—I swipe the wrong damn way.

And...I'm done. I refuse to pay for a Tinder subscription, which means I don't have access to the "rewind" button. Paying for a subscription would mean that I'm taking this app dating seriously, something I'm just not ready to do. Besides, the reality is that Devon is probably not as amazing as his photos. But the beignet one *was* really cute.

I toss the phone on top of my white comforter and look up at the popcorn ceiling of my bedroom. I should just delete this app tonight and move on with my real life. She may not be here now, but Maddie is really the only thing I should be focusing on. She still needs me. At least, she still needs me to drive her around. What does it say about me that I'm chauffeuring my thirteen-year-old daughter to the mall so she can hold hands in the food court with a boy from her school while I sit in the car and do crossword puzzles, hankering for a slice of Sbarro pizza? It's a sad state of affairs, that's what it is. Regardless, my needs aren't important right now; hers are. That's how a good mom should be. Isn't it...?

On the flip side, maybe I should be in a loving relationship to show her what a healthy adult partnership looks like. Patrick moved on four years ago, after we'd only been divorced for a year. He seems happy enough with Amber, who I actually like a lot which is a surprise even to me. She's one of those people I would love to hate, but she's sweet to Maddie, so I can't complain. But Maddie is at my house most of the time, and I worry she's missing out by not having a father figure here. I know what an important bond that can be, and I want that for Maddie. But that would mean I'd have to actually meet a guy. Go on a date. Start a relationship. Ugh.

Completely over myself and my lack of a love life, I pick up my phone again. But this time, instead of opening Tinder, I hold my thumb over the icon so it quivers and the *x* appears so I can delete it for good. Just as I'm about to hit the *x*, my phone lights up with an incoming call. I hesitate to answer because it's late, I'm half drunk, my nightgown is soaked in wine and I'm tired as hell, but it's Olivia so I answer.

"Hey, Liv," I say, sounding more cheery than I actually am.

"You're still up? Good! I was hoping I would catch you," she says with such an upbeat tone I'm instantly skeptical.

"What are you doing up? It's, what, six thirty in the morning in London? Are you going to work early? What's wrong?" I rattle off this litany of questions like a hyperactive dog digging for a bone. It's hard to imagine anything is wrong when she sounds so alive and vibrant, but she never calls this early, or late, as the case may be. In fact, she never seems to call at all; we mostly just exchange texts.

"Well, no...I'm just heading home."

My eyes narrow. "Why do I sense trouble in River City?" I can't help using song references. I was a musical theater nerd in high school.

After a moment, Liv lets out a melancholy sigh and my radar is pinged. She's put out the bait, so I'm definitely gonna bite. Liv's been happily married to Ethan for nine years. He's an okay guy, although I've never really thought he was right for Liv. But he's handsome and they live the big city life she always dreamed of having when we were younger. Which is why I'm confused by this "heading home" comment.

"Uh...okay. And where are you heading home from?" I'm white knuckling the phone. If she says anything other than an all-nighter at the office or saving a small child from a burning building, I may jump through the phone and strangle her skinny, swan-like throat.

In a voice barely above a whisper, she says, "Bex, please don't judge, okay?"

"Fine." I'm hoping she might have a reasonable explanation. She doesn't.

"So, there's this guy that I met a few months ago at this art thing and we've been texting and..."

"What?" I sit up abruptly, accidentally knocking my wine-glass into shards as it clinks against my bedside lamp. "Damn it," I mutter. Thank God the glass was empty. Hate to waste wine if I can help it.

"What's that noise? Are you drinking in bed?"

"Don't change the subject. We're talking about you." I put the broken bits into a pile on my *Real Simple* magazine. "Are you telling me you're heading home from a night with some random dude?" As stunned as I am by this revelation, I'm only human, which means I do love a bit of scandal.

"Well, yes and no. Yes, I'm heading home and no, he's not random...and look, it's not that big of a deal. This is like, a onetime thing. I just needed to get it out of my system."

"Uh-huh." My voice rings with doubt. Noticing she didn't really answer my question, I persist. "So, are you sleeping with this guy?"

Liv, ever the evader, ignores the question. "I've just been feeling so trapped and Ethan is out of town, again. And, um, the opportunity...presented itself."

If eye rolling made a sound, Liv would be temporarily deaf right now. I pick up the magazine with the wineglass shards and head to the wastebasket in the bathroom while saying with as much authority as I can, "Liv, you must be out of your mind right now. You've always said that Ethan is perfect for you. So, please, if that's true, don't mess it up. Take it from me, the single life ain't a walk in the park." I take a deep breath as the glass clatters into the metal bin. "Get your shit together."

I'm feeling pretty good about my lecture, seeing how she hasn't interrupted me once. I continue with vigor. "Delete all texts from Mr. Art-thing. In fact, delete him from your phone, your brain, and definitely your vagina and go back to your real life." I don't want to sound too preachy, so I soften up a bit. "You've made a mistake, and that's okay. Just don't do it again."

After an extended silence, I check my phone to make sure we're still connected.

"Yeah, okay, you're right. My husband is...perfect. That's what everyone seems to think," Liv says under her breath. "I said it was just a onetime thing and it is. I'll delete Francois."

Mr. Art-thing is named Francois? Oh boy. But, as much as I love hearing I'm right, I feel kinda bad for Liv. She's obviously going through something.

"How'd that date go last Wednesday with what's his name, Sean? It was Wednesday, wasn't it?" She's trying to change the subject again and this time I let her.

I burrow under my comforter and turn out the light. Where do I even start? Tell her I drove there, parked, and bailed? Even though I just gave her a lecture, I don't feel like one from Liv right now.

Fact is, there really isn't much to report on my dating life. I'm on Tinder, Match, Bumble, Plenty of Fish, and OkCupid. I've even contemplated signing up for JDate but I'm not Jewish, so there's that. When it comes to dating apps, I'm agnostic. I'm on all these apps, but I never actually go on dates. I'm on a predictable cycle of non-dating dating which goes something like this:

Phase 1 – Get excited and hopeful. I download all my previously deleted apps, ready to give this relationship thing a shot. For real this time!

Phase 2 – Swiping, matching, messaging, liking, and spending an exorbitant amount of time on my phone. I inevitably see some of the same guys that I matched with on other apps and realize there really aren't plenty of fish in the sea.

Phase 3 – Determined not to be derailed by the mundane bios (wine tasting, hiking, golf, and fine dining), the gym rats (flexing in the mirror is such a turn-off) and the downright appalling profile pics (was that guy in the bathtub!), I carry on, hoping there are some quality guys out there I might have missed the previous go-rounds.

Phase 4 – I'm in a messaging relationship with a few guys when one of five things inevitably happens.

1) Both of us are "too busy" to meet up.

2) A dick pic.

3) He tells me he's not looking for a relationship.

4) Another dick pic.

5) I decide I want to meet a man organically and that this whole thing is a waste of my time.

Phase 5 – Throw my hands up, yell "F this!" and delete all the apps from my phone. Again.

Phase 6 – See Phase 1.

Liv is well aware of this, yet she is eternally optimistic when it comes to my dating life. She says I self-sabotage, that I'm too picky, that I've never given anyone a chance. But she just doesn't get it. She's got the perfect relationship. At least, I thought she did, until this phone call.

I let out a huge sigh after reliving the trauma of Phases 1 - 6 in my mind and finally respond, "How was my date on Wednesday? I didn't go. I canceled."

Here we go—let the lecture commence. Liv takes a breath then cranks into high gear. "This is getting ridiculous, Bex! You say no to anyone that asks you out! You need to start saying yes. Be a yes person. No gets you *no*where."

I groan into my pillow, tired of this subject already. "I know. I'm just tired. I don't know what to do anymore. I'm freaking old, I'm a single mom. What do I have to offer?" I'm eyeing forty with disdain. It's one thing to be single in your thirties. At thirty-nine, at least I can say I'm still in my thirties, still youthful but with a certain appealing maturity. But forty, ugh. I'm crossing into being a real adult. I should have my life together and still look fit, stylish and "great for my age." Living in Los Angeles has done a number on my self-worth and I'm not even in "the business."

The jangle of Liv's keys distracts me from my depressing thoughts and with genuine kindness Liv says, "You're nuts, you know that? You are amazing. A total catch. And stop with this old crap. You're not old." Liv continues, on a roll, "Hell, you're not Blanche Devereaux yet. Stop with the pity party and just say *yes* for once." She pauses and I hear the click-clack of her high heels on the hardwood floors of her Chelsea flat. "I'm gonna come up with a plan," she says with such determination that I almost believe her. Almost.

"Bollocks!" she says and I hear a thud, then the muffled sounds of feet, fabric, and the clatter of her phone being picked up.

"Liv? You okay?"

"Yeah, shit, sorry, I dropped the phone. I'm kind of a hot mess right now." She giggles.

Is she drunk? I think to myself.

"What's with this 'bollocks' stuff? You've been living in London for too long," I say, the softness of my pillow lulling me into near sleep.

"I know...but at least I'm not faking an accent," she says, in a very bad fake accent. "I've got three hours to get it together and get to work. And you, what is it, like eleven p.m. over there? Don't you have to take Maddie to school in the morning? Are you working tomorrow?"

"Nope, it's summer. Maddie's at camp for the next ten days and it's slow season for my Etsy shop. Not a ton of orders comin' in right now. Just making new stuff for inventory when the holidays come around. Which can't be soon enough, considering my bank balance."

"Hello! So you can still go out. What's stopping you? Wake

up and say yes. Do not fire up *Outlander*. Get out of your sweats and into something sexy. Love you. Bye!"

And just like that, Liv in her usual way, tells me what to do while giving me a compliment, and totally managing to dodge any further discussion of her own life. I love that bossy bitch.

With my eyes already closing in sleep, I whisper, "Yup...going out sexy. Bye."

TRIPLE SHOT

LIV

Staring at myself in the mirror, I run my fingers through my long blond hair. The blowout I'd gotten yesterday afternoon has turned into a tangled mess, the strands heavy with the scent of cigarette smoke, damp with spilled champagne, and rustled by expensive hotel sheets. And Francois.

Bex was unnecessarily harsh about it. Doesn't she understand I'm only human? Besides, it's not something I plan to make into a habit. It just felt so good to make out. Too good. Kissing for hours, the delicious feeling of something new. I warm all over just remembering it. And before that moment when Francois and I were finally alone together, we'd teased each other with whispers of subtle innuendo, our glances deepening as the waiter began a well-rehearsed speech on the dessert menu. Halfway through a description of what sounded like a pretty damn good chocolate ganache cake, Francois threw £200 down on the table, grabbed me by the hand and we made for the exit. Just like that. The anticipation was almost too much to bear, and by the time the door had clicked behind us at the Savoy, I was weak with urgent desire.

"Dammit, what am I doing?" I whisper sharply, bringing myself back to reality, back to seven a.m. on a now rainy London

Thursday, exactly two and a half hours before I have to be in the office. I hastily undress and step into the shower, closing the glass door behind me. Of course, Bex was going to lecture me. Why had I called her when I knew she'd sleuth out what I'd been up to? Guilt? The need to confess, even though I hadn't done anything too crazy? Or had I...? Everyone says marriage is work, so I guess that means I have two full-time jobs. And Ethan only has one, and he's always at that job.

"Aaaahhh!" I let out a little shriek as the water instantly turns ice cold. "Shit!"

I hop away from the freezing water and almost tumble out of the shower, knocking my elbow against the glass door. When we redid the bathroom, Ethan insisted on a glass-enclosed shower cubicle. A shower-tub combination would have been fine for me, but Ethan hates bathtubs and wanted to have a separate shower. I went ahead with it because I have to choose my battles with him. Even at home, he attacks every argument with the relish of a lawyer who will never give up. Besides, it felt frivolous to fight about the luxury of a bathroom renovation. The whole time I was growing up, we never once renovated anything at home. I still remember the patterns of mold that seemed to be baked in to the aging caulk between the cracked lime green tiles in the one bathroom we all shared.

Most of the time I think London is the best city in the world, but what is so hard about keeping a hot shower hot for at least ten full minutes? That bathroom back home certainly can't compare to the snowy white marble that Ethan chose for this shower, but at least we had consistently hot running water. Just when I'm ready to give up and get out, the water turns hot again.

Am I expecting too much from a marriage? This is the time to hustle, isn't it? I'm forty, Ethan is forty-seven, so we're supposed to be working hard like this, saving and building a nest egg for when we retire. I guess that's when we'll finally spend time together.

But realistically, how much do we need to save without a

family of our own? We tried almost everything, but still, I've always been the *guest* at baby showers. Finally, I just started to decline invitations; it hurt too much to sit there and watch someone else unwrap tiny crocheted booties. And now, well, the chances are less than slim. There's no way Ethan will go through another IVF round with me. He doesn't want to talk about it anymore. I was such an emotional wreck; there were times when I'd cry uncontrollably for no reason. Ethan was mortified by the whole endeavor. He didn't want to admit there might be something that wasn't working on his side. Considering how things are between us now, maybe it's better that Ethan and I aren't parents.

I hold my face under the thankfully warm shower stream, a baptism to wash away the pain. The glass doors slowly steam up as I turn the faucet to hot. Soaping my torso, the soft, sudsy body wash slides down my thighs, and I remember the feeling of Francois' hands gliding over my skin right before he'd grabbed my legs and hoisted me onto him. I'd forgotten what it felt like to be so desired. I don't want to wait around until retirement for someone to pay attention to me.

I turn off the water, just as it's starting to turn cold again.

———————————•●•————————————

"Skinny triple shot extra hot latte for Liv! Spiced turmeric oat milk latte for Emily!" The barista's description of my coffee is a walk of shame in itself. Yes, I'm the middle-aged woman who needs three shots just to make it to lunch. A glossy new intern from this year's herd practically skips over to pick up the spiced turmeric oat milk latte. *What the hell is that? Does that even have caffeine?* I grumble to myself, thinking how much better it'd be to be back in that hotel room with Francois.

"Oh, hi! You're Liv!" Emily greets me with the enthusiasm of a puppy. "I loved the presentation you did at the departmental meeting last week. I am so excited to be here. We get free coffee. So cool. Well, this isn't coffee, but you know what I mean." She takes a swig of her turmeric latte, peering at me through chunky-framed glasses that I assume are trendy but would make anyone over the age of thirty look certifiable.

"Nice to meet you, too, Emily." Thank God the barista said her name because I would have never remembered it. HR circulates a kind of rap sheet of all the new interns each year, with their names, photos, and pithy biographies, but I hardly even look at it anymore. Their optimistic naivete and youthful ambition make me more depressed with each passing year.

"Yup, it's cool, isn't it." I try not to sound too sarcastic. Where do these kids get so much energy? How can she be this awake and not drink coffee? I wouldn't be surprised if she's nursing a hangover and still looks like a freshly blossomed rose.

I slowly trudge my way to my open plan desk. Just as I'm ready to face an in-box full of unnecessary "as per my previous message" and "looping in Liv who can give you more information" emails, my phone chimes. I welcome the distraction. It's a text from Francois. A hot and cold rush of adrenaline courses through me as I read:

Liv, you are magnifique. Until next time.

I slap my phone down on the desk, screen side down like closing a book. End of story. I can't go down this road. I'd witnessed the hell of Bex's divorce and, despite everything, I'm just not ready to go there with Ethan. I can't imagine starting over at this stage of my life. I turn to my computer, pretending to work, attempting to get back on track, but quickly succumb to the story of Francois.

Even though it was a fling, I can't help but want more texts, more dinners where we're each other's desserts, more attention, more *"magnifiques."* I do a Google image search of Francois Duval, not for the first time or the fifteenth time. I've lost count. It's become a compulsion since we first met a few months ago. I search images in the past week, past twenty-four hours. What the...? There's Francois with his hand around an undeniably cool young thing at a gallery opening he attended last night before he'd met me for dinner. *Who is that?* Must be some D-list British royal celebrity because she looks vaguely familiar. I can't keep track of all the titled Ladies, Dukes, and Duchesses and their pouty offspring who populate the gossip columns here more than most actresses.

I peer intently into the screen, squinting my eyes and trying to get a better look at the mystery woman. A dark shadow crosses my mind. What the—Is that Emily, the intern? She's wearing a black slinky cutout dress that shows off her toned physique, and a pair of chic gray ankle boots. A shiny curtain of chestnut hair cascades over her cheekbones, partially obscuring her face that's turned upward to Francois. They look cozy...too cozy. His hand is melded to her hip and in silhouette, they'd be one shrouded shape—no gaps, no distance between them. Bex is right. What *am* I doing? Did I think I was special? *Magnifique?*

I can't do this. I'm too old (and married!) to be swooning around after someone, especially a French artist. It's just too cliché. Bex was right, I need to get a grip and delete Francois. But that accent...that kiss.

Startled by my phone ringing, I jump. Ethan. Great, perfect timing. Swallowing my guilty conscience, I answer the phone.

"Hi, Ethan," I say with fake cheerfulness—*why hasn't this three-shot latte kicked in yet?* "How's the trip going?"

"Hello, darling. Listen, I'm terribly sorry, but this case is turning out to be more complex than we'd imagined. Alan thinks it's going to be at least another week in this desert oven. So I won't be able to meet you in Provence after all. I'm sorry, darling." Ethan's crisp delivery belies no trace of emotion other than extreme politeness. He's like a nervous, amateur actor doing a Hugh Grant imitation.

My heart sinks, though I'm not exactly surprised. This isn't the first time a weekend away has been spoiled by a case. I'd booked a beautiful suite in a renovated farmhouse in the lavender fields of Luberon. Ethan was going to fly from Dubai to Nice, rent a car and drive out to meet me. My flight was due to leave tomorrow from City airport. I knew he'd forgotten about the trip when we talked about it at the charity gala last week. And I held on to that hurt and anger in order to justify the night with Francois. Still, I didn't want to give up hope and in my foolish heart of hearts I thought maybe, just maybe, Ethan and I would actually get away together. Maybe distance from London and the rut we seem to be in could help turn things around for us. Certainly more so than those therapy sessions with Emma.

"Oh, um, that's okay, darling." I try to sound upbeat, while thinking that "darling" must be the most overused word in strained British marriages. "It sounds like a big case."

"Why don't you take Clarissa instead and have a shopping weekend? Alan's already checked with her and she's free."

Is he serious? Even after the snide remarks she made to me at the gala event he's still suggesting a girl's getaway with Clarissa, the mean girl of Treadwell & Sloane wives. Clarissa, who despite being ten years too old, is still mad that she's not Kate Middleton. Uh-uh, no way. Why is Ethan always trying to set us up anyway? Is it his and Alan's not-so-secret plan to fob us off on each other so they won't have an ounce of guilt about making these "Darling, I'm sorry" calls? That I'd be too busy shopping and brunching to notice my invisible husband is missing. Besides, what kind of shopping does he think Clarissa and I would do in the countryside of Provence? There's only so much lavender soap you can buy. The whole point of this long weekend away was for Ethan and me to get time together, for him to at least look me in the eye, talk to me about something other than a client or a case, and maybe even caress me, run his hands over my body instead of his damn laptop. After our failed therapy sessions, we're in do or die territory and he doesn't even seem to notice.

"Um." I'm stalling. I can't face being alone in the country with Clarissa. "I'd rather wait until we can go together. I should be able to cancel the reservation without a charge," I say, distracted by what's brewing in my subconscious. "Hope the case goes okay."

We hang up after exchanging a mutual "Bye, darling" in an *everything's fine and dandy* voice.

The prospect of a long three-day weekend suddenly free of any plans has me thinking, and not with my head. I swipe back to the text message from Francois and imagine what a "next time" would entail. "Liv, don't go there," I say to myself. But the freedom of a next time is so damn tempting. I think of Bex. I envy her freedom—she could do this any time. Which is why I don't get why she spends most of her nights with Netflix. Bex is gorgeous, so warm and charming. Could it really be that hard out there as a single woman? Isn't it a fun, secret sisterhood? Beyoncé's "Single Ladies" for God's sake! In our twenties, living together in Atlanta, we practically had to hire a bouncer to keep the guys away. Well, that *was* almost twenty years ago. I shiver at the thought.

"Hi, Liv." Emily waves to me as she prances by my desk. I hadn't really given her much notice in the office before. All the interns blur into one. It's not that I actively try to ignore them, it's just that their bright-eyed eagerness is salt in the wound to the fact that I'm getting burn-out with my so-called career. It's not like being in ad sales for a media company is my dream job. Does anybody do their dream job anyway?

I eye Emily suspiciously. Could she have been born in the 2000s? Maybe UK child labor laws are different than in the US. Spiced turmeric oat milk latte, my ass. She walks down the hall like it's a catwalk and I can't help but admire her fringed boots with a perfect heel—not too high, not too low, sturdy enough to trot around town but still with a sexy edge. The fringe tassels bounce to the rhythm of her stride, matched in movement by her smooth as glass mane that dances along with each step. Watching her, I start to feel sick.

I turn back to the computer screen and pull up the image search of Francois, leaning in to look at the gallery photo. She's not wearing those glasses, but I sure as hell recognize those boots. Dammit, it *is* her. Francois and Emily, the intern. My cheeks burn with indignation and embarrassment. Maybe she's his daughter? But no father holds his daughter like that. How many women (girls!) has Francois texted "*magnifique*" to in the last week? That's it. I delete Francois from my phone.

Okay, let's do the right thing. Let's be sensibly English. A weekend in Provence with Clarissa seems like the best option after all, even if she is a mean cow. What would I do otherwise? Sit at home and eat cheese puffs, watch the *Golden Girls*, and get lost in an Internet wormhole of stalking Emily and Francois? And what would Clarissa and I do away? I conjure up an image of Clarissa and me on a girl's trip, practically boring myself to sleep. *Now if it were Bex and me.* I smile at the thought, already hearing the percussion of popping corks and howls of laughter.

If it were Bex and me...

I tap at the keyboard. London to LA. Departing tomorrow—Friday. Screw Clarissa. Screw Ethan's case. And screw Francois. Well, maybe not, no screwing Francois. I can still be sensible and have fun. I need me some Bex time and Bex, well, she needs her some man time and I'm going to help her get it. Monday's already a public holiday here, and I can squeeze in four vacation days. It's August after all, and things are dead. A week in LA. How many dates can I get Bex to go on in that time? Go big or go home—seven for seven. Considering some of the conversations I overhear at the office about all these dating apps, it should be easy.

I reach into my Chanel handbag to retrieve my credit card. Ethan won't care if I buy the ticket. Hell, he doesn't even read the credit card statements. But, on second thought, I'm not going to use his money. Something about Francois, even if he is an intern dating lothario, has given me back a tiny bit of me. I'm going to do this my way. I used to juggle temp jobs during the day and a hostess gig at a Cajun restaurant in Atlanta. Before Ethan, before London, before I ever knew anyone like Clarissa, I survived just fine with my own money and purses from Target. And that was before Target was cool. I look around for a better price. With a layover in Zurich and a top up with miles, the price comes to £286 (damn those airport taxes).

The time on my phone says 1:23 p.m. So, 5:23 a.m. in LA, Bex is probably up by now. I know her too well, she wouldn't have gone out; instead, she'd have fallen asleep halfway through an episode of *Outlander*.

"So soon?" Bex answers groggily after three rings.

"Hey, are they still doing all that construction at LAX?"

"Yeah, it's a real shitshow." Bex groans. "No one knows where they're going and Ubers are everywhere," she says with increasing alertness, the topic of LA traffic setting her on edge. "Why are you asking? And why are you calling me so damn early?"

"I need you to pick me up."

"What? Now!" Bex says, fully awake.

"No, tomorrow. Friday at four thirty p.m. Don't forget to wear makeup and don't even think about wearing sweats. You never know who you might meet at the airport. Oh, and we're going out tomorrow night. You're officially back on the market, baby!"

Chapter Three

THE WEEPER

BEX

I'M DRIVING TO THE AIRPORT IN MY FRESHLY WASHED AND vacuumed Lexus SUV. It's an old one, the first hybrid model, peppered with a few dings and scratches, and still no AC, but with a good wash it looks presentable. *Kind of like me*, I half-laugh to myself.

Exhausted after a full day of errands, I run through my mental checklist of all the prep I've done for this last-minute surprise visit from Liv. The house is clean; the bedding has all been changed, and I even made Liv's favorite ranch dip. Oh, and I bought a month's supply of wine, which I doubt will be enough. And Advil.

Liv told me to put makeup on and to "not wear sweats." She says this like I wear sweats all the time. Which I don't. I wear workout clothes too. I believe "athleisure" is the name. I quickly look in the rearview mirror, checking to see if my cleavage situation isn't too much. It's been about a decade since I've worn this top, and well, let's just say gravity can do a lot over ten years. Thank God, it still fits. Working from home with little to no social life apart from going to Zumba and chauffeuring Maddie around means my regular attire has me looking like a hobo who found some leggings in a dumpster dive haul.

I don't know what Liv has planned, but honestly, I'm a little nervous. I can tell when Liv is in "go-mode" and she's full throttle right now. She hasn't lived in LA for a while and she doesn't know what it's like anymore. She has no idea what kind of hell it is to be single in this town.

Back when Liv and I lived in Atlanta, we hardly ever had a night alone. The amount of calls that came in to our answering machine nearly wore it out. We always ran out of tape (it *was* a long time ago). We gave out our number like evangelists give out bibles. Except we weren't saving souls...we were saving money! I don't think we bought a drink in four years.

We'd go out almost every night of the week, which always began with the same ritual: 7:30 p.m.—turn on the shower and turn up the music. One of us would bathe while the other put together outfits. The bathroom would become a fog of steam, perfume, and hairspray as we perfected our looks. 9:00 p.m.— out the door with two drinks under our belt and on a mission for trouble.

As I head to the airport in my best jeans and a skimpier than I'd like tank top, I wonder what it'll be like going out with Liv now. Things have really changed since those carefree Atlanta nights. I feel older, but none the wiser.

LAX traffic is as anticipated, slow as molasses, and inching forward to the terminal I see Liv waiting for me curbside with her bulky suitcase. She must have packed her entire closet. But she's wearing the same fitted leather jacket that she's worn for ages—which is still fashionable. That makes me smile, and I realize then that nothing has really changed at all. Any worries I had about her visit instantly vanish and I'm overcome with giddy excitement.

As I pull up to the curbside, I roll the windows down and turn up the first song on the playlist I made for "Liv and Bex Take LA," and sing along at the top of my lungs. "Get outta my dreams and into my car!"

"Hi!" Liv squeals and does a little jump up and down. She

heaves her suitcase into the back seat then jumps in the front seat beside me yelling, "Shotgun!"

We throw our arms around each other and I inhale her familiar perfume. It's hard to believe we're in the car together after so many years and miles apart. When we were little, Liv and I would always run out to my mom's car, racing to get the front seat. We could have easily ridden our bikes to the country club pool, but Liv liked riding in my mom's Mercedes. Liv came from a one-car family, and that one car was a total beater, so she loved riding in our convertible any chance she could. We'd always yell "Shotgun" at the same time, but Mom would say, in that slow southern drawl of hers, "Honey, let Livy ride up front."

And now, with Liv up front beside me, I know this week will be fabulous and just what I need.

"So," Liv cuts into my reverie and says in an authoritative tone, "first drinks, then some food, then we review your updated profiles."

Stop the train. Did I say fabulous? I take that back.

"What profiles?" I am suddenly afraid. Very afraid.

"Your dating profiles! Duh." She looks down at her perfect manicure, which means she's not looking at me. "I may have gone into your accounts and rewritten a few things."

I shoot her a sideways glare.

"Well, Sprinkles2407 worked! God, I loved that cat. He was so fluffy."

I make a mental note to change my password stat. My first cat's name and old Tennessee address obviously aren't foolproof.

We're at a stoplight and I take full advantage, giving her an eight second death stare. "Liv, really? That's a bit much. My profiles were just fine, thank you."

"Your profiles were not 'fine,'" she says, making air quotes. "They were terrible. Your photos didn't even look like you. That one of you at Disneyland in front of the tea cups?" She gives me a questioning look.

"What? I was trying to look adventurous and fun!"

"Adventurous and fun? More like wind-blown and cross-eyed, with mustard on your shirt."

"I had a corn dog that day. Sue me."

"Bex, it's time to move on from corn dogs and tap into your horn dog. Which is why you need my help. I found some much better pics from your Facebook account. I also rewrote your bio."

All I can do is shake my head and smile in resignation. This is so Liv—revamping my life in the first fifteen minutes of hitting the ground. You'd never know she just got off a twelve-hour flight. Sensing my unease, she forges on in a tone that means business. "Okay, I can tell you're not thrilled, but I'm here for seven days and I'm not going to leave any stone—or app —unturned."

I look over at my best friend who's flown all the way from London to be my wingwoman. She may be bossy, but I'll always jump into the deep end with her.

I hadn't been out for happy hour in what felt like ages and after a quick Yelp search, The Vacancy appeared on the list as a highly rated hot spot. I'd been there years ago and remember it being fun so thought it was worth a revisit. With food trucks out front on Friday nights, it's a bit of a dive bar in a very refreshing, not Hollywood way. Plus, apparently they have a great happy hour. And Liv and I *love* our happy hours.

Once inside the dark and moody space we climb onto the maroon faux leather bar stools, hang our purses on the hooks underneath the bar, then put our heads together as we browse the specialty cocktail menu. It's a well-coordinated exercise that we do in perfect unison, even after a long time away from each other. We're like the synchronized swimmers of happy hours.

"What can I get you two?" asks a smooth voice from across the bar. We both look up to see an attractive forty-something man with a mop of dark hair, coco-brown eyes and a perfectly chiseled jawline. He's wearing a button-down denim shirt that fits snuggly over his muscular chest and arms. I immediately give a quick glance to Liv with a hint of a smile.

Placing thick cardboard coasters in front of us, he continues. "Happy hour's on until eight. All house wine and beer on tap are five dollars, well drinks are six. And everything on the specialty menu is two for one."

"I love a twofer! Twofer!" I laugh too loudly while the bartender stands there waiting patiently for our orders. I catch myself awkwardly then turn to Liv. "What are you having, Liv?"

"Gin and Tonic with lime, please," she says decisively.

Predictable, I think to myself, *she always orders the same thing*.

"Okay, and what'll you have?" The bartender fixes his eyes on me, and I can feel the heat radiating off him. I run my finger down the menu, using a moment of pretend indecision to get a grip. I hope to God I'm not blushing. *He is so cute.* "I'll have the Kentucky sour. Two, please! Double fister!" I say, awkwardly holding up two fists like I'm some kind of amateur boxer. He's nice enough to smile and ignore my lame attempt at being witty, then turns to make our drinks.

Under her breath Liv hisses, "Okay, let's tone down the weirdness a notch or twofer. You act like you haven't seen an attractive man before. Did you just get out of lockdown in a women's supermax?" She shakes her head in disappointment. "Bex, we need to work on your game."

"Game! What game? I'm a single mom, I don't have time for game. Besides, we just got here. Like, five seconds ago. What do you want me to do? A burlesque show? He's not even my type."

"I'm sorry, good-looking and nice isn't your type?"

"No. Okay, well, he is good-looking and so far he does seem

nice, but, Liv, come on, I know this is going to sound bad but I don't want to date a..."

"Bartender," we both whisper it at the same time.

I feel like shit for even saying it out loud. But, really, the late night lifestyle of a bartender just wouldn't fit with Maddie and me.

"Which in this town means he's probably an actor. No way," I say with a groan.

Liv raises an eyebrow. "You don't know that. He could be a food chemist that's into mixology. He could be studying to be a sommelier. Hell, he could own the place." While she rattles off these outlandish possibilities, her voice rises in pitch. "You can't be so quick to shut things down before they even start."

"I guess." She does have a point. I'm always telling Maddie not to make assumptions about people before she gets to know them. I should be following my own advice, but I know where this road leads. A dead end.

The bartender places our drinks on the coasters and leans his elbows against the bar. "I haven't seen you two here before. Are you local?" It's the early side of happy hour and with so few customers around he's got a little time to chitchat. Lucky me!

"Oh, I am, but I don't get out too much. It's been a rough..."

"I just flew in from London today. Thought I'd take this one out on the town!" She gives a conspiratorial smile to the bartender. "Not married, I see." She gestures to his left hand. "Bex here is single too."

Oh my God. This is so embarrassing.

"Thank you, Yente."

"*Fiddler on the Roof*! I love that musical." The bartender grabs a rag and wipes off the recently evacuated bar top to the right of me, humming what sounds like "If I Were a Rich Man."

"Are you a singer?" I ask.

"I used to be. I auditioned for Fiddler years ago for summer stock. Met my ex-wife at that audition, actually." He looks right through me, seemingly into his past. "Wow, strange to think of those times...Anyway, now, I'm a substitute teacher by day, bartender by night." He takes a contemplative pause, which makes me curious for more of his story. There's a lot going on behind those eyes.

I take a sip of my drink, intent on letting the conversation breathe for a moment. But Liv has other ideas. "Bex is divorced, too. And a musical theater geek. You guys have a lot in common!"

Subtlety isn't really Liv's strong suit.

"Is that so?" he says with a laugh. "Bex is it? I'm Brandon. Nice to meet you." He extends his hand, and I give it a solid shake.

"And this is Yente. I mean, Liv," I rib.

The moment is interrupted when Brandon is flagged down by a customer on the opposite end of the bar. "I need to get back to it." He holds up a finger to the man, letting him know he'll be over in a moment. "Um, I hope this doesn't come off as strange, or overly forward considering we just met two minutes ago, but," he pauses and looks right into my eyes, "would you be interested in getting a bite after my shift tonight? I'm off at eight."

I freeze. Stunned. Speechless. He looks so hopeful. So optimistic. But I can't. I just met him. He could be crazy. Of course, he's crazy, he's an actor! But he seems nice and genuine and seemingly not crazy. Maybe I should...

"No. I'm sorry. I can't."

"What?" Liv interjects. "Can you give her a minute to think it over? She'll get back to you."

"Oh, sure. Okay. I'll just go take care of that guy. Let me know if you need anything else." Brandon turns away quickly with an air of defeat.

Liv swivels to face me and leans in close. "Bex." She slow blinks. "I cannot believe what I just heard. No, scratch that. I *can* believe it and it's got to stop. Now."

"What? I just met him. How am I already supposed to have dinner with him?" I protest.

"Listen to me. You know what you're missing? The yes factor. How long have you spent saying no to life, no to romance, or even potential romance, and no to just one date? It's time for a U-turn to become Yes-Bex."

One thing about Brandon I do know is that he must make a strong drink because Liv seems positively manic right now. Or maybe it's the jet lag.

She continues with urgency, as if she's telling me secret plans to invade Fort Knox. "For the next seven days while I'm in town, you're going to say yes. Yes to opportunity, yes to stepping out of your comfort zone, yes to adventure. Don't worry, I'll be your wingwoman. But, from here on out, you say *yes*."

Liv looks at me expectantly, waiting for me to say something as I let her words soak in. She's right. I've fooled myself into thinking that I've put myself out there when, in reality, I've just dipped my toe in the pool. I've patted myself on the back for signing up for dating apps, but then I never go on a date. I've had friends beg to set me up with someone. I reluctantly agree, but when it comes to scheduling, I'm always "busy." Poor Maddie has been used as an excuse time and again when, in fact, even Maddie has been encouraging me to date. And now, when I meet someone in the world, organically, like I've always wanted, the first word out of my mouth is "no."

If I don't stop saying no to the possibility of love, how will anything change? Maybe it is time to start saying—

"Yes?" I smile. "Fine, you're right. It's time to add the Yes Factor to the equation."

— ● —

Once I told Brandon that yes, I'd love to get a bite after his shift, he's been checking in with us at our little corner of the bar in between taking care of the steady stream of thirsty customers. We're really clicking. Who knew real-life encounters could be so easy?

"Still okay with those Kentucky sours?" Brandon says, as he plucks the little umbrella from my glass and moves to tuck it behind my right ear. I'm a little startled, but this small gesture is so playful that I lean in and let him do it. Liv squeezes my left thigh under the bar.

"Yes!" I say a little too loudly. "Um, yes, thank you." I raise my hand and touch the delicate paper of the umbrella to make sure it's still there. I feel like a teenager again, wanting to squeal with boy craziness.

Brandon leans over the bar. "All right, looks like I'm done here. Liv, do you want to join us? I realize you're only in town for such a short time. I don't want to take you away from your Bex. Come with us!"

"Thank you, but I'm so tired from the flight and need to get some rest. Jet lag!" she says, with no trace of fatigue in her voice. "You two go on. Bex, I've only had one drink so I can drive your car home and Brandon can drop you off later."

"Oh, no, just take an Uber. I'll drive my own car. Brandon and I can just go separately."

Brandon interrupts my babbling. "Great idea. I'll bring her home later. But not *too* late." Then with a wink. "I promise."

"Um, okay," I say to Brandon with a smile, although I'm starting to freak out. *Is this really happening?* "Can you give me a minute? We're just gonna run to the restroom."

In the privacy of the ladies', I'm still not able to get it all out. "Wha...You...I can't..." I utter in breathless staccato to Liv.

Liv puts up a hand. "The Yes Factor, remember? This is your first chance to say y-e-s. It's just some food with a nice guy." Off my doubtful look, she continues. "You aren't saying yes to marriage, you're not saying yes to sex—although maybe you will later. Just yes to sharing some food with another human."

40

Her hand goes up again as she knows I'm about to protest. "It's just a bite."

She knows she's right and I know she's right, as much as I don't want to admit it. So, I pull my lipstick out of my purse, slide on a fresh coat, give my hair a little ruffle and walk out the door.

"You have a daughter who's thirteen? What a blessing." Brandon's chin rests on his hand as he leans on the high table at the Tiki Taco, a Hawaiian/Mexican fusion joint. "I always wanted kids, but my ex just wasn't interested. That's why I started subbing. I love kids. But my ex really didn't want to have any." He doesn't sound bitter, just sad.

This is about the twentieth time he's brought up his ex. I should have suspected something was amiss right away when he mentioned meeting her at the Fiddler audition. That's not normally something most people would mention after meeting someone for all of ten seconds.

"I'm sorry about that, Brandon. That must have been hard for you." This conversation has been spiraling downward ever since we left The Vacancy. It's like the florescent lights of this taco joint have illuminated all of his sorrows. "How long ago did you get divorced?" His wounds seem so fresh, I'm guessing a year, tops.

"It's been eleven years. Seems like yesterday." He looks away and grabs a paper napkin from the metal container on the table-top. Are his eyes glassy?

"Uh...I'm sorry to hear that." This is all feeling a bit much. It's obvious his baggage is a heavy load he doesn't bear well. "Do you mind if we head out? I'm beat."

"Oh, sure. Sure." He finishes the remaining bite of his Maui Me taco and we head for the door. "It's been great hanging out with you, Bex. You are so easy to talk to." I return his watery smile with a tight-lipped grin. It's time for this date to end.

It's nearly eleven o'clock when we pull up in front of my house. I don't like the idea of someone I just met knowing my address, but Liv thought it would be fine if he gave me a ride home. After that disappointment of a date, I wish I hadn't. I sat in silence for the entire ride home except for saying "turn here" or "get in your left lane." The chemistry between us at The Vacancy has fizzled out like a Fourth of July sparkler.

"Oh, no, that's okay," I say with a bright voice after he offers to walk me to my front door. Realizing I've said *no* instead of *yes*, but the bucks gotta stop somewhere. I said yes once, and after the taco tedium, that's the only yes Brandon will be getting from me. "Liv will probably be asleep and I'm just gonna go to bed." It's a lame excuse but I can't bring myself to say no flat out.

He doesn't take the hint and is already opening his car door. "Really? But it's early. We can talk a little bit more."

I don't mean to, but I shake my head in disbelief. What else is there to talk about? Besides his ex-wife, of course.

Brandon opens my car door and takes me by the hand. He then proceeds to hold my hand, which I pull away as we walk toward the front door. The voice inside my head is now starting to get a little hysterical. *Is he going to try to kiss me? I haven't kissed anyone in years!* But then the reasonable voice says, *Bex, you're a grown woman. A kiss might do you good. Get you back in the game! Yes, he's got issues, but he is nice to look at. And at least he's a good guy, albeit one who can't get over his past.*

When we finally reach the door after what seems like the longest, most awkward walk of my life, Brandon reaches out to try to take my hand again. "I had a really good time with you tonight. I mean, like, a really, really good time. When can I see you again?"

I hesitate, thinking *never*. "Uh, I don't know. I'm really busy and Liv just got in to town, so—"

"How about next Monday?" he says with the eager optimism of a child.

I'm desperately thinking of an excuse. "No, Monday isn't good. I'm uh...starting a new project." I'm grasping at straws here.

"How about Tuesday?"

"Oh, Tuesday. Shoot. I can't on Tuesday either."

He has a sad droopy dog look on his face. "Really? Okay." But he recovers quick enough. "Well, let me get your number and I'll call you on Wednesday. We could maybe figure out a plan for next weekend." His voice lowers as he continues. "I really like you, Bex. I haven't had this kind of instant connection with someone since the day I met my ex."

"And look how that turned out!" My attempt at humor falls flat and the moment turns serious again.

For some reason I feel bad. Maybe it's female guilt or something, I don't know, but I recite my number and watch him type it into his phone, hoping beyond all hope that he'll type it in wrong...but he doesn't. Why did I gave him my real number? I should have just made something up. And he knows where I live. Exactly why I wanted to drive myself in the first place. All of a sudden he's about three inches from my face. I take a step back and reach into my purse for my house keys. Unfortunately, he stays toe to toe with me like a tango dancer preparing for his signature move. He leans closer and a waft of his hot, salsa breath hits me.

Oh shit. He's going for it!

I'm frozen like a deer in headlights as his lips gently press to mine. I give it a beat to see if I feel anything. Nope. The heavens don't open up. Fireworks don't explode. It was fine. Not bad. Not good. Just so-so. Fine. I pull away quickly.

Attempting to break the silence, I jingle the keys in my hand. "Well, thanks again for dinner, Brandon."

He turns his face away slightly and there, glinting in the incandescent porch light, I see a single alligator tear slide down his face.

He's crying!

I don't want to bring attention to the tear because then Brandon might want to talk about it and I'm so done with talking. But if I ignore the tear, does that make me a cold-hearted bitch?

I opt for cold-hearted bitch.

"Get home safely." I completely ignore his emotional theatrics.

Brandon turns his face square to the light now, not bothering to wipe away the tear or the new ones that are starting to fall down his face. "Bex, I've never had this kind of connection with anyone before. I thought the day I met my ex was special. That I'd never connect with anyone like that again. But then you sat down at my bar and said Yente and it was as if this was meant to be."

The tears keep coming as he hunches over, apparently too overcome with emotion to stay upright. Full on weeping like someone just died. *I* wanna die. Is this candid camera or something?

Oh, for fuck's sake. Why did I have to say "Yente"?

"I gotta go." I finally get some space between us and open the front door, quickly closing it behind me in a narrow escape. I want to shut the door on this whole night. How did Liv talk me into this fiasco? This is exactly why I don't date anymore.

I hear Brandon whimper quietly, "I'll call you."

"You've got to be kidding me!" Liv says with utter glee. She's enjoying this way too much and is riveted as I recount the night.

"I'm not kidding. He kissed me, then started crying." I flop back on the pillows. "My first kiss in years and the guy weeps! What is wrong with me? Why can't I find any 'normal' guys? You acted like the Yes Factor was gonna change everything but it's already turned into one big No."

Liv looks at me with compassion. "Come on, Bex, don't let The Weeper get you down. He wasn't the right fit. Let's move on, it's nothing to...cry about." She laughs. "Sorry, couldn't let that one go!" Seeing my lack of enthusiasm, she continues in a more conciliatory tone. "Listen, I've got something planned for tomorrow night that's gonna be great." I feel my eyebrows rise to my hairline with skepticism. If only I could afford Botox. "Trust me," she adds with a smile.

I've heard that from her before...Well, how much worse could it be?

Chapter Four

HOLLYWOOD ROCOCO NONO

LIV

I WAKE UP TO A KALEIDOSCOPE OF BRIGHT LA SUNSHINE streaming in through Bex's guest bedroom window. In my jet-lagged stupor, I'd forgotten to close the lace curtains, not that they'd have done much to stop this solar-powered spotlight. Leafy branches of an avocado tree sweep across the window-panes. God, this view, it's a tonic after the gray skies and dingy brick flats that I wake up to in London. I yawn and prop myself up on a few pillows to get a better look out the window. Grape-fruit hangs from a tree that is polka dotted with globes of the yellow fruit, too many to pick before they start to rot and fall to the ground, making a blanket of mushy bittersweet in the shade below. In comparison to the plastic-wrapped fruit in London grocery stores, Bex's backyard is a cornucopia of citrus, vibrant flavors and color. It's the picture-perfect California dream. And about a million pounds' worth of produce. I laugh to myself, thinking of the puny, green-gray avocados at the market near my flat that go for £3 a piece. It costs more than a bottle of wine just to make a decent bowl of guacamole. My parents would probably stop talking to me if they knew how much I spent on guac.

Feeling groggy and dazed, I wonder what time it is. Jet lag is a bitch. Was I dreaming that Bex told me the bartender started to weep? I'm all for men in tune with their emotional selves, but it seems like a major red flag to have an intense crying jag on the first date, regardless of gender. Bex definitely needs something more light-hearted, and what I have lined up for tonight will be perfect.

Lazily, I stretch and enjoy the luxurious comfort of the queen-sized mattress and starfish my arms and legs to all four corners of the bed. I can't help but enjoy this feeling of being alone in bed. No snoring Ethan, whenever he makes it to bed, and no half asleep wrestling to get more of the blanket. I used to laugh at the old black-and-white TV shows that had the husband and wife sleeping in separate beds. Maybe they were on to something after all.

Reaching up with another yawn, my hands bump into the polished oak headboard. Bex is a genius with rehabbing old furniture. I've told her a million times she should open her own shop, not just her online Etsy thing but an actual store. Her eye for unearthed treasures is better than those experts on *Antiques Roadshow*. I trace my fingers along the beautifully carved inlay of the headboard and smile, remembering the look on Bex's face when she first laid eyes on it.

We were grappling with vicious hangovers in the early stretch of a six-hour drive back to Atlanta in muggy August weather after a crazy weekend in New Orleans. Back then, in our college youth, a twelve-hour round trip drive for a Saturday night to meet up with cute Cajun guys and down some Hurricanes was no big deal. We'd made it past Slidell when Bex veered the car off the I-10, almost missing the exit.

"Did you see that sign?" She half turned to me under the weight of her hangover, then started saying repeatedly as if possessed, "Po'boys. Po'boys."

To this day, whenever we say "Po'boys," we both start to giggle.

It was a two stoplight town in Mississippi; I don't remember the name. I do remember those shrimp po'boys and sweet tea being the best damn hangover cure ever. As we were heading back to the car, Bex made a beeline across the street, having spotted an Antiques sign in the corner of a darkened storefront window. Before I knew it, she was inside. I followed just in time to see her stop in her tracks, a rapturous glow breaking the zombie look of her hangover.

"Amazing, it's perfect," she said.

I followed her gaze to see a beat-up, dusty piece of wood leaning against the wall that definitely did not look perfect to me. Bex sweet-talked the woman at the counter into letting her take it off her hands for fifteen dollars. We tied it to the roof of the car with some rope. It was heavy as hell, but the po'boys had given us strength. The following weekend Bex worked on it both days, resurrecting it from that cobwebbed corner of a forgotten store in Mississippi into a piece worthy of the Smithsonian. I love that she's kept it with her all these years. I wonder what this chunk of wood has witnessed in its lifetime. From forest roots to a carpenter's hand. Tender embraces, mean silences, arguments, and fights. How many cycles of a relationship has it been at the mast of.

"Wake up!" Bex hollers from downstairs. "I don't know what time it is in London, but it's too late for you to still be in bed. We need to at least do brunch before it's happy hour."

I grab my phone, 10:18 a.m. It's not that late. Bex is clearly still on Mom time, even with Maddie away at camp.

And no messages from Ethan. What did I expect? I hadn't even told him that I was here. He probably thinks that I'm with Clarissa, happily discussing the subtle nuances between French and English lavender.

"Okay, *Mom!*" I shout back. "I'm up! It's not even eleven!" Yelling from the bed like this makes me feel like a teenager again, but a happy one. I always loved spending the night at Bex's house when we were kids. Her mom would give me the fluffiest pink towels with satin trim and a matching robe. Those towels felt like pure silk compared to the nubby, sand paper thin ones we had at home.

Bex knocks on the door and peers in.

"Doesn't look like you're up to me." She dive bombs onto the bed, making the headboard rattle.

"Careful, this thing's old." I yawn. "Remember when we found it?"

"How could I forget? That was an insane weekend. And you know what the craziest thing about it is? We were only five years older than Maddie is now. I do not even want to think about her on a weekend trip to New Orleans! Let alone one with a fake ID!"

"Do as you say, not as you do?" I give her a wry look. "Why did you never open your own store? I swear you could have sold this headboard for six hundred dollars, even back then."

Bex leans back on the headboard beside me.

"I don't know. Well, I do know. It's called motherhood and divorce. I'm doing good just to make ends meet sometimes. God bless whichever millennial founded Etsy. Now I don't even need to open my own store, plus I can work in my pajamas."

"Speaking of." I give Bex a once-over. "That getup is not going to be getting you any. I think my grandmother had that exact same one."

"What?" Bex looks down at the nightgown. "It's comfortable."

"Exactly."

I was worried about it being too late for brunch, but this is America. Home of the all-day breakfast. And this is LA on a weekend, so basically the Disneyland of brunching. Pushing my sunglasses up like a headband, I soak in the relaxed atmosphere of the outdoor patio and warm sun that's melting away the London cold inside me.

"I'm so happy to be here," I say to Bex. "Thank you for letting me be your Fairy Godmother Wingwoman."

Bex clinks my mimosa glass with her own. "I still can't believe you came all the way from London to do this. And by the way, I changed all the passwords on my profiles. *Enjoys arthouse films, jazz, and cultivating heirloom tomatoes.* You do know me, don't you? That makes me sound like some twenty-three-year-old hipster growing his first beard!"

"Well, I had to put something! You'd hardly even filled them out. Anyway, forget about all that. Tonight is something different. Tonight is gonna be fun and upbeat. A party!" I say in a Valley girl accent.

"A party?" Bex takes the final bite of her French toast, holding her fork in the air in the utensil sign language for *seriously?*. "The last time I went to a party was, well." She pauses, deep in thought. "When *was* the last time?"

"Precisely. That's my point," I say like a schoolteacher.

"Whose party? And where?"

"Trust me." I wonder how many times I'll have to say that to Bex before I return to London. Coaxing her out into the dating world takes more work than I'd imagined. "Remember the mantra?"

"Say yes." Bex rolls her eyes, stabbing the air with her fork at each syllable. "But I wanted us to go to the Pasadena Society Estate Sale tomorrow morning. It's the last one of the season. I don't want to be out late tonight—I like to get up and out. Early bird catches the best antique bargain and all that. I need to find some distressed leather for a piece I'm working on for a client. Anyway, what time is this party?"

I'm not going to let her bail on this one. She might be able to weasel her way out of plans with her friends here, but I know her too well.

"Yes," I say.

"Yes, what?" Bex says in confusion.

"Yes. Yes, let's go to the Estate Sale thingy tomorrow morning. Yes, we'll still go to the party tonight. Yes. Yes..." I smile, on the verge of laughing. Mimosas, sunshine, and jet lag are a fun combination.

"Ah ha, I see what you're doing," Bex gives me a sarcastic look, but indulges me. "Yes," she says with a smile, "I'll go to the party."

———————◄•►———————

"Are you sure this looks okay?" Bex pulls nervously at the sweetheart neckline of her red body-hugging dress to tuck in an errant bra strap. "I should have worn a strapless bra. But they don't give me the lift I need, especially for a dress like this one."

"Stop complaining that you have boobs." I gesture to my almost B cups. "Check out this view," I marvel. "The city looks so beautiful from up here, I know it's cliché, but it *is* just like the movies. Those twinkling lights of lives and dreams. It almost makes me miss living in this crazy town."

"Yeah, it's really nice even though we did almost die getting here. This better be a fun party."

The twisty curves along Mulholland had been almost too much to bear, especially in the back seat of an Uber with a faulty suspension. I should have sprung for the executive car. The two double gin and tonics we'd enjoyed in Bex's backyard after mimosas at brunch were sloshing around in our stomachs as the car swerved and swayed. A near miss with an oncoming Range

Rover almost made us both throw up. The driver was thoughtful though and clearly protective of his 4.87 rating—there were handy wipes and a roll of paper towels tucked into the middle seat console. This driver was ready for anything. I'd told him to drop us off a couple of blocks away from the address so we could get some fresh air and walk off the nausea.

"I think this is going to be a big party. Look at all the cars. And nice ones too," I say.

"Come on, Liv." Bex rolls her eyes. "I don't care if a guy drives a pickup truck or a Porsche. You know, I'd actually prefer the pickup truck. You can't haul anything around in a sports car."

"Maybe there's an app for that. Pickup Truck Bucks," I say, racking my brain at all the dating sites I'd discovered while researching Bex's profiles. "You know there's even one for 'Uniform Dating.' How 'bout a fireman?"

Finally, after a pretty steep walk past a growing line of parked cars, our stilettos click-clacking up to the address, we arrive.

"Is this it?" Bex says.

"Yeah." I look at my phone to confirm that we're at the right number. "Yup, this is it. Shall we?" I raise my hand about to ring the doorbell.

"This is a house," Bex states. "I mean it's a nice house, but it's a *house*. I thought this was some kind of event, like at a warehouse or a gallery. How do you know these people?"

"Yes, it's a house. An amazing house," I say. "You just don't get this kind of place in London. This is so LA. Is that an infinity pool behind the gate?" I try my best to sound encouraging, sensing that Bex is about to turn tail and make a run for it.

"Are these friends of friends, or someone from Ethan's firm?" Bex says, switching into LAPD detective mode.

I can tell she's starting to get nervous. She's been hibernating for longer than I thought.

"Beeexxxxxx," I say, whining and stretching her name out beyond the one syllable to get my way. "Come on, you can't bail now. It was Saturday night, I guess that makes it all right," I sing out of key, knowing that the right lyrics will lure her into action.

"Oh, all right, fine, let's do it." When she sings back *What have I got to lose* I know I've got her hooked. "Hopefully, there won't be anyone crying," Bex says dramatically as she rings the doorbell.

We hear a high-pitched laugh from inside. "I'm coming!" a voice calls out with a slightly sarcastic edge as the door opens with a flourish.

"Hi, ladies, come in. Oh, I like the dress," a giggly woman in one of those Hervé Leger bandage dresses says to Bex. "Very *Dynasty*." We squeeze past her and walk inside.

"*Dynasty?* Why did she say that? Is it too fancy? Too Joan Collins? I mean, I got it from Anthropologie!" Bex whispers to me.

"Stop with the insecurity, you look amazing. You know you do. Okay, so let's get a drink then assess viable suitors to approach." I try to sound like I've got a plan when this party doesn't appear to have as many single guys as I'd hoped it would.

"Assess viable suitors to approach? Could you make that sound any less cool?" Bex says to me. She's right, but I'm not going to admit it.

We take a good look around. It's not exactly how I thought the event would be, but I'm going to make the most of it for Bex's sake. Two huge leather modular sofas form a semi-rectangular shape in the high-ceilinged living room. There's a beautiful fireplace, but nothing on the mantel. In fact, there are hardly any decorative touches, or much furniture, anywhere.

"Hmm, strange that it's so minimalist inside yet so Hollywood Hills rococo outside. I mean, did you see that water feature by the front door? It looked like something from Versailles," I say.

"Okay, just because you follow *Architectural Digest* on Instagram doesn't make you an interior design guru. Hey, there's the bar." Bex grabs me and we head for what appears to be a makeshift bar in the large, open-plan kitchen.

"Hi, could we have two G and Ts, please?" Bex says to the young bartender who isn't wearing a shirt.

"I do love California." I sigh, staring at his tan muscular arms. "He's cute," I whisper.

"Do not even go there. Do not try to set me up with another bartender," Bex says.

"Oh all right fine, but look at those biceps. So, we're sticking with the G and Ts then?"

"Yeah, I'm trying not to mix alcohol. Not that I always follow my own rules, of course." We both laugh, acknowledging without having to say it, the many times we used to see each other bowing to the porcelain god.

Hot Biceps serves us the drinks. "Have fun tonight," he says with a wink. "And I made them doubles so you won't have to come back here too soon."

"Well, I wouldn't mind coming back soon for a refill," I say quietly to Bex. "Those arms."

"Stop it. This is already hard enough for me. So can you take it seriously, please?"

"Okay, you're right. I'm sorry. Let's see, who do you think is cute?" I scan the room. "What about that—" I'm about to point out a guy across the room as I'm interrupted mid-sentence.

"Hi! I'm Candace and this is Chad. People call us *Chandace*." Candace, a bleach blond twenty-something sidles up close to Bex. "I lovvvve that dress!"

"Um, thanks," Bex says. "I wasn't sure about it. The woman at the door said it was *Dynasty*."

"Dynasty?" Candace says. "Oh, is that that new place on Sunset everyone's talking about? Isn't it owned by a Kardashian?"

Bex and I make eye contact, trying not to laugh.

"Hey, where's your man?" Candace says to Bex, lowering her voice conspiratorially.

"My man? Oh God, um, where do I even start," Bex drawls

theatrically. The double G and T is already hitting her hard. "We met, like, ages ago, a few years after college. He was so gorgeous, I mean, I was really swept off my feet. A fairy tale. But, I'm here to tell you that not all fairy tales have a happy ending."

Candace seems slightly confused. Meanwhile, Chad, a Ken to Candace's Barbie, leans in to me. "I get it, it's cool. She doesn't have a man, does she?"

"What? Well, I mean," I say, thinking to myself that this Chad guy is overstepping boundaries. But maybe he has a nice, successful friend here. "Dating in this day and age—especially at our age—has its challenges," I say. Chad is so close I know that he had something with garlic for dinner. I take a small step back. "Besides, some men are uneasy with a woman who won't settle and knows what she wants."

"But women know what women want, don't they?" Chad stares at Bex and me with a gaze that would give those full body X-ray things at the airport a run for their money. Maybe I've been around reserved English guys for too long, but Chad is just way too intense.

"You know, Chandace has done a lot of things. But we've never enjoyed the beauty of two women together."

Okay, why is he talking about Chandace in third person? This guy is starting to creep me out.

"Would you two like to join us upstairs? There are still a few free bedrooms," Chad says.

"Uh, thank you. But I think we'll finish our drinks down here for a while. It was nice to meet you and Candace. Nice to meet you...um...Chandace," I say haltingly, hardly believing what I think is happening.

I grab Bex by the arm and pull her away from Candace, who's babbling on about a bikini she bought for a trip that she and Chad are taking to an "adults only" resort in Florida.

"So sorry, Candace, it was lovely meeting you. Excuse us." I drag Bex away, not sure which way to turn.

"What's going on?" Bex says, apparently oblivious to the not-so-subtle Chandace divide and conquer MO.

I hurriedly walk through to the dining room with Bex in tow and see a couple making out in a corner, half hidden by an empty china cabinet that has a lone decorative bowl on top. Intertwined and clearly enjoying each other, the man turns the woman and gently pushes her on to the table, pressing down on her as the table almost topples over.

"Whoa," Bex says as we stand there frozen.

The guy continues kissing the woman as his arm reaches out, trying to find that bowl on top of the china cabinet. He topples it over and a confetti of condoms scatters across the floor. He grabs one, unzips his pants, and starts to unwrap the condom. This could potentially be hot. Except, they're not.

"Okkkaaaaay," I say in stunned shock. Bex and I are like deer in headlights. A nervous, panicky feeling starts in the pit of my stomach and quickly spreads throughout my whole psyche.

Suddenly, Bex snaps to it. "Liv. Liiiiivvvvv. Where did you find out about this party?"

"Um, I...it was an ad that popped up when I was researching dating apps," I say as a woman in lingerie runs by giggling.

"An ad? From a dating app? What kind of app?" A tone of impatient anger has edged into Bex's voice. "Let me see the invite." Bex grabs my phone and scrolls through to find the email.

Love the Lifestyle. Experience Hollywood high life at an out of this world party venue. Glamorous couples. Single ladies free. She lifts her eyes to mine and they narrow. "Liv..."

"I mean, who wouldn't want this lifestyle? A house in the hills!" *Shit, what have I done?* I think to myself. I'll never get Bex away from Netflix after this.

"Liv!" Bex whisper-shrieks. "I know you haven't been over here for a while, but what do you think *Lifestyle* means? We are at a swinger's party! You know, a sex party? What did you think it meant? *Glamorous Couples?* Free entry for *single ladies?* Do I need to spell it out for you in condoms?"

"I know! I'm sorry. I can't believe it. I didn't realize! I thought it was an exclusive dating event. A glamorous cocktail thing. Oh my God. And *Chandace* were all over us. He actually asked me if we wanted to go upstairs!" I am full-on panicking now.

"Let's get outta here. Get an Uber, stat." Bex orders in a voice as serious as a trauma surgeon. "I *cannot* believe I got all dressed up for what turns out to be a swinger's party. I just want to go home, get in my bathrobe and eat Ben & Jerry's. I'm done!"

"Come on, we can still go out somewhere. You look so nice," I gently plead, desperate to salvage what's turned out to be a total disaster of an evening.

Bex's dagger eyes dart sideways to look at me. "Is the car on its way?"

"Dammit, I can't get a signal here. My roaming coverage is awful, especially in these hills. Try yours."

Bex pulls out her phone and swipes to unlock it as the screen fades to black. "Of course, my battery is dead. I mean, why would anything go right at this stage?"

"Maybe we can just parachute down to Hollywood Boulevard?" I say, half-joking, half-serious. "Wait, what about the bartender, he seems nice? And I mean, he's working, so he can't try to kidnap us to a bedroom upstairs."

We go find Hot Biceps, who has now turned into our knight in shining, shirtless armor.

"How's your evening going, ladies? Chandace were just over here looking for you two. They said you're the most beautiful unicorns."

"Unicorns?" Bex and I say in unison and look at each other.

"Look, can you call us an Uber? My phone is dead and we need to leave. Now. This isn't our scene at all," Bex says.

"Okay, okay, I understand." He picks up his phone to order a ride.

"Here's twenty bucks for the fare." Bex puts the money on the bar.

"No, that's okay." He pushes the twenty-dollar bill back to Bex. "That's nice of you, but I'd hate for you to leave with a bad impression. You know, this isn't my thing either, but the tips are great. I'd rather wear a shirt, but the event organizers say it helps to create a 'party mood.'" His golden brown arms flex as he mimes air quotes. "I like my life to be more calm and authentic. My name's Alex." He extends his arm to Bex for a handshake. "I know this might sound strange but I don't care. I'll say it anyway." He's still holding on to Bex's hand as he continues. "I feel like you'd enjoy the spiritual journey of yoga. Have you ever tried a class? My friend Skip teaches at Loft Yoga and I can get you both comp passes."

I nudge Bex and pull her aside. "Say yes. I know this has been a total bust and I feel like such an idiot. But please, this night has got to come to something! He might be a new age Jeff Spicoli but he seems like a nice guy, and besides, those arms."

Bex elbows me sharply and I think I've blown the whole thing, that she'll never want to date anyone ever, but then she turns to Alex and says unenthusiastically, "Sure. Yes."

"All right! You're going to totally dig it, I promise. What's your name? You can pick up the passes from reception before class. They have an amazing class on Mondays. Super energy and vibe. A great way to spiritually detox from the weekend."

"Summer Moon Lotus," Bex says.

"Summer Moon...I dig it." Alex nods appraisingly, bowing to Bex with his hands in prayer position.

Back at Bex's house, blissfully decked out in our sweats, we stand side by side in the bathroom brushing our teeth.

"Oh my God, that was crazy!" Bex says with an edge of humor in her voice. This night will probably turn into a story she'll get a kick out of repeating.

"Ridiculous," I say, relieved that my mistake is something we can make fun of now that we're safely home and far from the likes of Chandace. "We've got Colgate rabies." I gurgle and foamy white toothpaste cascades from my mouth down into the sink.

I rinse my mouth and wipe it with a towel. "I miss you," I say with a sharp, bittersweet pang in my chest. It's true, God, how I miss this familiar companionship, the feeling of being with a friend who's a sister—family forged from love, laughter, and a shared journey from adolescence to adulthood.

I take my mouth guard out from its case and run it under the faucet.

"Why do you have that thing?" Bex says.

"I grind my teeth. Stress. Plus, it helps keep all that teenage orthodontic work from being all for nothing." I shrug, ignoring a rising wave of emotion that I don't want to surface.

"What do you have to be stressed about?" Bex says. "You and Ethan are okay, aren't you? I get that Francois is just a onetime blip on the radar. I know things can be up and down, but your life is basically *Notting Hill*. And now thanks to all that dental work, your teeth are almost as razzle dazzle as Julia's." She singsongs "razzle dazzle" a la *Chicago* the musical.

"Is any marriage ever really 'okay'? I wish grinding my teeth was the only thing that needed fixing." I shake the mouth guard dry and feel the tears starting to well up despite my best efforts to keep things breezy.

"What's going on?" Bex asks with concern.

"Nothing, come on. I don't want to talk about me. Let's talk about your hot yoga date," I say in an upbeat tone.

"Wait, hot yoga date as in hot date or as in hot yoga? Isn't that like over a hundred degrees, no way I'm doing that. Why can't this be a Zumba date? I love Zumba. And besides, I don't think he was asking me on a date. He just wants us to join his yoga cult or something." Bex gives me a gentle smile. I know her, and she knows I know her. She's giving me some space right now, which I'm grateful for. Maybe it's just the jet lag and leftover adrenaline, and gin, that's making me feel so emotional.

"This is LA, everyone's in some kind of cult or another. At least he didn't invite us to a Scientology meeting," I tease. "Hey, let's do pore strips and get grossed out. Doesn't Maddie have some?"

"No," Bex says "She's thirteen with perfect skin but she and all her friends use these filters and apps to look like poreless, porcelain mannequins. It's crazy."

"When is someone going to invent an app like that for life? There's so much in this world I'd love to get rid of," I say.

"I know." Bex starts listing, "War, poverty, hatred."

"Yes. And Chandace's breath." I take a swig of mouthwash then pass the bottle to Bex. "So, are you gonna go? The yoga date on Monday?"

"To culty yoga recommended by a shirtless bartender from a swinger's party? How could I say no?" she says. "Fine, why the hell not. But only if you come with me."

"I can't. I've never done yoga. And besides, I've lost a toenail."

"How can you lose a toenail? No one's going to be looking at your no-nail toenail." Bex laughs.

"I bought a pair of Stuart Weitzman boots at a sample sale that were a half size too small. But they were such a great deal," I say wistfully, then suddenly remembering Emily's fringed boots and the photo of her with Francois.

"A great deal that only cost you a toenail."

"So my toenail aside, you're really going to go?" I say. "It's a yes?"

"I don't know. Liv, I know you have the best intentions and I love you for being here, but do you see now that it's not so easy getting back out there? Saying yes doesn't automatically find me Mr. Right. Let's just enjoy the rest of the weekend and go to the Estate Sale tomorrow. I want to forget about guys and dating, at least for one day."

———————◆•◆———————

In the guest bedroom, I mindlessly read the jar of anti-wrinkle cream as I slather it on. *Gently sloughs away dead skin cells.* Hmm, well, slough away, I think as my phone chimes. It's a message from Ethan.

Darling, hope you're having a delightful time in Provence.

The message is nice, but impersonal. It's like our whole marriage has turned into a string of polite text messages. Sometimes I feel as single as Bex. I toss the phone onto the comforter, not even bothering to set an alarm for tomorrow morning, then flop back on to the pillow except I miss it. My head hits the headboard with a thud. I smile; serves me right.

Chapter Five

TREASURE HUNT

BEX

THE PASADENA SOCIETY ESTATE SALE IS JUST A FEW WEEKENDS a year and, in the past, has been full of unique finds. Normally, I'd be pounding the pavement by eight a.m., but with Liv's jet lag and my need to sleep off the nightmare called Chandace, we leave the house well after eleven.

I'm so close to finishing a project and need the antique gods to guide me to a leather statement piece to tie it all together. Although the process itself can be ugly, and most days my fingernails are darkened by stain or varnish, there's nothing I love more than the hard work that goes into creating beauty from something that's been neglected. There are a few antique markets around LA, but good pieces at a reasonable price are hard to find. Occasionally, I don't mind buying something that's already been restored, but if I find one more piece of old furniture that's been painted white or, God forbid, glued with decorative tiles, I might just take an axe to it. As far as I'm concerned, shabby-chic is a curse, not a trend.

I scan the stalls, hoping to find a few overlooked pieces while also trying to keep up with Liv who's flitting around like a drunk hummingbird.

"Liv! Wait up. What'd you find?" I shout out to Liv, who's

rifling through a cardboard box of scrap fabric with such focus that she doesn't hear me. "Olivia!" I finally call out in exasperation.

With a smile, Liv pulls out a gorgeous lavender, yellow, and white cloth like a magician pulling a rabbit out of a hat. "Look at this fabric! This would be perfect to recover that Victorian desk chair in your office. Isn't it great?"

"Shh." Doesn't she know anything about bargaining? I *was* wanting to cover the seat in an old suede, but it's been impossible to find something I like.

I reach out and finger the fabric. It's hand embroidered with wild flowers and birds on a thick wool backing, nicely discolored with age yet still sturdy enough to work with. My nose crinkles at the musty smell of dust, earth, and mothballs, like it's been kept in a basement trunk for decades. Maybe this could actually work on the chair. It's completely different than what I had in mind, but the colors would contrast so nicely with the cherry wood.

"You're right. I have to have this. Do you see a price tag on it?" I whisper.

Liv flips the fabric over looking for a tag and I see a small piece of blue painter's tape that reads $85. I cringe as reality seeps into my bones. This is slow season for my business, and I really shouldn't be spending money on myself when I came here looking to buy a piece for a client. Most importantly though, I need to save so I have some fun money for going out with Liv this week. But Mama didn't raise no fool.

I peel off the price tag, and stroll over to the stall owner with a casual attitude and say flippantly, "This is cute, I'll give you twenty bucks for it."

I may put on a brave face, but I can feel my underarms start to dampen. I'm desperate to make a deal. The woman looks at me over her purple rimmed glasses with suspicion. She fluffs her auburn bouffant and counters, "Fifty."

It's the final day of the last Pasadena Society Estate Sale of the year, and I know this lady wants to move the merch. I counter back, "Thirty. You probably bought this for twenty-five cents at a garage sale off some Altadena cat lady." I raise a confident eyebrow daring her to relent. She responds with an open palm, grudgingly accepting my price and waiting for the cash.

"Yes! You are a boss." Liv high fives me as we stroll away, the beautiful vintage fabric flung over my body like Miss America's victory sash.

I look over at Liv and smile. This is the perfect day. It's everything I love most—California, Liv, sunshine, and antiques. Old things and an old friend. The only thing missing is Maddie. A wave of bittersweet happiness floods me. Liv's only been here for two days and I'd forgotten how much joy she brings to my life. She reminds me of who I am, who I used to be, and what I aspire to be. It's like the ghost of Christmas past, present, and future showed up at my house with a bottle of wine to snap me back into really living.

"I don't want you to leave. Ever," I say. "How come we let so much time go by without seeing each other?"

Liv laughs her light bubbly laugh and rolls her eyes. "Aww, come on now. I just got here. We've got a lot more trouble to get into!" She puts on a 1930s flapper hat from a nearby rack, then shimmies her shoulders just to make me laugh.

"I'm serious. How did our relationship devolve into one sentence texts and funny memes? What happened to us?"

Liv pauses and puts the hat back on the rack, shrugging off the stern glare of the curmudgeonly stall owner. "I guess life happened? I don't know..."

"Life?"

"I guess part of me felt like I couldn't help you. Like, I had nothing to offer. Your struggles with Maddie in elementary school. All the drama with Patrick. I felt like I didn't know what to say. I don't even have a kid, so what would I know?"

"Really? You know me better than anyone and if anyone can give me some perspective, you can. I just figured my mundane life was boring to you. You, off in Europe with your cool job and cooler husband. Jet-setting and having late night cocktails in London hot spots. I just couldn't keep up."

The bustle of the market surrounding us, we stand in our vortex of silence as we let our truths sink in. Neither of us did anything wrong, we just let our differences divide us, momentarily forgetting that our bond is deeper than the daily struggles of life.

Liv breaks our reverie. "I'm sorry I wasn't there for you during the divorce. I should have come right away." There's pain in her eyes.

"Liv, it's okay." She starts to scoff, wanting to argue the opposite, but I don't let her. "No, really, it's okay. It was a hard time, but I'm okay. And anyway, you are here now. That's all that matters." I turn into the oncoming crowd and say over my shoulder, "Besides, somebody has to help me drink all the wine I just bought!"

"You know I'm up for that challenge!" Liv hooks her arm through mine.

"I love you." I lean against her shoulder.

"And I love you."

It's just that easy.

The world righted, we amble along in a comfortable silence, glancing from here to there at the assortment of wares. Old watches, dolls, dishes, and clothes, until we come upon a large tented area full of Hollywood memorabilia.

"Oh my God, speaking of *Dynasty*, look at this headshot of Joan Collins!" Liv squeals, running over to lift it out of the crate it's stacked in, the heavy emotion of our conversation left behind.

"What was that girl talking about? My dress looked nothing like that! The shoulders weren't nearly as puffy!" I say with a fake scowl.

"Puh-lease, you looked fabulously sexy. Nobody at that party was wearing enough clothes to know anything about fashion.

And anyway, Joan looks hot in this pic." Liv gives a final envious glance at the photo. "I'd kill for a dress and earrings like that."

I nod my head toward the sunshine. "Let's mosey on, shall we?"

Standing at the edge of the tent, staying in the shade until we get our bearings, we simultaneously inhale the aroma of churros and in unspoken agreement turn right, as if heading to Mecca, the breeze blowing the hair from our faces. We pass a stall of silhouette portraits, and another that's overflowing with hand-made soaps and lotions. Diagonal from the Santa Barbara Soap Co. I spot a gorgeous Eastlake mirror made of intricately carved mahogany. It's in near perfect condition, with only a hint of oxidation on the glass. Sweeping my gaze quickly over the items in this stall, I can see that this vendor has my kind of taste. Unpainted wooden furniture, that has either been painstakingly restored to its former glory, or left unfinished waiting for the right pair of loving hands to bring it back to life. I feel like the latter—a pair of loving hands would do wonders for my soul.

I look over at a sign hanging from the tent structure and smile as I read, "If You're Gonna Paint it – DON'T buy it." Obviously, the lady who owns this stall is a woman of my own heart. I inwardly chuckle with amusement and look around for the owner, assuming she'll be the twin I never knew I had.

Not seeing anyone, my attention is drawn back to the glorious Eastlake mirror, and I approach it for a closer inspection and catch a glimpse of myself. My cheeks are rosy from the heat, and even though I feel tired from last night's shenanigans, I don't look half bad. My makeup-less face and no fuss hair may not be glamorous, but I feel like myself. Despite the craziness, Liv's visit has already done wonders for me.

"Liv!" I call out, getting her attention. "Come look at this. It is to die for." I don't bother whispering or hiding my interest. There is no amount of bargaining that will bring this down to my price point.

"So gorgeous. Totally you."

Standing side by side, Liv lifts an invisible microphone to her mouth and busts

out, "I'm starting with the woman in the mirror!" changing man to woman because, well, that's what we always do whenever we sing this song together, which we've been doing since the sixth grade. As we round out the verse, a slow clap of applause strikes up behind us. We turn around, slightly embarrassed, but at the same time, not really giving a damn.

"You guys are awesome," a teenage girl with the vibe of a young Alicia Keys says with an approving nod. She has a soulful and organic beauty, seemingly comfortable in her own skin. "What do you think of the Eastlake? Awesome, huh?"

I look at her in surprise and ask, not masking how impressed I am, "You know a lot about antiques?"

"Oh yeah. It's in my DNA. We found this beauty last summer when my dad and I were on a road trip to visit my mom's grave in Louisiana. We spotted it at a garage sale near Lafayette. Got it for a song! But, don't tell him I told you." She leans in conspiratorially. My heart twists with compassion. This is a young girl who's been through a lot but it's obvious she's a fighter.

Liv and I are both enchanted by her. "Don't worry, we won't say anything!"

"I'm Chloe, by the way."

"Bex." I extend my hand.

Liv introduces herself and then asks, "So, this is your dad's booth?"

Oh, no. I can already see Liv's wheels turning. Maintaining my smile, I turn pointedly toward Liv, wanting her to know that I know what she's thinking. But Chloe doesn't know Liv like I do and innocently calls out, "Dad! Hey, Dad! Come over here and meet Bex and Liv. They're looking at the Eastlake." Chloe leans in close to us. "Please don't say anything about Lafayette and the garage sale, he'd kill me." She rolls her eyes skyward.

"Your secret is safe with us," I reassure her as both Liv and I nod in unison. Chloe gives us a smile then turns to greet a couple who are eyeing a mid-century modern coffee table.

Liv doesn't waste a second, hissing in my ear, "I don't know about you, but between this booth and that hunk of a man over there, I think we have a deal!" Liv gives me a little spank on the rear like we're in the NFL and she's motivating me to get out on the field for a winning touchdown.

"Don't get all worked up. Today's a day off. You can't keep pushing me into every man we meet."

"But—" Liv protests, so I stop her before she can go any further.

"Liv, I'll talk to him because it's rude to just leave, but this is not happening today. After last night, I need a break from saying yes."

Liv gives me an exaggerated pout and rolls her eyes.

I turn around to see the man who must be Chloe's dad. He's leaning over an account ledger, running his finger down the page, engaged enough that he doesn't notice me taking him in. He's around six foot two with a strong, sturdy build, a man that works with his hands. His complexion is darker than Chloe's. The simple aqua colored shirt he's wearing makes his skin appear luminescent. Liv wasn't wrong when she called him a hunk. But, wait. Hold on. I recognize this guy. "Oh my God," I mutter under my breath.

I turn back to face Liv, who's watching me with that knowing smirk of hers, but she doesn't know the half of it. "I'll be back in fifteen minutes, okay? I want to check out a few things. You're gonna talk to him, right? You can say yes to that, can't you?" Liv practically skips away, waving to Chloe as she disappears out of sight.

I look over to Chloe and then to her dad again. Yep, there is no mistaking it. Chloe is a little older than the Café du Monde photo, but it's obviously them. When I swiped left on him earlier this week, I felt like I had lost a real opportunity. I didn't get to read his whole bio, but there was something about him.

Something in his eyes and smile. Seeing him now, in the flesh, there's a calmness about him, like he's never rushed in his life, yet is never late. He exudes an air of powerful serenity, a stillness in this whirlwind of weekend deal-seekers and looky-loos. When I saw the Eastlake from afar, I'd expected a woman to be the mastermind of these beautifully restored pieces, but now that I see this man, it makes perfect sense. The wood sings at his pitch and frequency. I look around the stall, immersing myself in the energy of this song.

"Bex?"

I'm startled out of my reverie, gearing myself up to speak but suddenly feeling very nervous.

"I'm Devon. Nice to meet you." He reaches his hand out to me in greeting and with my eyes never leaving his warm smile, I reach out to shake his hand. This guy must think I'm an idiot because I'm moving so slowly, like a snail crawling through a bowl of Jell-O.

I start talking without realizing what I'm saying. Words tumble off my tongue.

"Hi, I'm Bex but you already know that ha ha I just love your stuff I'm a big fan of all things vintage and antique and I love that sign." I point to the wooden plaque and continue my ramble. "I mean *If You're Gonna Paint It Don't Buy it*—why ruin a good thing, right?" I'm sure my face looks like it's been painted bright red. I'm so hot and discombobulated I feel like I just drank a bottle of wine in a sauna.

Devon responds with an open and friendly laugh that realigns my senses and puts me at ease, bringing me back down to earth. With a twinkle in his eye and the lines around them slightly scrunched, he says, "Nothing brings me more pleasure than uncovering a hidden treasure."

I blink twice. *Damn. He is hot. And cool.*

"I know what you mean," I say, my nerves settling. "And the adventure leading to the treasure is just as rewarding, don't you think?"

"The journey, not the destination." He nods knowingly and taps his fingers on the teak table next to him. "You sound like a regular Indiana Jones."

My laugh comes easily and honestly. "I almost named my daughter Indiana, but my ex-husband was against it." I inwardly chastise myself for bringing up Patrick, The Weeper must have rubbed off on me with this ex-talk! I shake it off and get back on topic. "I took my daughter to Belize two years ago, and we did this crazy cave swim excursion thing where you end up in this big cavern and there is—"

"A Crystal Maiden?"

"Yes! Have you been there?" I say, eager to build on a connection.

"I have. Chloe and I went last year. What are the chances?" Devon leans over the table calling out to get Chloe's attention, "Chloe, what was the name of that cave in Belize? The one with all the Mayan pots and the skeleton?"

Chloe thinks for a minute, her eyes turned upward as she sorts through her memory. I can practically see the light bulb go on when she says confidently, "ATM." She gives him bug eyes, which I find cute and very endearing. I can appreciate that father-daughter bond.

Devon and I turn back to each other and long seconds tick by as we stare, smiling at each other. Anxious about what to say next, I unconsciously rub my lips together thinking I need some ChapStick. I'm not that good at talking to gorgeous men in person. I've been a strictly text conversationalist for too long now. Thankfully, Devon interjects my silence.

"Hey, do you wanna grab a coffee at the Chicory Cart down the way? We can swap vacation stories, plus, I could use a break."

Devon is so genuine that I find it hard to resist him. This is exactly what I've yearned for for so long. Meeting someone naturally, out in the world, finding a common interest and feeling an instant chemistry. Not all of that app dating crap, matchmaking drama, and random encounters at bars. I cringe as I momentarily recall the date with The Weeper. What was I thinking? This is how it's supposed to go down.

So then, why do I say, "I don't want to take you away from your booth. I'm sure you're really busy..." I trail off. But I can't take my eyes away from his, my lips parted, wanting to say yes, but I'm frozen.

Seeming to sense that my brush off was more out of politeness than lack of desire, he gently insists. "You really shouldn't miss their New Orleans iced latte."

This man is speaking my language. "You said the magic word —New Orleans," I respond and wiggle my eyebrows, trying to seem upbeat and carefree despite the explosion of nerves going on inside me. "Lead the way."

I'm enjoying every second of our leisurely pace over to the Chicory Cart. Devon is recounting a funny story about a Louisiana swamp tour escapade gone wrong. I wonder if it's the same trip as the beignet photo on his Tinder profile? Part of me wants to mention my swipe mishap, but another part of me feels like that would make me sound like a crazy stalker. So, I just listen and stay in the moment, noticing the way his glimmering, onyx eyes meet mine or how he smiles and touches my arm at a particularly funny part of the story. Our conversation flows so easily, like he's an old friend. Nothing feels put-on or like we're trying too hard. We just fit. Devon and The Weeper are night and day.

Delicious iced coffees in hand, Devon pulls out a seat for me at a small table under a towering oak tree.

"It's a perfect day." My voice sounds as relaxed as I feel in the shade with Devon. "My daughter would love this tree."

"How old is your daughter?"

"Ahh, Maddie. She's thirteen going on twenty-five. She still loves a good antique hunt, but she's away at camp. Junior counselor this year."

"That's cool. But, yeah, thirteen is rough. Still a kid, but ready to be an adult. Chloe got easier at sixteen. And it doesn't hurt that I don't have to schlep her around everywhere anymore. That driver's license has saved my sanity." Devon gives me a commiserating look and I smile. He really is adorable while also being hot as hell. I cross my legs, attempting to ignore my lady bits hollerin' at me.

We spend some time comparing notes about raising teenage daughters and I alternate between nervous babbling and relaxed serenity. I'm on the lookout for Liv since it's been about fifteen minutes since she left me at Devon's stall and I know she'll turn the place upside down to find me. I don't need a bull running through this china shop. But maybe I'm reading too much into this. I'm not one hundred percent sure that Devon is even into me. I mean, I think he is, but who knows. It's only been a few minutes and a cup of coffee. He was probably going to take a break anyway. Maybe this is just his way of sealing a deal, thinking I'll splurge on the mirror at his booth.

"Hey," Devon says suddenly under his breath as he puts his hand on my jeans clad knee, "Celebrity sighting, three o'clock."

The touch of his hand sends a jolt through me, and I forget how to tell time. *Where the hell is three o'clock?* I think, my eyes scanning the surroundings.

"Who? I don't see anyone," I say a little too loudly.

Devon leans in toward me and whispers softly, "Shh..." and I literally shiver. "Look over there, to the right. Diane Keaton. With the tan hat."

It's like my brain can't compute language anymore. Thinking only of his mouth whispering near my ear, my mouth, my neck.

A celebrity sighting, even one as good as Diane Keaton, can't derail the feeling brewing inside me. I pull back only an inch or two to meet his eyes, hoping he doesn't notice the electricity he's sparked, but also kind of hoping he does.

"Good one," I whisper, feeling myself melt into his touch.

Devon and I are jolted back to reality by the voice of an elderly man. "Excuse me."

The man is dapperly dressed in gray dress pants and a short-sleeved white button-down shirt. Blue suspenders top off his timeless look. "Sorry to bother you. Looks like you're having a nice time in this shade. But have either of you two seen that booth that sells records?"

Still recovering from the surprisingly intimate moment with Devon, I take a moment to unscramble my thoughts. "I passed it on the way in, I think." I look to Devon, hoping he can give more specific directions.

"Yes, sir, I know the place you mean. You aren't far from it. George's booth. It's two rows that way." Devon points west. "And about six or seven booths down toward the parking lot. He's got a great selection."

"Thank you kindly. I'm hoping to find a record by Ella and Louis. Have you heard of them? A lovely duo. My dear Mildred and I danced to one of their songs at our wedding and I plan on singing it to her at our anniversary party next month."

My heart glows looking at the joy on his face. Mildred is one lucky woman.

"I'm hoping to find that recording so I can practice," he says.

"That's very sweet. How long have you been married?" I glance over at Devon who is beaming at the man and seems just as charmed by him as I am. It's kinda adorable.

"Sixty wonderful years. I wish I could say we'll have sixty more, but no one lives forever." He sighs. "Enjoy every moment." He looks both of us in the eye and I blush, feeling embarrassed, like he knows something I don't.

"What song?" Devon says.

"'Our Love Is Here To Stay,' do you know it? It's a great tune. All you have to do is hold your lady close and sway. I'm not a very good dancer—two left feet, Mildred always says. What did you two dance to at your wedding?" The man thumbs his suspenders awaiting an answer.

Devon and I look at each other in surprised amusement, then turn back to the man, not quite knowing how to respond.

I stumble out the words. "Oh, we're not—" I hold up my ringless left hand, while Devon laughs and says, "We just met."

With a knowing smile the man says, "Well, don't wait too long, son. I can tell she's a keeper. Hold your lady close and sway."

The man hums that classic Ella and Louis tune and mimes a little dance. I can't help but wonder if his sixty years of marriage is showing him something I can't see yet. The man walks away toward the record booth, following Devon's directions, and I wonder if the whole encounter was even real. I feel so close to Devon, bonded in a way that I can't quite explain. With the melody of Ella and Louis in my head, and the magical words of that elderly man, I feel like I've seen a glimpse of the future.

Chapter Six

CHURRO-MANCE IN THE MAKING

LIV

AFTER MAKING MY ESCAPE FROM DEVON'S STALL, I SIGH IN both frustration and elation, tempted to look over my shoulder to make sure Bex didn't follow me. Why is she so shy? She should be all over a guy like that. They have the same interests; he is ridiculously handsome, and I can already picture them road tripping for antiques together. Bex better be saying more than just hello!

I shield my eyes against the beating sun, feeling like a lone figure in the Wild West pondering which way to go. All of a sudden, I want to run back to Bex, give her a hug, and tell her that I just want her to be happy, with or without a guy. I miss her already. We've been together almost nonstop since I landed in LA on Friday. I hadn't realized until now how lonely I really do feel back in London.

Walking down the little makeshift street of stalls, I see two young women walking side by side in the distance. As I get closer to them I see they're holding hands, and that they both have wireless ear buds in, each clutching a phone in their free hands. Are they listening to music? Is one of them on the phone to somebody? Could they even be on the phone to each other?

One of the girls has ripped jeans that look like they've been put through a blender. Her tan, taut legs are showing through the denim rips. She can't be older than nineteen, if that. Her friend is wearing cut-off shorts, suspenders over a faux vintage Rolling Stones T-shirt and knee-high striped socks. I guess this is the cool kid take on the '70s, a twenty-first century version of Farrah Fawcett. A young guy approaches them. *This must be the boyfriend,* I think to myself as he slips his hand around the waist of the girl with the ripped jeans and leans in to kiss her, an intense melting of the lips that only teen pheromones can produce. And all the while, the girls are still holding hands. He pulls back and the other girl leans in for a gentle peck on the lips. The whole scene is cozy, almost too cozy, this casual public intimacy something I never did in my youth. When did I get so cynical? Why is this making me feel so uncomfortable, almost jealous? *When did I start to feel so old...?*

I envy the freedom of this young trio. Their nonchalant blending of physicality, their openness, their who-gives-a-fuck attitude.

Bex and I, we're the last of the analogue Gen-Xers. We grew up with baby boomer parents who thought they were liberal, but at the end of the day, most of them still had the conservative norms of the '50s in their DNA. Girls didn't make the first move. It wasn't polite to kiss in public. You dressed nicely for outings. Ripped denim, public displays of affection—all of that was frowned upon. Especially in the South.

It's not even like I was raised in a strict household. I just accepted things the way they were before the Internet gave us a window into a million ways of being, of loving, of fucking.

If I didn't have that coding, or if I'd had the courage to ignore it, I'm sure I'd be a happier person now. Deep down, though, I know I'm just looking to blame anybody or anything but myself. Anything to ignore the fact that I seem to be stuck in perpetual quicksand. That I haven't had the energy, courage, or strength to make a change. That I'd rather spend my time googling Francois and daring myself to see him again. That I'd rather do anything than ask myself—or Ethan—the questions from which I run. An honest discussion, instead of denial, doubting, and excuses.

And to prove my point, I get in line at the churros stall that Bex and I passed earlier. Nothing like indulging in a feast of carbs and denial.

Balancing a flimsy paper plate, further weakened by the spreading grease stain from three churros, I wind my way back through the stalls looking for Bex. I should probably just give her a call but I want to give our best friend ESP a try. I pass table after table of stuff trying to backtrack to the stall with the mirror, but feel lost in a maze.

Finally, I see Bex in the distance, about five stalls away. She's sitting at a table, one of a few that are dotted around a coffee cart. She's doing that thing she does when she's flustered, waving her hands around as she's talking, and every few beats, brushing her hair behind her ears. *Is she on the phone or talking to herself?* I get closer, duck into the shade of a stall and hide behind a dream catcher that's dangling from a railing. I peer out and see that she's seated opposite the man from the antiques stall who's nodding and smiling at her as she talks. Ha! So this explains the erratic, pseudo sign language. She *did* manage to say more than a hello back at the stall. I'm proud of her but wonder if talking is all she'll do. Maybe she needs another nudge. Frozen in indecision, I want to run up and be the wingwoman I'm supposed to be. But I haven't exactly started out on the right foot with Chandace and the swinger's party. I laugh to myself, *how could I have been so stupid?*

"That's a beautiful choice."

I jump and turn around to see a full-figured woman in a tie-dyed sarong dress who's seemingly appeared out of nowhere.

"It sure does bring joy, doesn't it?" she says.

I'd been absentmindedly running my hands through the dangling ribbons of the dream catcher, mindlessly stroking trails of faux fur which are now probably coated with churro grease.

"Oh, um, yes, it's nice." I gingerly step away from the dream catcher.

"It's twenty-nine ninety-nine but I'll throw in a crystal for you. I sense you could use amethyst." She presents a display board of dusty gemstones that remind me of high school geology class.

"Thanks, but," I look at the dream catcher, "I'm not sure my energy is matching it."

I back away from the stall, deciding that maybe I should go see if Bex and Devon have at least exchanged phone numbers. I came to LA to help her get back out there, after all.

"Bex. Hey, Bex!" I run up to her, slightly out of breath after inhaling the churros.

"Oh, hi." She looks up in surprise, as if she's startled by my appearance.

"Are you going to introduce me?" I wink as I extend my hand.

She sighs, clearly not happy that I've interrupted her.

"Devon, this is Liv. Liv, Devon." Bex waves her coffee cup from Devon to me then back to Devon.

I sit down without waiting to be asked.

"Devon, your stuff is wonderful. I've been walking around and it's definitely the best. It's so huge, you've got, like, three stalls of to-die-for furniture. And the mirror. Bex, that's the kind you've been looking for, right? Eastfield, Eastwood?"

"Eastlake," Bex and Devon say in unison as they look at each other. There is a definite spark between them.

"Well, thank you. That's really kind of you to say. It's hard work, but I couldn't imagine doing anything else," Devon says with quiet confidence.

"Well, I salute you, Mr. Antique Man." I give a tip of an invisible hat. "Don't you think he's got great stuff, Bex?"

Bex gives me a cutting look and I can read her body language. Translation: *get the hell outta here.*

"Um, yes," Bex says. "That mirror is actually what drew me to your stall."

"Bex loves old furniture," I say to Devon. "You should see what she can do. She's a total magician." I tell him a shortened version of the Mississippi headboard story and feel proud of my wingwoman skills for once.

But I wonder if I've said too much, especially about us chasing Cajun guys in Louisiana. I didn't really need to include *that* in the story. I laugh nervously, aware that I'm lacking in subtle matchmaking skills. I should have stayed at the dream catcher stall and talked crystals with that tie-dyed pajama lady.

But Devon is gazing at Bex appreciatively. *Yes, maybe I should get his number for Bex after all.*

"So Devon, are you dat—" and before I can finish my question, Bex grabs my arm and starts to stand up.

"We have to go." Bex smiles in a way that seems to apologize for what I was about to ask.

Devon looks slightly confused.

"Oh, okay." He stands up and extends his hand to Bex, "It was a real pleasure meeting you, Bex". The veins on his forearm look like one of those raised topographic maps. A landscape of strength built from hard work. But Bex has already turned away from Devon, pushing me along by my elbow.

"Bex, what's the matter? Why are we rushing off?" I say to her quietly, even though I know why she is upset, because I probably overstepped boundaries. Again.

To cover, I look back over my shoulder and give Devon a half wave. He's holding his coffee and watching us walk away with a bemused look on his face.

"Come on, let's go!" Bex snaps. "The traffic is gonna be insane. And it's too hot to be stuck on the freeway."

"Don't you want to stay and talk to him longer? He seems really nice. I mean like genuinely cool. He has impeccable taste." Is Bex blind? Why am I pleading the case for what seems like her perfect match?

"No, let's just go. I'm tired." She keeps walking straight

ahead, not even looking at me, or back at Devon, a note of irritation creeping in to her voice.

"Hey, so what were y'all talking about before I got there?"

"Liv, do you have sun stroke or something? I said we need to go."

"Okay, fine." I decide not to press it any further, doing my best to keep up with her quick pace. I wish I could tell her that I only have her best interests at heart. *I guess everyone is allowed to be a bitch every once in a while*, I think to myself, perhaps too harshly.

Chapter Seven

SUNDAY KIND OF STUPID

BEX

"YOU KNOW WHAT?" LIV SAYS JUST AS I PUT MY KEY INTO THE ignition. "Sorry, but I need to make a quick run to the loo. The churros are starting to rumble." She cringes.

I audibly groan. Liv has a finicky stomach and I know that traffic will go from bad to worse because Liv can't be rushed in the bathroom.

"First of all, I told you to be careful with this market food. Second of all, it's called a bathroom, not a 'loo.' There were Port-a-Pottys right by the exit. Why didn't you go when we went by there?" I take the keys out of the ignition.

"First of all," Liv says, mocking me, "what's wrong with market food? It's Pasadena, for God's sake. Second of all, no, I'm not using a Port-a-Potty. I'll be back in five." She throws her purse over her shoulder and hops out of the car.

"You'll be back in twenty, but it's fine. I'll wait here. Catch the news on the radio," I yell as she slams the door a little too hard. She's always done that, and it's *always* gotten on my nerves. Why can't she close the door gently for once?

In reality, I'm glad for a few minutes alone with my reeling thoughts. I feel frazzled, frustrated, and intrigued by Devon. I don't even know how to process what happened there, and I don't want to talk about it with Liv because she'd probably march me back to ask him out. Plus, I'm not even sure he *was* really into me. He seemed so friendly and he did do that whole hand-on-the-knee thing...But, am I reading too much into it? Maybe he was angling for a sale.

Still, I think there *was* something there. Even that sweet old man saw something between us. And with sixty years of marriage, it's not like he doesn't know a thing or two about relationships.

When Devon talked about uncovering a hidden treasure, I felt it in my soul. Even now, my chest tightens just thinking about it. But in the midst of the moment, I acted like a dumbstruck teenager—talking too fast, or not talking at all, trying to impress him with my babbling. I forgot to ask for his business card so I could at least get his last name and Internet stalk him. *Did I even say bye?* Hashtag F-M-L. At least I know he lives in Sierra Madre, so that narrows it down from the Greater Los Angeles area. I shake my head in irritation. Maybe Maddie and I could drive out there for dinner one night, or every night, just in the off chance we might bump into each other.

The fact that I got a second chance with Devon and messed it up *again* is beyond discouraging. I had the opportunity to redeem my mistaken swipe with a real-life encounter, and I still fucked it up! I toss my head back against the headrest and groan. Ugh.

I don't know why I got so flustered when Liv joined us. I panicked because I was afraid she'd crank up into crazy matchmaker and ruin the magic. Which she did. She almost asked him if he was dating anyone! I could have died right there. She came to LA guns blazing on a mission for me to find love. She'll definitely take The Yes Factor to a nuclear level if she gets even a whiff of pheromones in the air.

In my fear, I bailed...not even bothering to say a decent goodbye to someone who's probably the coolest, and hottest, man I've met since my divorce.

I could kick myself.

Instead, I pick up my phone and search for The Pasadena Society Estate Sale just in case there's one more weekend I don't know about or maybe a directory of stall merchants. Nope. This is it, the last one of the season. It won't start up again until next spring.

"Dammit!" I cry out and slap the steering wheel. Liv's timing sucks. If she hadn't come over at that particular moment, maybe I would have harnessed the courage to believe, to be sure of what I was feeling, to make some kind of move to see Devon again. But why didn't he ask for *my* number? The old man told him I was "a keeper." Liv really shattered the moment.

This is *her* fault, not mine. Liv can be so controlling. Waltzing into my life like she knows how to fix it. How would she even know? We haven't seen each other in what feels like years. She acts like all I need to do is wear a push-up bra, go on Tinder, and voilà! I'll find my dream man.

I shouldn't have expected it to be any different though. Liv's always been this way. A Fixer. A fixer who loves to focus on other people but not on herself. She'll even try to fix things that don't need to be fixed. Like that time she *fixed* my perfectly good haircut, which then looked so bad I had to spend another seventy-five dollars at the salon to fix her fix!

I'm starting to wonder what it is that's wrong with *her*. We've both been so isolated in our own worlds that I have no idea what's going on in her life. All I know is that she came out here on a whim. Meanwhile, she's hardly even said three words about Ethan or her life in London. I know about that dalliance with Francois, but she hasn't said anything about it since our phone call. We should be spending time reconnecting with each other, not on this crazy dating scavenger hunt that's giving me bad flashbacks to wondering whether or not someone's going to ask me to prom.

Tears burn down my cheeks. I look into the rearview mirror to make sure I don't have mascara smeared all over my face, to see that I don't look like the hot mess that I feel like I am. I let out a big sigh, resigned to the truth of the matter. It wasn't Liv who messed things up. It was me. Self-sabotaging again. I could have told Liv to just give me a minute. I could have been confident enough to ask Devon for his number. I could have mentioned to Devon that I meant to match with him on Tinder, and that this real-life encounter feels like a second chance. I'm a grown woman, dammit. If I didn't make a move on Devon, it's because I chickened out, nobody's fault but my own.

Even so, I don't want to say sorry to Liv. That would mean explaining the connection with Devon. How could I even begin to explain the unexplainable? Recounting the whole thing will just make me feel like even more of a failure. If I hear Liv's *Just Say Yes* and *You Gotta Get Out There* lecture again, I might lose it once and for all. As much as I love Liv, she doesn't have life figured out any better than I do. Hell, nobody does.

I wipe away my tears and accept the reality of the situation. This mission for love isn't about me. It's about her. Something serious must be going on and she's not letting me in on it. Fine, I'll play along until she wakes up to it herself. In the meantime, why not go on a few dates? I'm probably crazy to be obsessing about Devon after only one coffee. We weren't even together for more than half an hour, max. But I can't deny that it felt like we'd been talking for hours.

Feeling lighter with this newfound clarity—I always feel better after a cry—I turn on the radio. I gaze at the Pasadena hills rising in the distance, squinting my eyes in the direction of Sierra Madre. Despite myself, I can't help but wonder what Devon's house is like. He probably has a perfectly restored Craftsman house, with a garage that's been converted into a wood shop.

I can just picture it...

"Sunday Kind of Love" comes on the radio right as I walk into the sunlit garage. Devon is leaning onto a sideboard, moving his arms back and forth in a strong, steady motion as he sands down its surface. Sweat

drips from his forehead and he's so intent on his work that he hasn't noticed me in the doorway. But he must feel my presence because he looks up and our eyes meet. He lets the piece of sandpaper he's been working with fall to the ground and never breaking my gaze, peels off his T-shirt. He approaches me with a slow, confident stride, a lion stalking his prey, his abs rippling with every breath he takes. A goofy smile spreads across my face because he's so damn sexy, but as he gets closer to me, I turn serious in heated anticipation. We breathe in unison, deep and heavy, and I can feel the fire between us before we even touch. Finally, his hands are on me. He lifts my yellow sundress up to run his fingers along my thighs and up to my hips, then caressing me over my panties, gently at first, then with an increasing pressure. He lifts me and sets me down on a nearby work-bench, leaning in to kiss me as I stare into his beautiful brown eyes. His lips lightly brush against mine as he slides my panties down my legs. Our kiss gets deeper, our tongues meet as I reach for his zipper...

"Okay, let's go. You ready?" Liv opens the car door and throws her purse onto the passenger seat floor as she climbs into the car.

Like a needle scratched from a record, my Devon fantasy screeches to a halt. Dammit, Liv. *Again!*

Chapter Eight

BREAK UP, MAKE UP

LIV

I HADN'T REALLY NEEDED TO USE THE BATHROOM. I WANTED to go back and find Devon to get his number, to somehow patch things up from the awkward goodbye. I shouldn't have interrupted Bex and Devon the way I did. So far, my track record as a wingwoman would only count as a success for a nun.

When I went back into the fray of the market, I got lost in the slow shuffle of the post-lunch crowd. I understand now why Bex had wanted to get there so early. Time was ticking and I couldn't navigate back to Devon's stall because I had no idea where it was. The market seemed to have acquired a life of its own with new tables and tents that I hadn't noticed beforehand. Finally, I gave up in frustration and fought my way back out of the maze, like a salmon swimming upstream against bargain hungry tourists, so I could run across the hot parking lot to Bex's car. And now, after running, I really *could* use the bathroom as the churros are starting to churn.

"Okay, let's go. You ready?" I open the car door and hop in. "You're the one who's been complaining about traffic. Let's get this show on the road."

Bex looks slightly drugged, like she's woken from a deep sleep.

"Hello? Earth to Bex?" I pull the car door shut then strap on my seatbelt.

"Jesus, you scared the hell out of me! Why do you have to slam the door so hard?" Startled, Bex turns the key and cranks up the car.

"Sorry, jeez. I didn't slam it."

We leave the parking lot behind only to hit the freeway, which by now is a parking lot itself.

"Dammit." Bex slaps the wheel. "I told you traffic was going to be crazy. We should have left earlier. And then you had to go and use the bathroom."

"Relax. You have a kid, you should be used to unscheduled bathroom breaks. At least I'm not asking 'Are we there yet?'" I hope Bex will smile, or at least blink. "Bex, what's going on, why are you acting like this?"

She doesn't say anything. The suffocating exhaust fumes from the traffic seem to have poured into the car. We're drowning in a toxic mess of passive aggressiveness.

My phone rings but I ignore it. Finally, the annoying xylophone sound stops as voicemail picks up the call. But then it starts to ring again. Whoever is calling doesn't sound like they're going to give up.

"Will you answer your phone or put it on silent? It's driving me crazy," Bex says.

I scrounge around in my purse to get out my phone while the ringing continues. Bex looks over and can clearly see Ethan on the screen as the caller ID. I hold it in my hand and let it ring.

"Go ahead, pick it up," Bex challenges me. "I wouldn't mind saying *bonjour* to him. How is he anyway? You haven't said much about him since you got here."

Bex sure knows how to cut deep. *Bonjour*. That one stings. I know she's judging me about Francois. No way I'm dealing with this now. I don't think Bex would say anything crazy while I'm on the phone with Ethan, or would she? Our fighting is making me paranoid. I turn the phone to silent and angrily throw my purse down.

"What the hell is wrong with you?" I spit out. I feel like rolling down the window to let out a big scream.

"What the hell is wrong with *you*? What's the matter, you can't 'just say yes' when your own husband calls?" Bex throws it back to me.

"Why are you acting like such a bitch?" I yell out in frustration.

I hate this. Why are we doing this to each other? It seems neither of us can stop. We've only ever had a few knock-down, drag-out fights before. And they were all back in our twenties. Our lives are too separate now to have these kinds of fights over the phone, or in texts. We only share snippets of a *hello, I miss you*. A blow up doesn't play into that. We've lost the rhythm of each other's moods, having hardly spent time together in person for so many years.

One time at our apartment in Atlanta, Bex actually threw my mattress out of the window. It hit the ground with a thud, shattering a bunch of terracotta potted plants in the yard of our downstairs neighbor. She looked at me, frozen in disbelief at herself, and at the boiling tension that'd arisen between us. Realizing how ridiculous our fight had been, we quickly snuck downstairs into the neighbor's yard to retrieve the mattress. We were laughing so hard we could barely get it back up the stairs. Life was simpler then. Now, both of us have emotional baggage that weighs more than a thousand mattresses. It's harder to let things go. Harder to say I'm sorry.

I curl up and stare out the passenger side window, making as much of an effort as I can to turn my back on Bex. She has both hands on the wheel, sitting upright, tense and ready to pounce.

"Car fights are the worst," I say quietly as a half-ass apology but Bex doesn't say anything.

We drive home in silence, like a married couple who've given up on fighting because stewing in resentment is more comfortable. After one hour of horribleness, we arrive back at Bex's house and I go straight to "my room" without saying a word. Maybe this trip was a mistake. Maybe I should have just stayed at home in London and spent some time thinking about my life. Or maybe I should have sucked it up and gone to Provence with Clarissa like Ethan had suggested. To continue the charade. To pretend that the way I was living my life was making me happy. I can't even fix my own life. Why did I think I could swoop in and fix Bex's?

I check my phone again to see if Ethan has called back or sent a text. No, nothing but that one missed call and his voicemail that I don't even want to listen to. His formal, nonpersonal check-in will just upset me even more. When did our marriage become so flat, so passionless? Speaking of passion, I open Instagram to scroll through Francois' page to see if there's anything new. I'm about to start stalking Emily when I hear Bex at the door.

"Lou Lou...Lou Lou," she whispers in a singsong voice, using my childhood nickname. Apart from my parents, nobody's called me that in decades.

Bex is holding out two glasses of wine from behind the door. Her apology.

I open the door wide and usher her in with a dramatic gesture and make a clearing on the bed. I take the peace offering and swallow a big gulp of wine in silence. We sit down on the bed, both cross-legged, just like we used to as teenagers except we didn't have wine back then, it was usually a phone between us, either making prank calls or agonizing over whether or not to call a crush.

I raise my glass to clink hers. "Fuck LA Traffic."

"Do you feel like we need some karma cleansing?" Bex says in mock seriousness.

I look at her in confusion, then it dawns on me what she means—the not-a-date yoga date on the cards for tomorrow.

"Yes, let's get our zen on." I move to put my hands on my knees in a meditation pose but accidentally knock over both our wineglasses.

"Sure you'll be okay, Miss Clumsy?" Bex tries to save what's left in her glass, as the Chardonnay soaks into the comforter.

I laugh, happy that the tension of the drive home has been dispelled. But why did she practically run away from that guy, Devon? I know I should let it go. I'm just happy she's going to get back on the saddle...or at least, the yoga mat.

Chapter Nine

GRIN AND BEAR IT

BEX

I LIE BACK IN BED AND MULL THROUGH THE DAY'S ROLLER coaster of emotions. The high of running in to Devon in person. The low of fighting with Liv. I still wish I'd gotten Devon's number, although there's nothing that can be done about it now. But, his lips so close to my ear...I tingle all over recalling that moment.

And, well, the fight with Liv. I'm not going to say I enjoyed it, but it did clear the air. Why can't relationships be like what Liv and I have? Things are so different with significant others than they are with friends. With friends we forgive so easily. They screw up; they say the wrong thing; they are who they are and we accept them. Sure there may be a few fights along the way but they quickly blow over and the friendship continues even stronger. With relationships, they screw up; they say the wrong thing, and we straight up lose our shit. Fights happen, resentment grows, bitterness creeps in and the relationship starts to rot from within.

I wish Patrick and I had had more of what Liv and I have. One wrong sentence from Patrick and I'd be wounded for a day, sulking, and stomping off to "work on a project" rather than try to resolve the situation. I nursed a grudge while he watched

ESPN, ignoring that there was even a problem. I'd stew about how he didn't give me enough attention when, in fact, maybe I bear some of the blame, too. I could have been more forgiving, less defensive, more open. I could have gone to him instead of waiting for him to come to me.

Liv and I can argue, apologize, let it all go and come back together stronger. But with Patrick, well, we just drifted and fizzled until there was nothing left, like a helium balloon that, after the party ends, eventually lands on the ground, wilted and lifeless. Once my marriage flatlined it couldn't be resuscitated.

I can't deny that I'm content, calling my own shots, and living life on my own terms. I like being in the driver's seat and having my life revolve around Maddie and me. Maybe, when it comes right down to it, I don't really want to meet someone, so I've been self-sabotaging all this time. I don't want a man to come in and take over my life and time, telling me what to do, like Patrick always did. And I know I don't want to be doing any more laundry than I'm already doing! But good sex and daily conversation with an adult would be nice. *Really* nice.

What's weighing on me more though is Liv. I need to figure out what's going on with her. Not taking Ethan's call in the car is very suspicious.

Meanwhile, why not go to yoga tomorrow. I guess I'm ready for it. There's no hiding the remnants of the baby weight pooch that I haven't been able to get rid of, even though I've had thirteen years to try. But, my legs are still in good shape and my muffin top is nothing a cute tank won't hide.

I grab my phone and search LoftYoga to get a look at what we're getting ourselves into tomorrow. I don't want any more surprises like the "house party." I'm not against yoga, but I'm more of a Zumba girl. I have a hard time quieting my mind for meditation, plus, chanting gives me the giggles. One glance at their website proves what I had suspected—cult yoga! "Guru Stan" looks like a mash-up of an '80s rocker and Richard Simmons before he went into hiding. With that amount of hairspray and spandex, it looks like he's spent more time seeking nirvana in the Hollywood Hills than the Himalayans. I click on Testimonials and settle into the covers like I'm about to start a binge watch of *Designing Women*. There are tons of frou-frou quotes from Guru Stan's devotees with names like Lark Angel, Moonwater, Willow Rain, and my personal favorite, Skip Stone. They've all written glowing reviews about how Guru Stan has led them on a path to "the Xanadu of Astral Planes," how he "holds space for the enlightenment of the tribe" and that his "Chakra centering left me feeling a buzz stronger than my last Wu Tang concert." That last one is written by the one and only Skip Stone —I gotta go to class just to see this guy in person!

Suddenly, my FaceTime pops up with a call from Maddie. It's late for her to be calling and I answer immediately, worried that something is wrong.

"Hey, hon, everything okay?"

Her response is a combination of a groan, cry, and grimace. "Mom..."

Knowing the camp counselor would only give her phone access if it was important, I sit up trying to cover my concern with a soothing voice. "Honey, what's going on? Did something happen? Talk to me."

"Mom, I started my period," she sobs out.

I know she's had some anxiety about when she would get her period, but I'm surprised she seems this upset. Several of her friends have already started, so it's not like this is totally unexpected. In fact, I think she was kind of looking forward to it, in a way. Although, I can understand how being away at camp and away from me might make it a little harder.

"Honey, it's going to be okay. You knew this would happen at some point and remember I packed you some pads in your duffel bag just in case. Check the inside zipper pocket. That should get you through the night then you can go get some tampons from Nurse Joanne in the morning so you can still go swimming!" I say the last part with a bright smile, attempting to lighten her mood.

When she doesn't respond, but just looks into the phone with her scrunched up, tear-stained face, I reiterate, "It's going to be okay."

"What? I can't put in a tampon! No! No way!" She breaks into hysterical sobs. "Mom," she gasps. "You have to come get me! I don't want to be here anymore. And I don't want to talk to Nurse Jo about it either."

I realize this is a scary time for her. That whether she was ready or not, she's taking her first step into the unknown and confusing road to womanhood. Of course, she's feeling vulnerable. I've done my best to raise her to be strong, fearless and independent, which means that I can't bail her out every single time she asks.

"Maddie, I love you and I know you can handle this. You've known Nurse Jo since you were eight. She can help you out. This is a natural and normal thing to happen. We've talked about it before. If you don't want to use a tampon, that's totally fine, we can cross that bridge when you get home. You can wear pads in the meantime, and I'll put in a call to make sure you have enough for the rest of camp. No big deal."

I think I'm handling this okay. Tough love is hard and yes, there is a part of me that wants to go pick her up so we can eat ice cream in bed together and watch *Mean Girls* for the millionth time, but she's going to have her period every month for the next few decades and I don't want to make it a dramatic, or traumatic, thing.

Maddie, on the other hand, doesn't seem consoled by my words in the slightest.

"Mom, how am I supposed to swim? And what about the relay? What is everyone going to think when I'm not in the water? I can't wear a pad!" Her momentary indignation collapses into tears again. "You have to come pick me up. Now!"

"Maddie, honey, calm down. You can handle this. I know you can. You can wear a pad, and not swim, or see Nurse Jo about a tampon." With a supportive smile I add, "You've got this, I know you do."

But Maddie isn't having any of it. She angrily wipes the back of her hand across her nose and with red eyes stares pointedly into the phone. "You're abandoning me when I need you the most! You are a horrible mother!" And with that, she hangs up.

Dramatic much? I think. She's treating me like I'm Joan Crawford!

I send her a quick text reminding her that I love her and that I am always here for her. I see the bubble of typing on her end, but she doesn't end up sending a reply back to me. I *do* feel like a horrible mother for a moment, but I've prepared her for this moment the best I could.

With a sigh, I roll over and turn off the bedside light, waves of alternating guilt and resoluteness washing over me. I reach out for the phone and send a message to Nurse Jo to let her know what's happened. Jo has seen Maddie through five years of summer camps and all the insect bites, sprained ankles, and upset stomachs that entails. I trust her with Maddie and know that she'll help her out.

God, sometimes I can't believe how tough it is to be a mom. It's hard to know what the right thing to do is. Looks like I'm going to need some yoga and meditation more than I could have imagined.

Chapter Ten

DOWNWARD (HOT)DOG

LIV

WITH A YAWN AND HALF-CLOSED EYES, I FEEL AROUND blindly for my phone in the tangled folds of the comforter. 9:42 a.m. *Damn you, jet lag.* I've been in LA since Friday and I still feel like I've been hit by an eighteen wheeler. And yet, I'd rather feel this way than be slinking into the office for a Monday morning of forced cheerfulness.

I pad downstairs in a borrowed robe from the guest room closet. It's almost like I'm back in Bex's childhood home. I half expect to see her mom at the kitchen table, plumes of smoke streaming from her ebony cigarette holder.

Bex's chatter from the kitchen grows louder with each step. Standing in front of the kitchen counter, one hand resting on her hip, the other holding a cup of coffee, Bex is staring intently into the iPad on FaceTime with Maddie.

"So, are you sure you're okay? I knew you could handle this. Now go have fun." Bex gives a firm nod and smiles into the screen at Maddie.

I love to see Bex in mom mode. There's so much of her life that I've missed out on. She's bossy but in a good way, a firm hand at the helm on what has surely been choppy waters.

"What? Don't make that face," she says, and for a second I

96

think she is talking to me. She hands me a mug of coffee across the counter without even asking if I want one. The morning choreography of a real friend who knows I'm not exactly the rise and shine type, with or without jet lag.

"Thanks." I blow softly into the mug to cool the coffee. "Hi, Maddie." I peer into the screen, trying not to say what everyone says when they see a kid after a long time. But the resemblance to Bex *is* crazy and Maddie really *is* growing up.

"Hi, Miss Liv." Maddie waves at me.

"You know you can just call me Liv. Your mom and I aren't that old," I say, even though without makeup I'm sure I look about eighty-two. "How's camp?" I cringe at such a lame question. What do you talk to a thirteen-year-old about?

"It's okay. So, did you find Mom a boyfriend yet?" Maddie sounds only slightly enthused.

"Working on it."

"Cool. Okay, I gotta go."

"Hey," Bex calls out. "Don't forget to write Grandma a postcard. Not a text but an actual postcard, paper with a stamp. You know how much she loves hearing from you at camp," Bex gently commands. "And, I love you. I'm proud of you."

"Okay, I won't forget, jeez. Love you, too, Mom. Bye, Miss Liv," Maddie says it sarcastically but also sweetly, waving bye with a smile.

Bex takes a swallow of coffee. "That's about as much as I get these days, a two-minute call. Even when she's here at the house, it's like she has zero attention span for human interaction. But put a phone in her hands and she'll text to no end."

"She's a teenager. Remember how we were at that age? We were on the phone with each other all the time, and that was before cell phones. I guess it's not easy when they start to pull away. You're a wonderful mom." I feel pride bursting through my heart for Bex, thinking of the highs and lows she must go through on her own with Maddie.

"There are times when I sure don't feel like one."

"What's up? What happened?" I say in between sips of coffee.

"Maddie started her period last night."

"Wait, what? Wow. I can't believe she's growing up so quickly."

"She was in a state. Wanted me to come pick her up from camp. She was crying and everything. But we've talked about this moment a million times and I knew she could handle it on her own." Bex sounds as if she's trying to convince herself.

"It's okay. Remember how weird and scary it was getting your period for the first time? It's like all of a sudden we weren't in control of our bodies anymore."

"Please don't remind me. I still don't want to think about it. Even to this day I hate the sight of a volleyball," Bex says. "And Coach Bryant was way out of his depth. Told me to get cleaned up and get back on the court like a man. What a dinosaur."

"Look, I'm sure Maddie is in good hands at camp. Thankfully, things have evolved since we were in seventh grade volleyball with Coach Bryant. I think you're a badass mom, you know that." I walk around the kitchen island to give Bex a hug.

"Thanks, that means a lot. It really does." Bex gives me a quick hug back, then seems to shake off the emotional heaviness. "I'll tell you what, this badass mom could do with some more coffee. I feel like I have a hangover."

"I know. Me, too. It's a sad day when a few glasses of Chardonnay leave you feeling this way. I blame it on wandering around the estate sale in the sun and that damn traffic. But, you know what's good for a hangover? Bex's blueberry pancakes. With lots of bacon."

"I don't feel like cooking this morning." Bex scrunches up her nose.

"Pleeeeeaaaaase. You don't know how impossible it is to get good pancakes in London. Or American style bacon, for that matter."

"Come on, Maddie's away and I could use a break from being

a short-order cook. Don't make me cook when I don't have to. Besides, I don't have buttermilk. Here, eat this. It's healthier." Bex hands me a plate with a grapefruit cut in two.

I take a bite and recoil, overwhelmed by the bitter taste.

Bex takes a big scoop out of hers. "It's an acquired taste. Put some salt on it." She slides a little bowl of sea salt across to me.

"Salt? Don't you mean sugar?" I stare at her like she's lost her mind. "You've been living in California for too long."

"No, I mean salt. NPR did a story on it last year and the salt cuts the bitter flavor. Try it. You'll see," she says with the authority of Julia Child.

"Boo! I need carbs! Pancakes, please, please, please, make your pancakes." I sound like a grumpy four-year-old, but I don't care.

"There might be some bread in the pantry, just have some toast. Besides, we don't have time for pancakes. We're going to yoga."

"Really? So you're still up for it!"

Bex laughs. "Yup. We need to be there by eleven, so we should leave the house soon. Let's get moving."

Upstairs in the guest bedroom, I heave my suitcase onto the bed. I wasn't planning to work out during this trip, nor am I what you'd call a practicing yogi. I do my fair share of walking (more like running to keep up with the fast moving chaos of London sidewalks) but that's basically the extent of my fitness routine. The dreary weather, the pubs, the fact that most of the year people are clothed in layers upon layers. Winter coats can hide a lot of sins. And let's just say, I have a few winter coats.

I have no workout clothes on me but I did pack a swimsuit. Who doesn't bring a swimsuit to LA? I dig around and fish out the bikini top. I guess this triangle top will have to do for a sports bra, not like I need much support, sadly. I throw on an old T-shirt that I sleep in and pull on a pair of sweatpants. This is gonna have to do.

I hurry out of the room and nearly crash into Bex on the upstairs landing.

"Is that what you're wearing?" Bex looks at me in bemusement.

"Is that what *you're* wearing?" I eye Bex up and down. She has on a purple tank top, with straps that crisscross over her shoulders into an intricate pattern on the back. The matching purple leggings have a stripe of lace inlay running down the side of each leg. "Does everyone in LA have haute couture sportswear?"

"Oh, come on. I got it at the outlets. Does everyone in London have—well, I'm not sure how to describe your sportswear. 'I heart sports, birds, and beer'?"

I look down at my ensemble that's bordering more on grumpy old man loungewear than gym bunny. "What? I didn't bring any workout stuff. Isn't yoga supposed to be non-judgmental and non-materialistic? Besides, this T-shirt is really comfortable. It's an old thing Ethan wore for one of his friend's bachelor parties ages ago."

"Birdwatching and beer? That's what British guys do for bachelor parties? Sounds *crazy,*" Bex says.

"No, birds as in girls. You know, slang for girls."

"Hmm." Bex squints at me. "Well, these birds are going to be late for class. And does Ethan even let you in bed with that thing on?"

I know where she's going with that question, so I ignore it. And yes, I do sleep in it. Half the time Ethan comes and goes without even waking me up. He doesn't know what I am (or not) wearing in bed. It's an issue, to say the least.

We hustle into Bex's car and in her haste to put her phone in the hands-free holder, the entire contraption falls off the dashboard.

"Shit, here hold this." She hands me the phone as she backs out of the driveway. "I already typed in the address. It should be fine. Just tell me which way to go because the navigation voice thing isn't working."

We drive for a while through the heavy traffic of a late Monday morning, passing block after block of taco stands, nail salons, health food stores, and the occasional psychic storefront. All under the umbrella of that bright blue LA sky, fringed every now and then with towering palm trees.

"Are you sure this is the right way?" Bex says. "I thought it was somewhere off Olympic. Here, give me my phone, let me see." She reaches out to grab the phone.

"Hold on, hold on!" I squeal, pulling the phone close to me like a hand of cards I don't want anyone else to see. "Hands free, it's the law! We don't want to get pulled over. Um, okay, Olympic, where are we..." I try to switch back to the navigation map. I've been secretly looking through the dating apps on Bex's phone. She may have changed her passwords, but all's fair if she gives me her phone. "Yeah, left here and then take a right at the next light."

"Okaaaay." Bex turns up the radio and sings along to "You Can Go Your Own Way." "Yoga cult, here we come."

I quickly scroll back to Tinder and adjust Bex's criteria, lowering the age range to twenty-five. Bex had it at forty to fifty! I practically shout it out loud. Bex is in her thirties—thirty-nine still counts as thirties!—so she should definitely see what's on the market below forty. Why should it only be older guys who can date below their decade? Didn't Demi Moore make this a trend? And Kylie Minogue? *Okay, let's go shopping*, I think to myself as I look through the growing number of potential matches that are now coming through. I see a guy that kind of looks like Channing Tatum. Yes, that'll do just fine. I swipe to indicate interest and almost instantaneously the phone chimes with a loud ding.

"What's that?" Bex gives me a quizzical glance.

"Oh, I think the navigation alerts are working again. Keep going straight." I quickly mute her phone.

Whoever Jason aka Mr. Channing Tatum Look-alike is, he's definitely on his phone all the time. He's a match with Bex! I send a message.

Hi! You look hot.

God, I think to myself, how is this supposed to work. This is like sending notes back and forth in junior high. Should I write "circle yes or no"?

Immediately a response comes through,

Hi there. Drinks on Wednesday? Come to the upstairs bar at Glamour & State. 9:30.

I message back. *See you then and there!*

Maybe my wingwoman skills are improving. So that's Wednesday night sorted. Tuesday I have something in the works, and as for today, well, I think we can consider Monday morning yoga courtesy of Hot Biceps Alex a *Yes* even if it's not a date.

"What?" Bex catches me looking at her.

"Nothing, just feeling happy on a beautiful LA day with my best friend." I flick back to the navigation map. "I think we're almost there. Just up two more blocks on the right."

"Okay, I see it. Loft Yoga. Now, where are we going to find parking? Wish my car could do yoga and bend into a spot on the sidewalk. I don't see any street parking. Looks like it's going to be valet. There's only, like, five minutes until class starts."

"Valet? At a yoga studio? What kind of place is this?"

As we would soon find out, it's the kind of place with two-hundred-dollar yoga leggings and a menu of international bottled water. I wouldn't be surprised if they had a water sommelier on staff.

"Namaste and welcome to Loft Yoga," A slender, super toned

and tanned young woman purrs to Bex and me as we enter the airy reception space, almost bowled over by a wall of incense-laden air that smells like the lobby of a medicinal marijuana dispensary.

"Hi," Bex says with a fake smile.

"Wow, what's that smell?" I say, trying to decide if I love it or hate it.

"It's palo santo and sage. Isn't it beautiful? Totally chakra cleansing and it clears out all the negative energy. Not that we have negative energy here. Guru Stan provides such a positive space. We sell it for twenty-five dollars per stick if you'd like to clear your domestic dwelling." She displays an incense stick like it's an Oscar statue.

Bex's eyes bulge at the price and her fake smile gets even faker. "Um, that's nice, but no thank you. Alex left me two guest passes for the yoga class at eleven o'clock."

"Alex...such a pure soul." The woman sighs. "What's your name?"

"Summer," Bex says.

"Her name's Summer Moon Lotus," I step in and say somewhat loudly. There's no way I'm letting Bex out of this one. "And I'm her spiritual sister, Kitty Aura." I stifle a laugh and try to keep my face as deadpan as possible.

"Okay, here you go, Summer Moon. What a beautiful name. Who gifted it to you? I'm waiting for Guru Stan to gift me with a name. Until then, I'm Jennifer." She says it with such sadness that I almost feel sorry for her. "You and Kitty are booked in for Skip Stone's eleven a.m. Hot Karma Movement and Meditation. Guru Stan will join to lead the meditation."

"Hot?" Bex says.

"Yes, we have an infrared studio. It warms your body from the inside. You're going to feel amazing. It's not like other studios that just blow hot air, like you're under a blow dryer. This really gets into your body, your soul. You will feel like you're glowing," Jennifer enthuses in her airy voice.

"Glowing like an ember in hell," I say under my breath to Bex.

"I didn't know it was hot yoga. That seems a little intense for me." Bex takes two steps back toward the door.

"Yes, we didn't know it was oven yoga. Please tell Alex thank you from us." I think to myself that we could be at a diner eating pancakes in less than fifteen minutes.

"Are you sure? Infrared heat improves skin tone and also promotes weight loss," Jennifer says.

"Okay!" Bex and I quickly say at the same time, then laugh. Well, what have we got to lose—a few pounds and a few wrinkles? I guess it would be good to sweat out the wine from yesterday, and the G and Ts from Saturday.

"Here are your mats, a complimentary perspiration towel and my blessings for a good class. If you'd like another towel, it's five dollars. A vegan lunch will be served after meditation. Guru Stan encourages all of his devotees to embrace the vegan path."

Bex leans in to whisper to me as we make our way up to the studio. "A perspiration towel! Vegan lunch? Oh boy, this is gonna be fun."

"Hey, at least you look hot before we get hot." I playfully pull on the strap of her tank top. "Skip Stone? Sounds like a sexy construction worker on a soap opera."

———————————◗•◖———————————

"Breathe in to the count of four, breathe out to the count of four. Expel anything in your life that you don't want. Breathe in two...three...four. Out...two...three...four. Now longer. Six counts in, six counts out. You're entering a new world of consciousness with each breath."

In the midst of Skip's breathing instructions, he motions to Bex and me as we pause tentatively in the doorway. The class is packed. If parking a car in LA is hard, then parking a yoga mat is even harder. *Maybe we will be eating pancakes soon, after all*, I think optimistically. He signals that we should come up to the front of the studio and put our mats down beside his. We both shake our heads and survey the studio, hoping that miraculously some space will have opened up, preferably at the back.

There's one space open, I nudge Bex to go for it and indicate that I'll wait in the lobby. She looks at me with a killer "don't you even think about it" stare.

"Summer Lotus! You made it! What's up, girl?" Alex whispers as he squeezes past us with a wink. "Glad you two are here. Don't worry, Skip won't bite. Go on up to the front."

In resignation, we carefully tiptoe our way to the front of the class, past row after row of toned bodies lying on their mats, breathing intensely and apparently releasing toxins. Does that mean we're inhaling them? I hold my breath until we make it to the front of the studio.

We unfurl our mats and get into position, basically the position I get into when I crash into bed after a night of partying. Arms out to the side, hands facing upward in a "God forgive me pose," legs straight out, eyes closed. Hmm, I could get used to this. *Except*, I think to myself as if noticing it for the first time since we walked into the room, *it's hot*. I mean really hot. I don't know what infrared is, but it's at least the third circle of Dante's Hell. I'm already beginning to sweat and see that the "perspiration towel" is more like a washcloth. I'm going to need something the size of an industrial tarp to wipe up my sweat.

But if Skip is an endorsement for this yoga path, then maybe I should just feel the flow. He's lean and muscled like a lightweight boxer, while the deep tan and bleach blond dreads make him appear more surfer than yogi. Bex is checking him out too.

Maybe I could get Ethan to do yoga? Would it help us to align our chakras, whatever that means. If I couldn't get him to stick to therapy, then I know there's a snowball's chance in hell of us going to a yoga class together, but I still think it might be fun. Something totally different for us to do together. Something that's not networking at one of his work cocktail events.

As Skip gradually builds up the pace of the class and we move through more poses, I'm impressed by Bex. She's fit and barely seems to be sweating. It's hard to tell she's even had a kid. Sure, she has a little bit of flab around her waist but at our age don't we all. And her purple ensemble really does look good. Meanwhile, I peel off my T-shirt, which has been sweatily hanging on me like I've just taken a not-so-refreshing dip in the pool. The sweatpants are a problem, and I'm desperately trying to remember what underwear I have on in case they can pass as yoga bottoms. I look around the class and can't believe what I'm seeing. Every tight and toned fame seeker in town must be here, and they're all an eleven out of ten. In the midst of all this athletic exhibitionism, I feel like a turtle stripped of its shell.

While suffering through a downward dog stretch, I see a curtain of flowing blond locks on the mat behind us. *This is hot yoga, put the hair extensions away!* I think to myself. Beside blondie, two bro types, who look like aspiring *Men's Health* cover models, are trying to topple each other over during a balancing pose. Meanwhile, I roll my soggy sweatpants up around my knees.

"And one long exhale through the mouth. Sigh everything out. One, two, three. Aaaaahhhhhhhh." I ran out of breath thirty seconds ago but the people around me continue to drone on with their aaaahhhh. The last remaining "ahh-er" finishes and smiles like he just received a medal of honor when Skip commands, "And relax into savasana."

Everyone begins to unfold back onto their mats, lying down as they were in the beginning of class. I look around, not knowing what savasana means, then gladly relax as I see it's the "passed out drunk" pose from the very beginning of class. Skip walks around the mats, stopping every now and then to adjust someone's leg or arm. He kneels over Bex and places his hands on her shoulders, right near her collarbones and presses gently, then brushes his hands down her arms. I thought he was finished but no. He holds her head in his hands and slowly moves it from side to side.

"There's so much tension in this life. Let it all roll away. Roll away. Open yourself to peace, to love." Is Skip Stone hitting on Bex? From that angle he's got a clear view down her tank top. Maybe this was a date after all, but with someone other than we thought. I smirk to myself as Bex is sending me SOS eyes.

The door to the studio opens and a whiff of that marijuana/rainforest incense comes pouring in. Could this be the infamous Guru Stan? The class seems to silently rouse itself with anticipation and reverence. People move their mats closer to the front of the studio. Some have brought little pillows to sit on and proceed to sit cross-legged, straight backs in an exaggerated state of attention. Bex and I are surrounded, caught in a sea of searching souls at a Hollywood yoga studio.

As he enters the studio, he runs his hands over his scalp and tightens his one-inch ponytail. "Namaste and welcome to the beginning of enlightenment. It will always be a beginning. Enlightenment is something you will never know you've achieved. The journey *is* the enlightenment." Guru Stan says this with the seriousness of an undertaker while looking like a lost, balding member of Kajagoogoo.

"Thank you for leading the class, Skip. I sense we have some new energy here today. Welcome." Guru Stan nods to Bex and me, keeping his eyes on Bex as Skip spritzes scented rose water around her.

I'm seriously starting to feel dizzy, like I'm hallucinating, the hot air and heavy incense going to my head. I better leave this infrared heat a size four and without one wrinkle on my face because this is torture. My perspiration towel and T-shirt are balled up in a wet pile at the top of my mat, and the bikini top that's a sorry excuse for a sports bra is itching like hell. Bex meanwhile still looks fresh. Maybe I should think about buying some proper sportswear after all.

"Now, everyone, close your eyes. Embrace the release of letting go." Guru Stan waves his hand as if it is a magic wand. I can't help but close my eyes.

"Everyone, tap into the deep well of your subconsciousness. Release the first word that comes to your mind."

Amidst a chorus of "Love," "Harmony," and "Peace," I blurt out "Bacon!" I clasp my hand over my mouth. I can't believe I just said that out loud. The girl with the blond mane of extensions actually starts to move her mat away from me. Guru Stan looks physically repulsed, and out of the corner of my eye I see that other students are shaking their heads in disappointment. Skip looks at Bex, then me, then back at Bex with a confused look on his face as if he's been betrayed.

Without even having to say a word to each other, Bex and I pick up our things and make our way out of the studio, trying to disappear in an awkward series of backward steps. We've hardly closed the studio door behind us when we both burst out laughing. Making a fast escape, we head downstairs and almost make it out of reception.

"Are you okay?" Jennifer says. "Guru Stan's meditation lasts for one more hour. The vegan buffet hasn't even been set up yet. Do you want to try some dried rosemary kale? It's got roasted chia seeds. We sell them for eight fifty a box..." Her voice fades as we race out to Bex's car, that even without air-conditioning feels like an ice box compared to the hot yoga studio.

———————◆•◆———————

"ONE WITH EXTRA BACON!" Bex leans into the counter. "And a side of chili fries and onion rings. Oh, and two cokes please. Thank you!" We couldn't have made it to Pink's faster than we did. We were practically levitating through traffic. A glorious escape!

"See what happens when you don't make me pancakes?"

"Well, this still counts as carbs. Namaste." Bex takes a huge bite of her chili cheese dog.

"Bon appetite." *Damn, this hot dog tastes good.* "Do you ever think about becoming vegetarian? Or vegan?"

"Sometimes. I tried being vegetarian for a few months. Some of Maddie's friends are vegan. I do admire them for being so disciplined and conscientious at such a young age. But no, come on, we grew up in Tennessee. I'm not sure I could live without bar-b-que!"

"I suppose we'll have to try Guru Stan's vegan brunch another time. Hey, on Wednesday night I want to check out this place called Glamour & State. Have you heard of it?" I say, in between a bite of my extra bacon hotdog, hoping that my suggestion sounds casual.

"You'll fit right in. You look really glamorous right now." Bex points to sauerkraut that's dripping down my face. "How do you know about Glamour & State? It opened like a month ago."

"Uh, I read about it in a *Conde Nast* travel blog. Isn't it supposed to be really trendy? I need a bit of Hollywood glamour. I'm a tourist, you know." I didn't read it in a *Conde Nast* travel blog, and I have no idea if it's trendy or not. But if Jason the Channing Tatum Look-Alike wants to meet Bex there on Wednesday night, then it's the trendiest joint in town. Besides, what's a little white lie to help out a friend?

"How could I say no?" Bex says. "To Bacon!" We clink our Coke cans and take a swig.

Chapter Eleven

WHO WANTS TO DATE A MILLIONAIRE?

BEX

"Liv! Look what I bought!" I toss my keys down on the kitchen counter and wave a pair of quarters in the air.

"Scratchers? Yes!" Liv eagerly reaches out for one. "I have a good feeling about this."

Liv has been doing scratchers for as long as I've known her, and yet she still isn't a millionaire. She told me she won a hundred dollars on a Lucky Fortune once, but I have my doubts.

I sit down at the table across from her and dramatically fan out the scratchers like a magician preparing a card trick, six in total, three for her and three for me. "You go first. You may choose three, and only three, so choose wisely."

Liv proceeds to do her usual song and dance of flipping the scratchers over, holding them up to the light as if there is a chance she might see something, and chanting "Cungee, Cungee, Cungee" over and over.

Still perplexed by this strange ritual I know by heart, I ask for the fiftieth time, "Liv, what the hell does *Cungee* mean and why do you insist on repeating it? It drives me crazy. I've never heard anything more ridiculous."

She stops me with a look. "Please. You know it was my great

aunt Maeve's good luck chant. She always won at bingo. If it worked for her why, won't it work for me?"

Not seeing the correlation between scratchers and bingo, I shake my head and mutter, "Why not?" and grab a quarter to begin scratching at Liv's cast off "loser" cards. After all this time, one of us is bound to win something, right? I'd run out earlier this morning to pick up some milk for coffee, and when I saw the colorful rolls of scratchers next to the cash register at 7-Eleven, I thought *What the hell*. I knew it'd give Liv a thrill. Back in Atlanta, after rent was paid, we'd spend our last few dollars on scratchers hoping for a miracle. Liv would only ever buy them at 7-Eleven—she was convinced that was *the* place to buy them if you wanted to win.

"Hey," I say, looking to Liv mid-scratch, "if either of us wins, we split it fifty-fifty. You in?"

Scratching away at her card, she grunts, "Yup." Then she looks up and stops mid-scratch, her voice a bit unsure, "Actually, it's funny you bought these because I wasn't sure how to tell you this..."

I narrow my eyes, trying to guess what she's about to say. Either she's already won the lottery, or she's got something up her sleeve I'm not going to like. Judging by the guilty look on her face, my money's on the latter.

"You know that show? The one with that woman, Stella Bancock who runs the—"

"The dating service?" I say in disgust while Liv nods slowly. "What. Did. You. Do?" I ask in staccato.

Liv bites her lip like she can't quite bring herself to speak. I don't blame her.

"Did you sign me up for a reality TV show?" My screech increasing in volume and panic.

She rolls her eyes as if I've just said the stupidest thing ever. "No! Come on! I would never do that. You know I hate that crap," says the woman who I know is secretly addicted to *The Real Housewives of Atlanta*.

"Just tell me what you did. You're starting to scare me." Liv's response is a mocking "who me?" look. "I'm dead serious here, Liv. What's going on?" My patience is wearing thin.

Liv sounds a little too upbeat. "I signed you up for Stella's matchmaking service!" I protest, but she keeps talking, just louder. "Don't worry, it was free to sign you up since you're an *attractive single woman*. It's the millionaire men who have to pay a small fortune to Stella."

Like the money is what I'm most worried about! I'm too flabbergasted to speak. I thought Liv couldn't top herself after the "house party" but apparently I was wrong. She is the wingwoman from hell.

"Liv, in the future, don't sign me up for things where single women get in for free!" I throw my hands up in exasperation. "Did you learn nothing from the Chandace experience?"

"Relax, it's no big deal. I don't see how it's any different from dating apps you've already been on. You have your first date tonight at six p.m. with Brad at The Pearl and The Girl." Liv crosses her arms and smiles like she's just delivered amazing news. Which she kind of has. I've been dying to go to The Pearl and The Girl and have never had the opportunity, or the money. The food is supposed to be stellar and the LA Times ranked it as having the best cocktails in the city. But Liv doesn't need to know it's been on my culinary bucket list. I can't let her get away with this that easily.

I dive in. "First off, that Stella woman is batshit crazy. I know reality TV isn't real, but if she's half as crazy as she is on TV, then we have a problem. Secondly, I already told you, I don't care about dating someone with money. Hello! Have we met?" I shake my hand in bewilderment. "This whole thing makes me feel like a piece of meat, and frankly, I'm a little shocked you'd go there."

Liv has pushed beyond my limits on this one. Liv has always been self-conscious about the financial struggles her family had when she was growing up. But she's never seemed so preoccupied with money and status as she seems now. Ever since she moved to London with Ethan, it's gotten worse. Things like this make me feel like I don't even know who she is anymore. Where are her priorities?

She lets out a hard sigh. "Bex, I came here to leave no stone unturned. If you're gonna fall in love, why not do it with someone rich? You just spent thirty dollars on scratchers, for God's sake. So don't tell me that you wouldn't mind having money."

Well, she isn't totally wrong, I mean, who wouldn't want to win the lottery. But I am *not* a gold digger. This big bucks Brad is probably just looking for an obedient piece of arm candy. What kind of guy wants to date a woman who's interested in him for his money? Despite my reservations about it all, I know Liv won't let me say no and I don't want to get into another fight with her. And I can't deny that there's a little part of me that's curious and a bigger part of me that wants to be wined and dined at The Pearl and the Girl.

"Fine. One date with Stella's service. That's all I'm gonna give you on this one. After tonight, you remove me from the site and we never speak of it again. Deal?"

Liv smiles in pure triumph. "Deal."

"So did you win anything?" I blow away the silvery shavings off my scratchers.

"No. Where did you buy these from?" she asks suspiciously. "Did you get them from the gas station?"

"They're from 7-Eleven," I say in an "I told you so" voice.

"Humph." Liv shrugs her shoulders. "That's weird. Well, it doesn't matter. We might just end up millionaires tonight anyway!"

I roll my eyes. Why do I let her get away with these schemes?

Liv is sprawled out on my bed watching me put on my makeup. Women are funny that way; we seem to love watching each other put on makeup, looking to see how we do things differently, if someone has a special trick to achieve the perfect cat eye. As I'm finishing my eyeliner flick I call out, "Liv, what do we know about Brad? Show me everything Stella sent over. I want pics, bio, everything."

Liv laughs uneasily, which means she's going to drop another bomb on me.

"Uh, well, that's the thing about Stella's service. She doesn't send any photos, just a short bio, not even a last name. She tries to make things as un-google-able as possible. Keeping it old-school so it's about the immediate chemistry and connection."

"And the money," I grumble as I comb my eyelashes to remove a few clumps. I need some new mascara. I feel like I've been using this same pink and green tube of Maybelline since my twenties. But then, why am I even caring about how I look for this date? "No pics, huh? That doesn't leave me with a very optimistic feeling. What does his bio say?" I guess Stella's philosophy is when you're dating a millionaire, *his* looks don't matter.

Liv scrolls through her phone to find Stella's email with the information on Brad. She reads out loud as I finish up my final touches. "Brad B. is originally from Seminole, Oklahoma. He is the heir to a successful oil drilling company that's been in his family for generations. He's often in California for business and recently opened a West Coast office. Brad B. enjoys golf, documentaries, and Tex-Mex."

I put down my powder brush to give Liv a slow two-clap

applause for her rousing delivery of the most boring bio I've ever heard. But he does like Tex-Mex. And I never say no to queso, so at least we have that in common.

I clear my throat. "Is that the best Stella can do? Jeez. I was hoping this would be more exciting. Like, a movie producer or something. Have you tried looking for him on Facebook?"

"Can't! I told you Stella doesn't give out last names. How am I supposed to find a 'Brad' on Facebook? It's a mystery, an old-school blind date. Come on, it's fun!" She's clapping her hands like one of those performing sea lions at Sea World, which is exactly how this date is making me feel.

———— •●• ————

I'm walking in my three-inch heels at a fairly brisk pace as I review the game plan in my head. I told Liv on the drive over that I was only going through with this if she promised to tag along and rescue me if things got weird. I mean, we don't know anything about this guy and after watching a rerun of Stella's show, my faith in her is dismally low, as are my expectations for this date.

I check myself out one last time in the reflection of the restaurant glass, which I know is lame, but I can't help myself. I still want to look good, even if this is one big joke. The red dress I've accessorized with a vintage bag looks sexy and put together, but not like I'm trying too hard. I don't usually use this bag because it's got a rock hard resin shell and is on the small side, kind of like a pearlized crystal ball, but Liv thought it was perfect. I take a deep breath to remind myself that I'm *not* like those women on *Who Wants to Date a Millionaire!*.

115

I slow down as I approach the restaurant entrance and look around hesitantly for what I imagine a millionaire who'd use a dating service would look like: an old, fat, white guy with bad plastic surgery who's channeling the swagger of a thirty-year-old despite his eighty-year-old chicken neck. I spot just the man as he feebly tosses the keys of his sparkling white Bentley to the valet. I smile at him, swallowing the lump that's suddenly risen in my throat, when suddenly from the open doorway of the restaurant, I hear a deep, smooth voice call out, "Rebecca?"

I stop in my tracks, looking around to see who's calling my name. When I hear it a second time, I walk into the restaurant and see a fairly attractive man smiling and waving at me as if we're old friends. *Maybe we went to high school together?* I glance around the restaurant one last time to make sure he's actually addressing me and when he smiles and nods, I head in his direction.

Assuming this is *the* Brad B., I'm relieved to see he's mid-forties, around five foot ten, not too heavy, almost athletic, with a full head of hair (a plus). Then not so relieved to see that he's wearing an ugly navy and white gingham shirt (a negative—screams preppy good ole boy) paired with the most ridiculous fishing vest I've ever seen. I can't imagine what he keeps in all of those pockets! I inwardly scold myself to not be so judgy. I can overlook bad fashion choices—things like that are fixable. His smile and youthful energy make me feel more optimistic, despite my doubts about this whole evening.

I extend my hand. "You must be Brad. I'm Rebecca. But, everyone calls me Bex for short."

He laughs good-naturedly and says in a subtle Okie accent, "Bex! No wonder you looked confused when I called your name. I'm sorry if that was awkward. Stella told me Rebecca, so..." he tapers off and I can tell he's embarrassed.

Perching on a high-backed chair at the posh bar, I jump in to save him because it's not his fault he called the wrong name. I guess Stella's bio of me was just as short, although there was clearly a picture of me included.

"Don't worry about it, Brad." And then I give him a playful look. "You don't go by Bra for short, do you?" *What am I saying? Why do I feel so nervous?* Fortunately, for me, Brad laughs off my weak joke and hands me the menu.

"Wow, it all looks delicious. I want to order one of everything." I try not to drool looking at the menu. I absolutely go weak in the knees for Cajun food.

The bartender asks if we'd like to dine at the bar and Brad and I both answer at the same time, "Sure!" We look at each other and laugh.

"Did you have a reservation for a table? I'll tell the hostess to cancel it and that you'll be dining at the bar." The bartender has a casual, friendly style which puts me at ease.

"Thanks, that'd be great. Yes, the reservation is under the name Brad Blunderwood."

Okay, so Blunderwood isn't exactly the sexiest last name and Bex Ophelia Blunderwood would leave me as B.O.B. or technically R.O.B...but let's not get ahead of ourselves.

"We'll start with a dozen oysters on the half shell and the grilled blackened alligator appetizer. Does that sound all right with you, Bex?" I nod and relax back into my chair. We take a moment to discuss the cocktail menu, which is even better than I hoped for, and as Brad continues his easy chatter with the bartender about our food choices, I see Liv saunter into the restaurant as planned. She's trying to look inconspicuous, but that's nearly impossible for Liv. I give her credit for trying, but wearing sunglasses inside isn't helping her attempt at incognito. As she takes a seat on the other side of the bar I can tell she's looking to me for a sign. I give her a subtle nod and smile to let her know everything is A-OK. I'm only ten minutes into this date but I actually have a good feeling. Maybe it's just the relief that he's not eighty, but Brad is so much better than I expected.

We're polishing off our first round of Hurricane Camilles (which I imagine are as strong as the real one) and finishing up the last of the oysters when I get a text alert. I know it's Liv, because this was part of The Plan, so I excuse myself to the ladies'.

I waltz into the bathroom with a sly grin on my face and Liv practically jumps me as soon as the door shuts behind me.

"You little minx! You *like* him!" she says in a singsong voice.

"I know this is crazy and totally not what I was expecting. But, I do!" My excitement is contagious seeing how Liv's smile grows as wide as mine. I don't know if she looks so happy because she's happy for me or if it's because she's about to burst out with an "I told you so," but it doesn't matter. I *do* feel good.

"Okay, give me all the deets and make it quick. I'm dying to know! And, PS, why is he wearing a fishing vest? Where's the canoe?" She blurts all of that out in one breathless stream of consciousness.

"Right? I know. We can work on that. No biggie." I wave the fishing vest issue away as if it were a bad smell. "Okay, so, his name is Brad Blunderwood."

Liv cringes slightly.

"I know, you don't have to say it. He travels a bunch and owns a boat in Marina. He doesn't have any kids and, uh, I don't know...What else? I don't know. We've just been chitchatting. He's a super nice guy with a great sense of humor and a weird last name! But, I like him. Time for the main course!"

Liv looks at me like she has no idea what I'm talking about. "What's the main course?"

"Crawfish étouffée, what else would it be!" I slide past her to push open the bathroom door, then look back over my shoulder to give her an over-the-top wink. "And there may even be dessert!"

So, when I said dessert, I really *was* talking about Key lime pie. But after Brad paid the bill and invited me across the street to see the view from his penthouse suite at the new swanky Spade Hotel, I couldn't resist, thinking that a different kind of dessert might be in store.

I didn't want to tell Liv I was going to his room, so when I texted her to let her know I was hopping over to "the rooftop" at the Spade to watch the sunset, she responded immediately.

Liv: 3 drink rule!

Me: Yep. Only had 2. Will be 30 min tops.

We enter Brad's luxurious suite and I take a look around. I don't like this kind of glossy contemporary furniture, but I recognize the quality. No expense has been spared in this room —it must cost a fortune. Afraid I might break the glass coffee table with my lipstick-carrying mini bowling ball of a purse, I gently place it and my phone down on the lacquered credenza.

With a look of lust in his eyes, Brad grabs my hand and leads me out to the balcony to admire the sweeping view. It's a stunningly clear evening and there's a glimmer of the ocean and the buildings of Century City in the distance. *Maybe dating a millionaire isn't a bad idea after all!* As that thought crosses my mind, Brad wraps his arms around my waist and the pockets of his vest press against my back. Okay, well, I could do without that reminder of his sartorial (non)sense but still lean back into him, resting my head on his left shoulder and breathe in the scent of his cologne as we bask in the orange glow of the sunset. *Is that Stetson cologne?* I think to myself. Well, we've got to work on the clothing and the cologne (he smells like 1991!). My mental shopping list is growing longer.

"I really like you, Bex. There's nowhere else I'd rather be than right here with you, right now," Brad whispers in my ear. There might as well be a halo hanging over this man's head because he's saying everything right.

"I like you too, Brad." My voice comes out slow and whispery like I'm auditioning to be a phone sex operator. This whole scene feels so surreal. Am I just getting swept up in the glamour of it? But dinner felt so easy and relaxed. I might actually like this man.

I slowly turn around, looking up at the salt and pepper scruff on his face as Brad pulls me in gently for a kiss. His lips are warm and soft on mine, and I exhale into him, reveling in his caress. God, it's been so long since I've done this. He's a great kisser, alternating between softness and a rough urgency that has my knees weak and wanting more. Feeling bold, I playfully push him back into the suite's living room with an eagerness I haven't felt in years. As my fingers slide down to his belt buckle and our feet are shuffling on the thick pile rug, my mind is reeling. *Does he have condoms in any of those pockets? What underwear am I wearing and are they still wet from when I sneeze/peed—sneed at the bar? Ahh, the glamorous side effects of childbirth.* I try to calculate the time I've been up in Brad's suite, knowing that Liv is expecting me in about fifteen minutes and she'll go completely insane if I'm not back at the restaurant on time. But I *like* Brad. He's such a gentleman—kind, attentive, sweet. Maybe it's time I stepped off this frozen tundra that is my sex life and got tropical.

Panting with need, I whisper, "Brad, I don't have a condom. Do you?"

He kisses me deeply, looks into my eyes and responds in a breathy low rumble. "No, but I'm fine with a blow job."

Huh. Hold on, what...? He's fine with a blow job? Admittedly, that is not the most romantic thing I've ever heard, and is totally presumptuous, but honestly, I'm kind of relieved. I was never really the type to have sex on the first date. But I do like Brad enough that a blow job isn't an insane idea. Patrick always told me I was talented at that particular skill, so what the hell, let's see if I've still got it.

Brad kisses my neck hungrily as I lower his zipper one millimeter at a time. He groans into my shoulder and I smile with the knowledge that I'm turning him on so much. I slowly lower myself onto my knees and pull his pants down his legs as he plops down, none too gracefully, on the gray couch, navy boxers still covering his manly parts. I scoot my knees over the rough pile to wedge myself between his legs, when Brad looks down at me, his voice heavy with raw lust. "Goddamn, you are beautiful."

I feel a sense of empowerment that I haven't felt in years. Yes, I *am* the one on the giving end, but I'm overcome by a feeling of confidence as I control this man with his pants around his ankles and his shirt disheveled in lust. I'm in the driver's seat and he's the willing passenger I'm going to take on a wild ride.

My mouth watering in anticipation, I reach toward him, high on the control I have over him as my fingers disappear into the front seam of his boxers. My body is singing like Marvin Gaye, soulful and willful, when suddenly the needle scratches off the record in my head...because what I've grabbed can only be described as a *hot dog*. Long, thin, and blotchy red. Trying to shake off thoughts of yesterday's lunch at Pink's, my sexy meter dials back more than a few notches and I take a moment to gather my quickly fading enthusiasm. Those feelings I had just moments ago, Confidence and Empowerment, are now running down the hall screaming. Maybe I'm not as hungry as I thought...

Pulling me back into the moment, Brad reaches down and strokes my cheek with his thumb and gazes deep into my eyes. Shit. *Come on, Bex, you can't make him feel bad because he has a frankfurter for a penis!* It's not what you have, but how you use it, right? I can't give this genuinely nice man a complex because his package resembles Oscar Mayer rather than something I'd buy at a Bavarian meat market! He can't help it. It's the lottery of life.

121

Resolutely, I lick my lips and descend, closing my eyes and parting my lips when...

DING! My phone on the credenza chimes loudly.

"Do you need to get that?" Brad opens his eyes with concern.

"No, it's fine," I mumble, determined to stay in the sexy zone.

With relief, Brad drops his head back on the couch cushion. I begin my second approach only stopping for a moment when I breathe in his aroma of sour beer. I can't help feeling disappointed. Why can't this be like the romance novels I beach read where men smell like cedar and musk after chopping wood shirtless? Christian Grey he is not. Oh well...

I touch the edge of my tongue to him when...

DING! My phone chimes again, which gives me mild "mom anxiety." What if it's Maddie having another meltdown? But, no, she said on FaceTime that she had it all handled. Anyway, whoever it is, I'm sure they can wait a few minutes.

Licking my lips a final time I...

DING!

DING!

DING!

DING!

Okay, that is *definitely* Liv. Only she would send me back-to-back texts that sound like church bells, making me momentarily question my morality. Not wanting to be deterred from breaking my sexual drought—regardless of how unsexy it's all turning out to be—my sense of urgency increases with each *DING!* and I'm even more determined to give Brad the blow job of his life. This isn't about him anymore, this is about me. I'm bringing sexy back, damn it!

My lips close for the first time over Oscar and with one smooth plunge, Brad jerks and moans, he grabs his swollen wiener with his right hand and showers his boxers before I even have a chance to grasp the reality of what just happened. I pull back in surprise and confusion.

"Baby, that was incredible." Brad grunts.

I stare wide-eyed at his lap as Oscar bends over his hand, ready for a nap.

"I'm just gonna..." I wave my hand toward the en suite bathroom and hear my knees creak as I push myself to standing.

Still in my heels, I stand facing myself in the bathroom mirror wondering what the hell just happened. I turn on the hot water and look for a clean washcloth to wipe my face. Did I even give a blow job? Does that count as anything? And, jeez, poor Brad must have a premature ejaculation problem. That blows. Literally.

There's a tube of toothpaste on the counter so I briskly finger brush my teeth. Is this what it's come down to, middle age dating? I look at my knees, red with indentions from the carpet like I've been kneeling on gravel. This wasn't how I thought my first ride back at the rodeo would be. Not nearly as sexy or gratifying as I'd imagined it. *Not how it would have been with Devon...*

"Bex, your phone is blowing up!" Brad calls out with a worried tone, interrupting my Devon daydream.

Exiting the bathroom I retrieve my phone to I see I have about ten texts from Liv. A string of "NOW" "WHERE ARE YOU" and "9-1-1" with a series of question marks and exclamation points. I still have two minutes to spare, so I don't know what she's going on about. I'm a big girl.

"Is everything all right?" Brad looks at me with concern, his eyes droopy with satiated lust, his pants still half off.

"Yeah, fine. Should we head down?" I grab my purse and walk toward the door.

"Sure. Let's grab one more cocktail. This has been a great date and I have a feeling it's the first of more to come!" He says this with such honest enthusiasm as he's rushing to pull up his pants that I can't help but like the guy despite his lack of thunder down under. Maybe it's just first date nerves?

My phone dings a final time and as I draw my gaze away from Brad's brown eyes I see...a mug shot of Brad looking like he got hit by a truck at a roadside boiled peanut stand in Jackson, Mississippi.

"Bex! There you are! Come over here!" Liv calls out to me in the lobby of the Spade, the echo of her heels tapping across the shiny floor with military efficiency. She looks distressed and disturbed.

I look awkwardly at Brad, still unsure what to make of the last text from Liv. I gesture from Brad to Liv making introductions. "Brad, this is my friend Liv. Liv, this is..."

"I need you. Now." She glares at Brad so harshly that I blush with embarrassment. Brad grins warmly at us as Liv drags me toward a semi-private alcove in the hotel lobby.

Confused, I hover over Liv's cell phone as she rapidly fills me in on the details of Mr. Blunderwood. "So far I've found five mug shots of him from different states. He has warrants out for his arrest for credit card fraud, check fraud, embezzlement, two DUIs, and there appears to be multiple lawsuits against him and his company. There's even a blog started by some lady in Oklahoma who says he conned her out of her land then put oil wells on it, and there are about eight people who say it's happened to them too! He is not a good guy." Liv is out of breath and I'm instantly out of hope.

I slide down the wall and sit on the floor with my head in my hands and let the tears fall freely. I am such an idiot! I should have known this was too good to be true. I just wanted something good. I just wanted to feel sexy. To meet a nice guy who laughed easily and looked at me like I was special. But here I am, blinded by a swindler who's a convict with a record as long as my last CVS receipt. Liv sits down next to me and puts her arm around my shoulders. Her gesture is comforting and I lean into her as I sob out quietly, "I gave that motherfucker a blow job." I wipe the snot trailing from my nose and rub it onto my red dress.

Liv tries to soothe me. "It's ok, honey. It's no big deal..."

"Literally." I groan. "It was literally *not* a big deal."

Liv leans in and gives me a tighter hug but then pulls back. "Ugh, you smell like the floor of a brewery."

I cry even harder.

Liv's voice rises with vengeance. "This is on Stella. Does she have interns doing her background checks? Is she even doing background checks? I'm calling TMZ on her ass. They'll eat this up."

I look at her through my tears. Liv is nuts and I love her for it, but I feel too defeated to even laugh about this right now.

She digs a wad of tissues out of her purse. "Don't ruin your dress! Come on, get up. Pull yourself together and don't let him see you cry." As she grabs my elbow and hauls me up off the floor, I tense at the sound of approaching footsteps.

"Is everything okay over there, ladies?" Brad's voice now just sounds fake and overly friendly. What used to appear as genuine I now see as smarmy and sinister.

I glare at him with the strength of a thousand daggers, and Liv responds with a knowing smile. "We were just looking at a few of photos of you. Looks like wearing that fishing vest isn't the only crime you've committed!" She flashes the screen of her phone his way and he gasps, taking a step back, confronted with one of his own mug shots.

I'm looking at a man who tricked me into believing a relationship, or at least dating, might be possible again. Who made me think that a future might be something I was ready to tackle. Who made me want to break out of my shell and feel sexy again. And it was all one big fraud.

What an asshole. And that's apart from all the other bad shit he's done to so many other people.

I'm so mad I could spit. I could curse. I could scream at the top of my lungs! But I don't do any of those things. I look down at my purse and smile, inwardly thanking Liv for convincing me to bring it tonight. Then I swing it round in a circle like I'm Conan the Barbarian and aim straight for Little Oscar and the Peanut Twins.

Chapter Twelve

ENCORE COUTURE

LIV

"WELL, HERE WE ARE AGAIN. TWO MIDDLE-AGED WOMEN OUT for brunch. I refuse to talk any more about last night, or about dating. I'm over it." Bex takes a gulp of her Bloody Mary.

"Come on, we are not middle-aged. And what's so bad about brunch?" I can see she's still in shock about what happened with Brad, even though she's putting on a strong game face. That she ordered a Bloody Mary instead of a mimosa says it all.

"Look, it could have been worse," I continue in a weak attempt to cheer her up. How do you console a friend who went out on a blind date with a felon wanted in multiple states? "You totally dodged that bullet, um, bait. Sorry, couldn't help that one. I guess his outfit should have been a sign! What sane man wears a fishing vest on dry land, let alone to a place like The Pearl and The Girl? I should have pulled an intervention right from hello," I say, taking responsibility for what was, yet again, a disaster of my own making.

"The thing that scares me the most is that even with the fishing vest, I thought we could have had something. I'm tired of this game. I don't think I can handle any more of it. I'm single and that's fine by me."

"Well, you and your bag handled yourself just fine last night.

When did you get such a strong arm? You wound that thing up like Babe Ruth. Brad won't be running to home base any time soon!" It may be too soon to joke about it but Bex's bowling ball revenge was one of the best things I've seen in my life. I wanted to cheer and applaud right there in the lobby of the Spade.

Bex cracks a small smile in spite of herself. "I told you, I don't want to talk about it. I still can't believe I let you get me into that mess. Why would you even think that I'd be okay with a millionaire matchmaking service? I've told you countless times that I don't care about all that." She pauses and gives me a cold look. "I know it means a lot to you. Look at your bag." Bex points to my Chanel purse. "That probably costs more than my monthly mortgage."

Bex is taking her anger out on me and after what she went through last night, I don't blame her. I look at my purse and sigh deeply. She's right, it probably did cost more than her monthly mortgage. It's my crutch in London, my little status symbol that helps me deal with women like Clarissa who wield their designer wares as if we live in a logo'd caste system. The purse has become a piece of my armor. Armor I've been building around me so slowly, yet so strongly, it's taken me this time with Bex to see that it's suffocating me. The LA sunshine and this roller-coaster ride I'm on with Bex is bringing me back to *me*. For the first time, it feels like I'm taking a long hard look at myself, and I'm a stranger.

"You want to know the story of this purse?" I challenge. A knot is starting to twist in the pit of my stomach, but I ignore it. It's time to tell Bex the truth. She deserves it, and I don't think I can hold it in anymore.

"Another sample sale? Hopefully, you haven't lost another toenail because of it."

"I wish. I would rather have lost all ten toenails than how I ended up with it." Bex's clenched jaw relaxes as she turns toward me with interest, and I continue. "Ethan was in Paris on a huge case that'd he'd brought in shortly after making partner. He felt that this was his moment to prove his worth. I don't remember what it was all about. A bank in Monaco had been doing dodgy transactions with high net worth clients in France. Some tax thing.

"I was back in London, still unpacking boxes at our new flat in Chelsea. The upstairs neighbors were doing renovations and it was a mess. Workers were stomping in and out of the building all the time. Then, on a Sunday of all days, one of them cracked a main pipe, and I woke up to a gushing cascade of water and crumbling sheet rock that flooded our kitchen. It was a nightmare. Ethan usually deals with the house stuff and I had no idea what to do."

"What does this have to do with the damn purse?" Bex impatiently takes another sip of her Bloody Mary.

"I'm getting there, hold on. So, the neighbors didn't think that they should pay for the repairs and tried to offload all the liability to the builders who wouldn't even speak to me when I'd try to approach them about it. I knew Ethan was busy in Paris building a case against tax scammers, but I needed him to build a case against the builders..." The memory of this still frustrates me.

"I'd texted Ethan dozens of times, but he hadn't gotten back to me. I know how he can disappear into cases, so I wasn't too worried. I finally called his hotel, since I wasn't getting through to him on his cell, and in my best/worst high school French asked to be connected to Ethan, but the front desk refused to put any calls through unless I knew his room number. Which, of course, I didn't. In my garbled French, I went on to explain that I was Ethan's wife, Madame Davis. The clerk replied that he couldn't connect me to the room of Monsieur et Madame Davis and asked again if I knew the room number. I guess because of my bad French he thought that I was asking for Ethan's wife, not that *I* was his wife."

Bex nearly chokes on her celery stick as she inhales sharply. "What!"

I keep going, even though recounting this is killing me.

"I was in shock. Ethan had checked in to the hotel with his so-called wife, probably some twenty-something paralegal or a Parisian temptress he'd picked up there. I called Clarissa in tears, but she didn't understand why I was so upset. She said it was part of the trade-off. That Ethan and Alan worked so hard, who cared if they had an out-of-town fling. *I* was Madame Davis, not that random woman in the hotel room, who by now I envisioned to look like Gigi Hadid.

"I sent SOS texts to Ethan, and he finally called back. When I confronted him, he confessed, saying it was no big deal. *Like eating a cheeseburger*. Those were his exact words! Not something you do all the time, but every now and then you get a craving. When he came back from Paris, he brought me this bag." I plonk the purse onto the table, "So, this is my consolation prize."

"Are you fucking kidding me? A cheeseburger!" Bex is outraged. "Why didn't you tell me any of this? Why'd you call Clarissa instead of me?"

"Because it would have sounded like whining. You're so busy with Maddie and when it happened you were at the tail end of your divorce, and I didn't want to bother you with my stupid drama. Besides, the whole thing is just too midlife crisis cliché to talk about." I lean back in my chair, emotionally exhausted.

"Liv, it's not stupid drama. And fuck *mid*life crisis. *Life* is crisis. We're all living our own crisis, midlife or otherwise. And don't use Maddie as an excuse. You know you can call me anytime."

"Thank you," I say, genuinely grateful.

"How come you aren't furious? The Liv I know would have had Ethan's stuff in trash bags on the curb. You sound almost...at peace with it." Bex shakes her head, perplexed.

"I wanted to go to couples counseling, but Ethan didn't think we needed it. He said it wasn't a big deal and I guess I just accepted that as normal. I didn't have many people in London I could confide in at the time. I was still trying to fit in with his crowd where everyone thought it was vulgar to show emotion. Stiff upper lip and all of that English emotional suppression. I'd moved halfway around the world to build a life with Ethan, I didn't want to throw it all away. And you know me, I'm stubborn."

Bex nods her head. "Yup, you are, especially since you're still with him."

"I don't know how to explain it. Something inside me died, the dream I had about marriage. It became a wound in my heart that scabbed into a hard stone. I pushed any hurt away from me —didn't even process it. Just batted it all away. I learned how to live with numbness." I stare down into my now empty mimosa glass, which is the perfect mirror of how I feel. Empty.

"Liv, when did you get so lost? You're my ride or die partner in crime. You should not be feeling like this. I had hoped every-thing was okay with you and Ethan, I mean, as much as any marriage is good. When you told me about Francois, I was abso-lutely floored. But now, knowing all of this, I can see it's been a long time coming."

Bex pauses to poke around at the bottom of her glass with the half-eaten celery stick before she continues quietly. "I should have told you this a long time ago, but, Ethan hit on me at your engagement party."

"What?" I stutter in disbelief.

"I'm so sorry. I should have told you, but I waved it off as him being drunk. You were so happy and I didn't want to ruin that by saying something."

"Oh my God..." I am completely mortified. It's one thing for Ethan to "sow his oats" when he's out of town or when it's with people I don't know. It's another thing entirely when it's my best friend.

"He seemed so perfect in every way, your very own Hugh Grant, that I just chalked it up to sloppy drunkenness. In hind-sight, I should have told you about it a long time ago. It was a mistake for me not to. I'm sorry, Liv. I guess we were both wrong about him." Bex pauses in deep thought as she wipes the condensation off her Bloody Mary glass. "Listen, I know we're bff's and I want you to visit me all the time, hell, I want you to move in, but you have to admit it's a little crazy that you just dropped everything to come here. You can't run from your life over there, Liv. You have to face the truth about you and Ethan. Things can't go on like this. You know that, don't you?"

I wipe the tears from my eyes. I feel sheepish for dumping all of this on Bex right now. She had dinner last night with a felon, for God's sake.

"Maybe I *will* just move in with you." I signal to the waiter to bring over another mimosa, doing my best to move on from what's become a very difficult and painful conversation.

"And one last thing." Bex points to the Chanel. "I hate that purse."

"I hate it too!" I say, half-laughing, half-choking on my tears.

———————— ➤•◄ ————————

"That was sooo good. I love brunch life! You know, this whole mimosas on a weekday thing is great. I don't want it to end." I lean over and clumsily hug Bex as she's craning her neck to see if the road is clear to pull away from the valet stand and into traffic.

"Hold on, I'm trying to drive here. How many did you have anyway? Four?" she says to me in mock reproach, adjusting the rearview mirror and joining the stream of cars on Wilshire Boulevard. "I love it, too. We're lucky to have this time together, even if we haven't been lucky lately. Reminds me of the good old days. Before all this life and marriage crap got in the way."

"I miss those Southern boys!" I wail, feeling a little tipsy. It's not just the mimosas, I'm strangely elated after telling Bex about my problems with Ethan. And also after what she told me about him. I feel lighter, like the burden and internalized shame that's been smothering me is finally starting to evaporate. "So, where to next?" I clap my hands. "What about the Grove? I really need to find some new jeans."

"The Grove." Bex sneers. "That's amateur hour."

After a twenty-minute drive through twisting streets, we pull into a strip mall somewhere off Ventura Blvd.

"No valet? Guess this isn't a popular place."

"Just you wait. It's very popular." Bex hops out of the car. "Come on."

Behind the small storefront of Encore Couture is a mosaic wonderland of designer labels. Layer upon layer of red soled stilettos that retail for upward of five hundred dollars a pair line one part of the wall. Toward the back, a jungle of fur coats hangs next to a beveled glass display case of handbags straight from the pages of *Vogue*. An adjacent round table is packed two feet high with stacks of designer jeans in every shade imaginable. There's even a small bargain box tucked away in a corner simply labeled Miscellaneous Cashmere and Silk.

"What is this place?" I say, my eyes slowly scanning the store, hardly believing the Aladdin's den of upscale loot. "It's like the aftermath of Carrie Bradshaw reading Marie Kondo."

"It's incredible, I know." Then in a half-whisper as if we're in a holy place of worship, Bex continues. "This is the place everyone knows about, but nobody talks about. Holmby Hills socialites come in here to hock their vintage Dior, as if they need the money, and every Oscar nominated starlet comes here to find a gown that no one else will have. This is where a Best Actress nominee got that vintage Halston for last year's ceremony."

"So how do *you* know about this place?" I wonder when Bex —who I had to warn not to wear sweats to the airport—developed such an affinity for high fashion.

"Remember Bernice, my mother-in-law from hell? She had two amazing vintage Gucci dresses. Let's just say that when Patrick and I were married I borrowed them and after the divorce 'forgot' to give them back."

"Bex! You didn't!"

"I know, it's terrible, but I don't feel guilty. She never wore them, just kept them in storage. So I borrowed them, brought them here, and then Maddie got to go to volleyball camp *and* science camp. Patrick was being so difficult and we were still hashing out the divorce settlement. I was pinching pennies wherever I could."

"More like pinching Gucci." I marvel at her tenacity. "So does Maddie still want to be an astronaut?"

"Who knows. All she talks about lately is wanting to be a YouTube star. I don't even know what that means! Anyway, put your stuff in here." Focused on the mission at hand, Bex takes my Chanel bag and turns it upside down, shaking its contents into a plastic Target bag she's pulled from her own purse.

"Bex..." I say, finally realizing what she's up to. "Bex, what are you doing with my bag?"

"Do you really want to carry around this albatross of adultery any longer?" she hisses. "I can't believe you let him see you with this thing. Does he think he can just buy himself out of betraying you?"

She's right. I know she's right. I watch her stroll up to the very soigné sixty-something woman behind the counter and start talking about the purse. I turn around and mindlessly riffle through the bargain box, pulling out random sleeves of ridiculously thick cashmere sweaters and slinky silk scarves. I don't want to explain anything about the purse to the store clerk. Now that Bex—God bless her—has told it like it is, I'm almost ashamed of myself, the way I so easily accepted Ethan's infidelity or simply chose to ignore it, like a buzzing bee that I'd hoped would go away and not sting me. If Bex only knew about everything else...I scrunch up the cashmere sweater in my hands and squeeze it hard like a stress ball. *I don't have to tell Bex everything all at once.* But I know deep down that I can't keep living my life the way I am now.

"Oh no, sweetie, that's a sad color." A woman in a bright purple '80s jumpsuit with a glittery belt takes the pale gray balled up sweater from my hands. "This is California. Look outside! Blue sky, yellow sun. Here." She drapes a fluorescent Pucci style scarf around my head and nods with approval. "Oh yes. This is so Talitha Getty with a dash of Isadora Duncan. Now, give me your yacht face. You're looking starboard, the Mediterranean wind blowing across your tanned skin, you're dreaming about the Italian deckhand and wondering if this is the summer your eighty-nine-year-old billionaire husband will finally keel over with a heart attack." She laughs wickedly. "Now, what else can we do with you?"

"I'm not here for shopping." I pull the scarf from my head.

"Honey, we are all here in this life for shopping."

"Really, I'm not." I gesture to Bex, who's at the counter, in deep discussion with the woman who's holding up the purse and inspecting the stitching.

"Oh, now *that* is a Chanel. Where did you get that? They didn't even distribute that model in the US. My name's Sharlene." She extends a multi-ringed hand, clearly thinking I'm a big spender she needs to woo.

"Nice to meet you, Sharlene." I turn back to the bargain box.

"Now why is a woman with a purse like that so sad?"

"It's a long story."

"Hey." Bex comes up behind me, looking over my shoulder into the bargain box at a sweater I'm thumbing like a rosary. Thank God she's back, Sharlene is getting a little too intense. "Do you want that sweater? Because we could buy it even if it's not in the bargain box." Bex gives a triumphant smile and discreetly flashes a handful of bills.

"Whoever buys that purse is going to be one happy person. But I don't know why on earth you'd ever want to sell it. It is class," Sharlene says.

"That purse was bought as an attempted peace offering by her philandering husband." Bex comes to my defense, seeing that Sharlene is being a bit too pushy.

"Oh my goodness, oh honey, that's why you couldn't channel that yacht energy I was trying to give you. I could see that you weren't receptive to it. That you're lost at sea instead of feeling the femme fatale power of the sexy Siren that you are." Sharlene has suddenly turned as sympathetic as Mother Teresa, and as dramatic as Shirley MacLaine. What is it with this town and "energy"?

"We're fine." Bex turns to Sharlene. "We're just on our way out."

"Ladies, ladies. I've seen this before and I want to help. I won't take no for an answer. It's on the house." Sharlene leans in conspiratorially. "And knowing Victoria at the counter and how tough she can be with pricing, you ladies are probably due a little something extra anyway."

Sharlene drags Bex and me over to the evening gown section. "Now I know it looks a little over the top, but trust me, this will bring out your inner vixen." Sharlene pulls out a slinky Bob Mackie dress with beaded fringe. Somehow, despite being covered in sequins, the dress is understated and glam. "It's got a bit of stretch and hugs all the right places," Sharlene says with a wink, and pushes the dress into my arms.

———————•:•———————

I reach out my arm and Bex passes me the bottle. We're side by side on loungers underneath the leafy canopy of her backyard. If I reach up, I could almost pluck an avocado from the tree. I slowly fill our wineglasses with the crisp dry white from a vineyard somewhere near Santa Barbara.

"Twenty, Thirty, Forty, One, Two, Three, Four, Five. One thousand eight hundred and forty-five bucks." Bex hands me the money.

"Is that the price of my marriage?" I take a sip of wine and stare upward into the clear sky, cradling the wineglass against my chest and ignoring the bills in Bex's outstretched arm.

"Well, considering what Ethan makes, I'd say your marriage has a much higher price than that."

"Take out eight hundred dollars for a shopping trip with Maddie. As long as she stops calling me Miss Liv. And the rest, well, what does that buy these days in Hollywood?" I turn with a weary smile to Bex.

"A hell of a lot of fun. We're still going out tonight, aren't we? Glamour & State, right? The place you read about in *Conde Nast?*" Bex is enthusiastic, and now she's the one egging me on.

I get a sinking feeling in my stomach as I remember Jason aka Channing Tatum Look-alike and the date I've lined up for Bex. After Millionaire Mayhem and the drama at brunch, I'd completely forgotten about it.

"Um, yes." I know I should just fess up and tell her about it but I chicken out. Maybe Jason will be a no-show? I'm too messed up from the emotional craziness of today to even think straight. "Sure, let's do it, we've got spending money after all."

Chapter Thirteen

GLAMOUR & STATE

LIV

GLAMOUR & STATE TAKES UP A HUGE SWATHE OF TWO BLOCKS in what's now the Hollywood that everyone comes to for vacation. At some point these formerly scuzzy blocks of urban decay turned into a Vegas style playland for adults.

"Where do all the strippers go now to buy their heels and fluorescent fishnets? And where did all the pawn shops go?" I turn around in confusion, looking up and down the block. "When I lived in LA, this was the last place I'd want to stop at a red light, let alone get out of the car."

"Welcome to the new and improved city of dreams. Brought to you by commercial real estate developers." Bex waves her arm like a girl unveiling a convertible at a car show.

She looks amazing. The Bob Mackie dress that Sharlene gave me had a hard time hugging my A-cup curves. I would have needed two padded bras to fill it out. I convinced Bex to try it on and it was meant to be. Her inner vixen was ready to roar.

A group of twenty-something guys hustles past us, and one of them turns around and gives Bex a whistle.

"It's Wednesday night. Don't these people have jobs? Or school?" I hadn't expected Glamour & State to be so popular...or so young.

But then I wasn't the one who suggested it. I have twenty-six-year-old Jason to thank for this hotspot. *Dear God, please don't let this night turn out like Chandace, or worse, like last night.* I'm skating on thin ice with Bex right now, and so far, my wing-woman skills have been disastrous. I should have told her during our backyard wine session that tonight we, or she, were going to meet someone I found on her Tinder, but I couldn't bring myself to do it. I want her to have fun, and hell, I want to have some fun, too, after this afternoon's confession of my mess of a life.

"Come on, let's get some drinks—bottle service maybe?" Bex excitedly takes my hand and we join the decked out crowd making their way up the red-carpeted sidewalk to Glamour & State. It feels good to see that she's got a spring in her step again.

The place is huge inside, a high-ceilinged fortress of bricks that must have been an old factory or warehouse. In its current incarnation, it's the watering hole of every trend seeking, Instagram posting wannabe out to see and be seen.

"This place is insane," I whisper to Bex as we walk past the three young hostesses in super tight and super short black dresses guarding the foyer entrance, illuminated by an oversized glass chandelier. They're almost too young to be pretty, with puppy fat faces and exaggerated makeup that looks like they're playing dress up.

"Not a girl, not yet a woman," Bex says, finding the perfect lyric as usual to sum up a situation.

"Or is it just that we're old? Either way, they were definitely born after Britney's first hit." I wonder if it was a mistake to have lowered Bex's age range on Tinder. Glamour & State should be renamed Glamour & Steak, it's such a meat market.

"We're not old," Bex corrects me. "We're women."

She gives the girls a smooth hello and saunters past, making a low-key but confident entrance like a female version of Clint Eastwood in a western. Maybe Sharlene is some kind of vintage voodoo witch doctor because that dress has transformed Bex into a sex kitten.

The low lit main dining room is a crowded sea of round tables. It's an eclectic mix of today's LA—Hollywood industry types with suspiciously younger arm candy so you're not sure who's a daughter and who's a date; boisterous guys vying for attention from bored looking girls checking their phones; a table of tourists who seem a bit overwhelmed; a suited up group of young professionals who must be in either real estate or insurance sales. And swimming through it all is a synchronized crew of sharp, casting-ready waitstaff. You definitely had to have a headshot to get hired at this place.

"Let's go check out the upstairs bar." I look at my phone to see what time it is. 8:23p.m. Good, we're doing okay for time. Jason said around nine thirty. I have two text notifications on my lock screen.

Darling, still busy in Dubai. Alan said that Clarissa... From Ethan then, *Sweets! Where are you? Did you go...* from Clarissa. I sigh and put my phone away. No need to read either of those texts any further, certainly not now.

We leave the main dining room and walk back through the entrance foyer to ascend a wide staircase that leads to the upstairs bar. It's an airy, less crowded space, an intimate setting that feels much more exclusive than downstairs. I'm pleasantly surprised. Maybe Jason won't be so bad after all. We slide into a cozy, semi-circular booth, one of six that line the side of the room, the other side anchored by a long bar of thick, rounded marble. Two bartenders are making cocktails in focused concentration, quickly turning and reaching every now and then to pull a bottle from the mirrored shelves behind that go all the way to the ceiling, myriad liquor labels, and bottle shapes forming a 3-D mural of twenty-one-and-up delights.

Bex squints her eyes looking at the bar. "Maker's, Four Roses, Blanton's, Woodford. Oh my God, wow. They have Pappy Van Winkle. I'm impressed, Liv. Nice choice with this place. I should start reading *Conde Nast!*" She gives me an approving smile. I cringe.

A cute waiter appears out of nowhere. "Hi, how are you two doing? Here's our cocktail menu, and I see you've noticed we have a wide selection of ultra-premium spirits. Pappy is one of my personal favorites." The waiter looks at Bex and gives her a warm smile. "I admire a woman who knows her bourbon."

"You know, why not? We'll take two Pappy's," Bex orders decisively.

"Coming up." The waiter turns as I leaf through the cocktail menu.

"Pappy's? I'm not sure I'm going to like that. This elderflower gin fizz sounds really good. What tha—Bex, Pappy is eighty dollars a glass." I drop the menu in shock.

"I know. We've got a few coins burning a hole in our pockets, so don't worry about the price. And trust me, you'll love it. Forget your Kool-Aid gin. This is for big girls."

The waiter returns with our order. Served in a hefty crystal glass that seems to weigh at least four pounds, the Pappy is indeed delicious. With each sip, I feel warmer and more relaxed.

"Told you it was good." Bex laughs.

"So...the waiter's cute." I give Bex a look.

"Do not even go there. After The Weeper, I'm done with chasing after the waitstaff." Bex crosses her arms.

"Okay, fine. But what about yoga teachers?" I tease her.

We're not even halfway through our drinks when the waiter appears with two more glasses of Pappy on a tray.

"Ladies, this is from your neighbors over there." The waiter points to a pair of hot guys two booths over. Even though they're sitting down, I can tell they're tall and fit, their shirts pulled taut over rippled muscles and broad shoulders. One of them turns to us and nods, lifting his own glass in a silent "cheers." The chunky titanium watch wrapped around his wrist is surely more expensive than a hundred bottles of Pappy.

Bex smiles, raises the fresh glass in a return "cheers" and as she goes to take a sip says like a ventriloquist, "I'm dying, I think that's...I don't know his name, from the Lakers."

"You know I have no idea about sports. The only thing I know about the Lakers is Paula Abdul. Wasn't she a Laker Girl? Those guys are Lakers? For real?" The Pappy is tasting better and better.

"Hey. I'm Jason." Bex looks up, expecting to see Mr. Laker, but instead she's staring up at a tall, lean, brown-haired guy who looks like he could be Channing Tatum's brother (siblings of celebrities aren't ever as hot as their famous brother or sister). Still, there's no doubt he's attractive, and with that slim fitting V-neck sweater you can see he has the tight body of an Olympic swimmer. *Bex, meet Jason, your date that you don't know is your date. And who's also not a Laker.*

"Hi," Bex says somewhat unsure as she looks over at the Laker booth.

"I'm Toby." Jason's friend steps up to extend a hand. Toby has the kind of arrogant jerk appeal of an '80s era James Spader. He's cute and he knows it.

"Hi, I'm Liv. And this is Bex."

Interpreting this as an invitation, Toby sits down beside me in the booth while Jason slides in next to Bex. We're now sandwiched in between these two man-children.

"Bex, you're hot. Even better than your photo." Okaaay, well, Jason doesn't beat around the bush. Does this generation even know how to flirt?

"My photo?"

"Yeah." Jason whips out his phone from his jeans pocket and opens Tinder. He turns the phone to Bex and I can see her photo and a preview frame of their conversation on the screen.

"I wasn't too sure if you'd show up tonight. I mean, I figured at your age you probably have kids or something."

Suddenly Bex is downing the Pappy like it's water. Under the table, I feel a sharp stiletto bearing down on my foot. Yup, I'm in trouble.

"Oh, right, you know, I *did* almost forget. That early onset

Alzheimer's is getting to me." Bex turns to me in a harsh whisper. "What the hell have you done now?"

"It's fine," I whisper back, fully cowed. "Just think of it as the last of my matchmaking. Trust me."

"Do not say trust me, because I don't," Bex hisses, then turns back to the table to face Jason and Toby.

"So," she says to Jason in a fake upbeat voice, "we met on Tinder and here we are in person!"

"I know, cool isn't it? Hey, what was it like when you were dating at our age? Would people really put ads in newspapers? Like paper newspapers?" Jason seems dumbstruck, and I realize that despite the insensitivity, he's being serious. I also realize that hot bod of his doesn't have much of a brain.

"No, we'd send out carrier pigeons with notes attached." Bex goes to take a swig of her bourbon, then frowns when she sees the glass is empty.

"And what about video dating? My mom said she did that one time. Hired a makeup artist and everything." Toby says this with a tone of disbelief, like it'd be more believable if his mom had said she'd been kidnapped by aliens. "Whatever, man, I'm just glad we have these apps now, it helps to cull the herd. I'll get us a round." Full of largesse, Toby motions for the waiter.

"Finished with the Pappy?" the waiter says to Bex. "Another round?"

"No thanks, man, we'll change it up and have four Jack and Cokes," Toby says.

Upon hearing Jack and Coke, the waiter gives Bex a glance as if to say, "For real?"

"Did you fine women want those Cokes to be diet?" Toby looks at Bex and me. God, this was a mistake. I'm surprised he didn't call us ma'am.

"I'm good, I don't need another drink." Bex's face has turned as hard as stone.

"Go ahead and bring four," Toby says. "No harm in me having yours if you don't want it. So," he turns to me, "what are you on?"

What am I on? Is this guy for real?

"I've only had a couple of drinks. I'm not on anything." I sniff at him, losing my ability to be nice. Why do we women feel like we have to be nice to everyone anyway? These guys are redefining the word jerk.

He laughs and pulls out his phone. "No, I mean like what apps are you on? Seems like you're up for it, too." He gives me a sleazy look. "I'm on Tinder, Bumble, Match, The Society. Pretty much everything. I think it's good to diversify. You know, like stocks."

Toby is swiping through the photos on his phone. "I met her on The Society, it's the invitation only one. I think you might be out of the age bracket." He looks up and intently assesses my face. "It's very high class, very exclusive. She is total second wife material."

"Second wife material?"

"Yeah, you know. First wife material is the kind of girl you want as the mother of your children. Reliable, nice, good-looking but not too sexy, so she'll stay at home and raise the kids."

"Raise the kids?" I'm in total shock. I can't believe the words I'm hearing from this jerk's mouth. If Toby is the future of what it means to be a man, I can only hope that every woman becomes a lesbian. I thought this younger generation was supposed to be past stereotyped gender roles. Toby sounds like he's straight out of a 1950s misogynist guidebook.

He continues on, oblivious. "Whereas second wife material is the hot girl, the girl every guy in the room wants to fu—"

"Okay, I get it," I snap.

"First wife—Jennifer Garner. Second wife—Jennifer Lawrence," Jason chimes in and lays it all out as a simple equation.

"Exactly, bro!" Toby reaches across the table to give Jason an enthusiastic high five.

"Liv, I need to run to the ladies'. Come with me." Bex grabs my arm.

We both sit there and wait for either Jason or Toby to move out of our way so we can leave the booth. Jason is staring at his phone. Toby finally gets up so we can leave and says with tacky innuendo, "Don't have too much fun without us. Or if you do, take photos."

"Liv, who the hell are these morons? How does he have my photo?" Bex talk-shouts to me over her shoulder, furious. She's walking so fast I can hardly keep up. "Have you been on my phone? I changed all the passwords for my profiles. I told you not to mess with anything! Where is the damn bathroom?"

"Um, you gave me your phone to help navigate to yoga, remember?" I quietly reply. "I might have gone on Tinder."

"I can't believe you! I really can't." Bex pushes open the door of the women's bathroom.

"I mean, he's cute," I say in weak defense. "And he's probably too young to be a felon?" I'm floundering and I know it.

"How could you do this to me after last night? He's an asshole, and his friend is even more of an asshole. He's nowhere near as cute as *those men* who sent over the drinks. And that just happened organically, analog-ally! Jack and Coke, my ass." Bex is indignant, then looks around slightly bewildered. "Is this the bathroom?"

"It's looks like a Mary Kay cosmetics showroom." I'm confused, or maybe drunk. "Let's talk, okay? Please don't be mad. I just thought it'd be fun to see what else is out there. You had your age range set at forty to fifty-five! I'm surprised you didn't just go up to sixty. So, I lowered it a bit. Look, there's actually a sofa in here."

We plop down on the pink velour sofa; the bourbon hitting both of us hard. Suddenly, two glasses of rose champagne float in front of us. "Complimentary bubbles?" a young woman asks. We exchange side glances, and a "what the hell" look and take the glasses. "Well, we sure as hell didn't get served free champagne in bathrooms when we used to go bar hopping." Bex's voice is still brimming with irritation.

"This is a *Lounge,* not a bathroom," I correct her sarcastically, trying to lift her mood.

"I'm still mad at you, by the way." Bex begrudgingly clinks my champagne glass with hers. "I would rather join a convent than deal with guys like that."

"Bex, you basically already live like you're in a convent. When was the last time you even had a guy over? It took me flying out here to get you to even go out on dates."

"Excuse me?" Bex takes a big swallow of the champagne. "What do you mean *It took you flying out here?* I didn't ask you to come out here. I'm doing just fine. I'm not your little project. Maybe you're the one who needs to look in the mirror!"

"Look, I'm sorry. I may not have gone about it the right way. I don't know how to date these days either. But I do know that Patrick was a long time ago. Your marriage didn't work out, and that's okay. You've got to let go and move on." Doesn't she know what a catch she is?

Bex slams down her champagne flute on the glass coffee table, making me jump in my seat. "Do not go there, Liv. Do. Not. I have let go! I have moved on! Just not in the way you want me to. And do not even talk to me about marriage, or dating, or relationships like you are some kind of expert!" She makes an immediate move for the exit.

Shit, is she really leaving? I rush out to follow her.

"Bex, wait!"

She turns around and spits out, "Don't follow me. I'm leaving. There is nothing wrong with my life. I don't need fixing. You do!" Then, as she whips back around to make her way through the lobby, she bumps right in to Jason and Toby who seem to be on their way out, too.

"Oh, hey. I, uh, I thought you left. Have you been in the bathroom this whole time?" Jason says, sounding confused.

Are Jason and Toby ditching us? Shit, it's supposed to be the other way around.

"Yeah, I got a call from home." I step in to respond because

Bex is standing there, too angry to say anything. And I know it's not anger at Jason and Toby, she's angry at me, which is even worse. These guys, they don't mean anything to us, so I don't even know why I'm making excuses to them.

Bex starts digging around in her purse looking for her phone. Then, from seemingly out of nowhere, a trio of young women bounce up and one of them excitedly puts her hand on Toby's shoulder. "You're going to totally love it. It's like the new Glamour before Glamour got overrun with wannabes." She flicks her freshly blown out mane and looks up and down at Bex and me. Did Jason and Toby pick up these girls while we were in the bathroom?

Another girl, spray tanned to an orange sheen of nearly burnt toast, pipes up. "Who's Jason talking to? Jason, ohmygod, is this your mom? That is so sweet, Jason, taking your mom to a pre-party. Hi, I'm Sarah," Sarah preens, extending her hand to Bex.

This isn't happening. This cannot be happening.

Bex looks up from her phone and locks eyes with me. It's as if all of Glamour & State is suspended in freeze frame. Sarah keeps her hand out, a dare, a staking of her claim to Jason. I can tell by the smug look on her face that she knows exactly what she's doing. We look eight years older than these girls, tops! And after the torture of wrinkle reducing infrared hot yoga, maybe only five years older.

Sarah's not budging, Bex is dead still, frozen like a cheetah stalking prey. I'm not sure what will happen next. I envision a telenovela style slap, or maybe a thrown drink. But Bex, trooper that she is, sucks it up and casually extends her arm to shake Sarah's hand. Phew, so everything will be fine. We're grown-ups, after all.

"So nice to meet you too, Sarah." Bex smiles, killing her with kindness and a saccharine Southern tinge to her voice that I haven't heard since she sweet-talked a Georgia state trooper out of a speeding ticket. I'm now back to seriously worried about what Bex has up her sleeve. Finally, letting go of Sarah's hand, Bex turns to Jason.

"Now, Jason honey, you be good tonight. Mommy doesn't want you out too late." Bex leans in slowly and plants a long wet kiss on Jason's lips. "Bye boys, y'all have fun tonight."

Sarah and her two friends look completely freaked out. Jason is simply dumbstruck while Toby is laughing and rubbing his hands together in bro'd out glee. I'm just as stunned as Jason.

I think I might have pushed Bex completely over the edge. Oh. Shit.

I follow her as she struts out of the restaurant. "Bex, what the hell? That was crazy, but also kind of amazing," I say in disbelief at what I just witnessed.

"Screw 'em," Bex says, in a detached voice. And I know she's not just talking about Jason and Toby, but about Mr. Felon-aire Millionaire, the Weeper, and even Ethan and Patrick. "And Liv," she turns to me dead serious, "you've gone too far."

Phone still in her hand, I can see that Bex is deleting all of her dating apps.

"Come on, Bex, what are you doing? Don't overreact. I'm worried about you," I plead. "Let's go back in and have a drink, just you and me. Or let's go someplace else."

"No. I told you I'm done. I'm going off the grid. The only app I'm going to be using is Lyft. Ravi will be here in two minutes. Why don't you go get a drink by yourself and see what it's like to be single?"

"Bex, stop. Please." I'm practically begging.

We stare at each other in silence. Bex won't say a word.

A Corolla pulls up and honks.

"That's me. Bye. You can find your own way home, can't you? Unless, of course, you meet someone. Don't worry, I won't tell Ethan, or Francois." Bex slams the door, the pain of her words hurts so much it's like she slammed the door on my fingers.

I watch the car pull away and stop myself from calling her. I should give her some space. I sure as hell don't want to have a drink at the bar here though. I can tell the night is heating up and the place is probably teeming with millions of Tobys and Jasons.

I make my way back to the bathroom where at least nobody will bother me. I can take a break from this craziness then order a car back home. Hopefully, Bex will have cooled off.

I sit on the same pink sofa where Bex and I were just sitting. The bathroom champagne girl is gone and I'm feeling especially alone and angry with myself. I lean back with a sigh and thank God I'm no longer twenty-one as I watch a gaggle of young Hollywood wannabes flounce in and out of the bathroom. They stop and take a group selfie with pursed duck-face lips. Does anybody smile in pictures anymore? Everyone seems to be doing everything but being present in the moment. Nobody is even making eye contact with their friends, they're all too absorbed in their phones.

I watch a girl in over-the-knee boots, a miniskirt, and bolero hat loudly exclaim as she's staring at her phone screen, "Your eyes are closed again! We don't have time to keep retaking this. Just stay out of this one for now." Bolero hat girl laughs as she turns her back on her friend to rejoin the rest of her group who are already posing, lips in the ready position.

The girl who'd committed the apparently mortal sin of closing her eyes in a photo crashes down next to me on the sofa. She's obviously a little tipsy and her handbag topples off her lap, landing with a dull thud on the floor as the contents scatter everywhere.

"Oh my God, I'm so sorry, ohmygod," the girl slurs an apology.

"It's okay." I lean over to help the girl with her stuff, spying a driver's license that I pick up. Looking at the driver's license photo of "Nia Griffiths" and then at the girl's face, it's obvious they aren't one and the same. Then it hits me, this girl isn't Nia Griffiths, whoever that is, it's Chloe from the estate sale!

"Chloe?" I look into her overly mascaraed eyes, hardly

believing what's happening. The universe has given me a get out of jail free card.

"My name's Nia," Chloe stumbles over the words.

"It's okay. I'm not going to say anything. I met you on Sunday at the Pasadena Estate Sale. I was with my friend Bex."

Chloe nods in slow recognition then looks back at her friend, the mean Bolero girl, who's calling out to her.

"Come on, let's go, the car is here," the girl orders, doing her best model stomp out of the bathroom. Chloe turns to me with a look both vulnerable and defiant. "I have to go."

"Is she really your friend?" I say and lightly touch her arm. "You know you're worth way more than those girls." I look at Chloe and see how young she is underneath the makeup she's put on for this night out with her fake ID and fake friends. "Will you just give me two minutes? I know it sounds crazy, but I really need to talk to you." I do my best to not sound like some kind of creepy middle-aged woman sitting in a bathroom pleading for a teenager with a fake ID to talk to her.

"What do you want talk about? I know she's not my real friend. I can handle it. Didn't you do stupid stuff when you were a teenager?" Chloe says to me in a voice edged with defiance.

"I'm still doing stupid stuff. But I'm really hoping I can make up for it. Can I have your dad's phone number?"

"What? You said you weren't going to say anything about the ID!"

"No, no, it's not that. It's for my friend Bex. Remember her?"

Chloe softens with understanding. "Yeah, I do. And my dad remembers her, too. Here, give me your phone."

I unlock my phone and hand it over to Chloe who adds her dad's number to my contacts. "There you go." She hands me back the phone. Yes! Now I better not screw this up.

"Thank you, Chloe. This means a lot, more than you know. Oh, and do me a favor. I won't say anything about the ID if you don't tell your dad about running in to me. Deal?"

"Deal. Look, I gotta go. Jasmine's probably already left for the club."

"Jasmine. Well, she doesn't live up to her name. Not sure there's anything sweet about her. Be careful with that pack of she-wolves. Watch out for yourself."

Chloe surprises me with a quick hug. "I'm my own pack. I'll be okay."

She slips out of the bathroom like a ghost into the night. I feel a pang deep inside and wish that she were my daughter. That I could prevent life's ugliness from hurting her. But, if I've learned anything these last few days, it's that my meddling only makes things more of a mess. Chloe's already out in the ugly world, and I trust that she'll be fine.

Chapter Fourteen

DETOX/RETOX

BEX

As we back out of the driveway, a wave of relief washes over me. This cloudless, picture perfect, seventy and sunny day is not about dates or men, it's about Liv and me. I said I was going off the grid, and I meant it in more ways than one. I wanna get out of the city for a day and get into what's going on with Liv.

The tension from last night is still buzzing between us but at a lower frequency, and I can't think of a better way to dissipate it than a day at Sunny Dale Hot Springs. It may not be the most glamorous spa in the world but they do serve alcohol. Need I say more?

Sitting in somewhat un-companionable silence, listening to the radio with the windows cracked in the sweltering heat, we're ten minutes into an hour-and-a-half drive when my phone rings. Liv reaches to grab it since I'm driving, but I quickly spit, "Don't touch that," and she snaps her hand back into her lap. I deflate with remorse, I know she was just trying to help. I relent. "Fine. Just look and see who it is. No app surfing!"

Liv jumps at the chance to make amends. "The number doesn't have a name attached. But it's a three one zero area code. Should I answer it?"

I'm puzzled because I don't get many random calls. However, I *do* have a kid and when you have a kid, you pick up the phone.

"Yeah, answer it. But put it on speaker," I tell her after the fourth ring. "Hello?" I say, concern edging my voice. Liv hears my tone and stares at me intently while chewing on her bottom lip.

"Hey! Is this Bex? How *are* you?" says a male voice which sounds familiar, although I can't quite place it. I look over at Liv and give her a questioning shrug. She shrugs back.

I proceed with caution. "Yes, this is Bex. I'm sorry, I don't have your number saved in my phone. Who is this?"

"You don't remember me? This is Brandon from The Vacancy!" I look at Liv, my eyes not blinking, my heart racing in a fight-or-flight reflex. He charges on, "So, hey, I've been thinking of you nonstop since the other night and was wondering if you want to go up to Big Bear next weekend with me. I rented a cabin. It'll be fun!"

My mouth is frozen as I try to gather my thoughts, which are spinning like a Tilt-A-Whirl. Should I play nice and kick the can down the road? Or just tell him the truth, however harsh it is? I'm so over all of this. I take a deep breath and decide on honesty. Let's just rip off the Band-Aid, which is what I should have done at the end of our so-called date.

"Brandon, thank you so much for inviting me, but I just don't think that you and I are the right fit." I sound like a Hollywood agent. Out of the corner of my eye, I see that Liv is nodding vigorously for me to continue on this course. "I wish you all the best. You're a really nice guy."

As Brandon drones on and on about his disappointment and how he thought what we had was real, I tune him out as his tone becomes more desperate. Is he going to start weeping again? I can't help myself and rudely cut him off, losing patience as the words rush out. "Okay, Brandon, thanks for calling. Bye!"

Liv instantly blurts out, "Oh my God, what a weirdo! I'm blocking him from your phone." On instinct she reaches for my phone in the cupholder but I beat her to it. She looks at me. "I'm sorry. I'm sorry about everything. I over-stepped and I know I've made mistakes in trying to help."

Feeling somber, I keep my eyes on the road. "See what I'm dealing with? This is the landscape of dating. It's crazy apps and crazy guys. I know you were just trying to help, but you pushed too hard. You flew out here with these grand plans, that The Yes Factor was the key to it all, but *this* is the reality of the situation." My voice drops to nearly a whisper and I feel tears spring in my eyes. "But it's not *all* on you. I'm such a mess that I couldn't even ask that Devon guy for his number. That was organic. That was exactly the way I want to meet someone and...I messed it up and ran off like an idiot.

"I didn't tell you this, but I actually saw him on Tinder, the night you called me about Francois. I saw him and I thought, *that guy looks like a perfect match for me,* and then I swiped the wrong way, and lost my chance. Seeing him again felt like kismet, but I botched that too. I just can't seem to..."

"Bex, it's gonna be—"

"No!" I interrupt her brusquely, blinking the tears back and focusing on the road. "You know what? I don't want to talk about me or any of this bullshit." My tone softens. "I forgive you. But, can we please change the subject and talk about you? I feel like you've only revealed the tip of the iceberg yesterday when you told me about Ethan." I take a quick glance at her and she's practically turned her back to me looking at the roadside mini-malls like they're the most interesting thing she's ever seen. I give her a gentle nudge. "Liv, hello? I know you don't have Ross Dress For Less in London but I promise you, it's not worth a pit stop."

She swivels around to face front once more. "I think I need a big glass of wine and a spa soak before I can talk about the Titanic that is my marriage." I nod, understanding her completely.

"That's fine. Put on some tunes then, will ya? This is a road trip after all." I try to sound cheery.

When Liv puts on Bonnie Raitt, "I Can't Make You Love Me," I know we're in for a real doozy of a conversation. I wonder if we can order wine by the bottle and Uber back?

"This place is absolute Heaven. How have I not been here before?"

Liv and I are sprawled out on plastic recliners, covered in mud from head to toe. She takes a sip of her Sauvignon Blanc, which she's loaded with ice, and closes her eyes.

Sunny Dale Hot Springs isn't too crowded since it's a Thursday. The deck area is dotted with clusters of mostly older women in bathrobes, enjoying the California sunshine and more importantly the California wine. Fortunately, there are very few men in sight. After the surprise call from The Weeper and the chaos of the last few days, I'm perfectly content spending a day without men. The mineral baths, sulfur springs, and special mud are the body and soul cleansing that I need.

"Guru Stan, would be proud of how Zen we are right now!" I laugh.

Liv smirks and the mud cracks along her laugh lines. "Yeah, although I'm not sure he'd approve of the wine. As over the top as that place was, I wish I could find something similar in London. I was thinking maybe Ethan and I could start doing yoga together on Sunday mornings. He doesn't want to go to counseling anymore, but maybe yoga would help us. If he were ever around." She mutters that last part under her breath.

And there's my cue. I dive right in.

"Speaking of." I pause to see if she'll open up without any further prodding. She doesn't. "Ethan," I say definitively. "Spill. Troof."

Ever since our obsession with *Da Ali G Show* in the early 2000s, we picked up his exaggerated way of saying truth and ran with it.

Liv rolls on her side to face me, her eyes open, looking like two oyster pearls nestled in Dauphin Island, Alabama clay. "Troof? I don't know."

Slightly frustrated, the need to call her out gets the better of me. "You know. Talk it out." I wave my hand to encourage her to continue.

Taking another sip of icy liquid courage, she says, "I know from the outside it seems like I have this great life and everything. Living in London, a successful husband, my so-called 'glamorous job,' but, I'm miserable. I don't think I can move past his cheating. I feel like I just don't have the energy to keep up with the charade any longer."

I reach down to adjust my forest green bikini bottoms and inadvertently reveal a bit of skin that's so white I immediately smear it with mud so I don't blind myself, or anyone else.

"I just feel so ignored." *Sip.* "Invisible." *Sip.* "Insecure." *Sip.* "Unlovable." *Sip.* "Under sexed." *Gulp.*

Of course, I hate hearing my best friend say these words and I want to comfort her, but doesn't every woman feel these things at some point? Could this just be the cycle of the relationship? My grandmother always said, "This too shall pass." Maybe it will pass? But, before I can respond, she says, "It's been this way for nearly seven years."

"Wait, you've been married for nine!" I do the math in my head.

"Things have never really gelled with us. Like, round peg, square hole kind of situation. We just don't fit. I've tried and tried for years. Talking about it. Not talking about it. When I got on the flight here, I was ready to give up. That little dalliance with Francois boosted my confidence. I was on the plane thinking I was going to see how fun and amazing being single is." I cough mid-drink at Liv's naivete. "And now I'm seeing it's just kind of...pathetic." Liv almost whispers the last word.

"Oh, wow. Thanks." Well, I asked for the *troof* and I got it.

"Now I'm thinking, maybe I should just go back and try to make it work, no matter what. Everyone has affairs, don't they?" She sounds so non-committal and depressed. So unlike her.

"Okay, I'm playing devil's advocate here, but maybe y'all are in a slump? All the things you said are shitty, really shitty. But maybe they can be worked through. Talked out. Maybe *beg* him to stay in therapy? You and Ethan fell in love for a reason. Can you get back to the beginning? Do you remember the beginning?" She gives me a muddy side eye. "Ethan's affair in France was probably a onetime thing. Like, maybe he's a vegetarian now and doesn't like cheeseburgers anymore." It's the best analogy I could come up with on the fly.

Liv doesn't move. Doesn't even blink. Doesn't even lift the glass to her lips for a final sip. I expected her to at least crack another mud smile at my lame attempt at a joke, but nada. The weight of her silence is a heavy blanket over my whole body. In the suddenly oppressive stillness I say in a barely-there voice, "It *was* a onetime thing, right?"

She nervously winds her fingers around the tie strings of her bikini bottom. "Well, I don't know for sure. I found out that he had an Ashley Madison account." She mistakes my gasp for a sound of confusion. "You know, that website where married people have affairs." I'm nodding my head slowly, taking this all in. "When their site was hacked a while ago, I looked through the data and found the last four of his credit card number alongside our post code."

I'm wide eyed with disbelief. "Is that how he met the woman in France?"

"Probably."

I lean in to her more closely. "So, you don't trust him." It's a statement, not a question.

"No. I don't. In a weird way, it kinda made me feel better when I found out he has this double life. Like the past suddenly made sense. It put all his late nights, last-minute travel plans, and his emotional distance into perspective. Not to mention all the ridiculous gifts he's brought home to me."

"The puzzle pieces all fell into place," I say with understanding.

Her fingers stop their fidgeting. "Exactly. That knowledge should give me the freedom to think about my own decisions, to try to understand what I want. But I just seem stuck. I don't know what's wrong with me."

"And what do you want?" I look over at my friend and see the strength and vulnerability warring within her as she tilts her head up to the clear blue California sky, closes her eyes, and exhales. "Why didn't you just leave him?"

"Do you know how many times I've asked myself that? I've thought through all of my exit strategies, but I just can't bring myself to do it. It feels so complicated."

"But why? If he's been cheating on you repeatedly, what is complicated about that? You deserve better!" I say indignantly.

"Do I? This life with Ethan is so much better than my life growing up, my mom and dad barely being able to cover the bills. I always wanted to escape, and I've done that with Ethan. This is the life I've always wanted." She pauses. "Or that I thought I wanted."

"But, Liv, your parents loved each other. Who cares about the rest of it?"

We sit in silence, although both of our wheels are turning at breakneck speed.

"There's still so much of me tied up in Ethan. I know I deserve to be treated better. But it's like, I'm waiting for him to leave me. Like that will somehow make it easier."

I try to process what she's saying. I can't judge because that's pretty much how I felt about my relationship with Patrick. It was easier for me to be the victim than for me to take control of my own happiness. Until I did.

Jesus, what a web we weave for ourselves.

Having washed the mud off, we're back to our previously pasty selves as we settle into the sulfur hot springs with a final glass of wine. The smell of rotten eggs may not be my standard aromatherapy go-to, but all five senses are now relaxed.

Liv holds her glass up to the light and releases a satisfied sigh. "Ahh, detox and retox. Story of my life."

We both laugh and look around at the dwindling crowd, surveying the bodies of the other women. Isn't it something all women do without even really being aware of it? I know it's terrible, and I'm not judging, but I can't help but compare myself to everyone else around me. The lady in the pink tankini has a perfect butt, not a dimple of cellulite, but that tankini is covering a tummy that's just a little too pouchy. A young woman with fake boobs and too much lip filler has actually made herself look older than she probably is. I look at my own body and make a mental list of the many things I want to change (thighs, lank hair, age spots on my chest) but being in the midst of these different shapes and sizes, I give myself a break from it and acknowledge that nobody is perfect. We're all doing the best that we can.

"Listen, I know you'll make the right decision," I say.

She groans. "Can we talk about something else? Like Charlie Hunnam's hot bod? Or more importantly, can we find any good gumbo in LA?"

"Look, one last thing, and then we can definitely talk gumbo." I pause to summarize my thoughts. "Leaving is hard, but staying is harder. I know that firsthand. I just want you to be happy." She rolls her eyes at that. "I do! You deserve love and respect and all the best things. I'm here for you."

Liv looks me in the eye. "What do you think I should do? Troof."

Giving someone relationship advice is tricky. The only people that really know what's going on in the relationship are the two people in it. Only they know the ins and outs, the good and the bad, what they can or can't live with. But I do know Liv.

"Leave his ass." I dunk my head under the hot water, holding my wineglass aloft so it doesn't spill, not wanting to hear what Liv might say in response to my no holds barred *troof*.

Driving home against traffic is always a delightful feeling. I'm stone-cold sober since I stopped drinking a couple of hours ago, but Liv is living up to her name and *living* in the passenger seat with the windows rolled down, a big smile on her face and sing-yelling at the top of her lungs "Girls Just Wanna Have Fun."

"I want to be the one to walk in the sun!" I look at her and feel bittersweet hope as she belts out those words. The mourning of the past and the optimism for the future. It's how I feel right now, too. Sad about the lost dream of my marriage, no matter how long ago it was, but hopeful for better things ahead.

Sometimes, when I drop Maddie off at Patrick's house, I wonder if we were right to divorce. There were so many good things about Patrick. Did I try hard enough? Maybe we should have gone to therapy, put our egos aside and given it a solid go.

Gone the distance for the sake of Maddie. Maybe I was selfish. Maybe I thought I deserved more. Because I didn't *fight* for my marriage, I just walked away in defeat. And, sadly, I still feel that way after all these years. Yes, I have guilt, but more than that there's a sadness in me that's holding me back from opening up to someone new. Until Liv showed up, I hadn't put any energy into my own heart, let alone out into the world. I've been closed off, defensive, and solitary. I've found joy in Maddie, but she is not and should not be my whole world. I know it isn't healthy and looking at Liv singing with her eyes squeezed tight gives me a feeling that I haven't felt in a long time.

When the song ends, Liv turns to me excitedly. "What's next, Ms. DJ?"

Ahead, I see the beautiful glow of the In-N-Out sign calling my name.

"Well, I think it's time you get yourself a Cheeseburger of your own!" I blast Jimmy Buffett's "Cheeseburger in Paradise" just to bring my point home.

I lurch the car into the driveway after our intense but refreshing day at the spa, only a little sunburned and savoring that wonderful paradox of exhaustion that comes from a day of relaxing. The wine under a hot sun and in even hotter mud and water has made me groggy. And the barebones discussion of everything going on between Ethan and Liv has tired out the both of us.

"I'm so ready to—"

"Get into sweats and hibernate?" Liv finishes my sentence.

"Yes! What should we do, *Bridesmaids* or *Dirty Dancing?*"

"Is that even a question?" Liv gives me a "seriously" look as she gets the last of our bags out of the back seat, slams the car door shut with her hip then does a little Baby dancing on the bridge as she sings the words from "Love Is Strange," "How do you call your lover boy?"

Chapter Fifteen

DUBAI, DARLING

LIV

OUR BEDROOM DOORS HAD CLOSED ALMOST IN UNISON. IN affectionate half-sentence grunts, we both agreed we were too dead to watch a movie, even too beat for Patrick Swayze and *Dirty Dancing*, which I didn't think was possible. Baby would have to stay in a corner, at least for tonight. Maybe, for Bex, it was the sun, the mud, the wine, or the drive. But for me, it was the talk. There it was, all my dirty laundry for Bex to see.

But it was still a good day. Bex's support for me, our support for each other, is as strong as it ever was. Yes, we drive each other crazy sometimes, but she's the sister I never had.

I lie down on the bed, curled up on my side, clutching my phone, staring blankly into the screen. My eyes go dry as I mindlessly scroll through the news, then switch to the weather, then my pedometer app, then back to the news, all the while willing myself not to look at Instagram or Facebook. I have two unread texts that I've been ignoring since the night out at Glamour & State. One from Ethan, one from Clarissa. Might as well dive in.

Darling, still busy in Dubai. Alan said that Clarissa never heard from you. What's going on?

Perfunctory. To the point. Well, I guess that's what texts should be. But still, would it kill him to drop in an emoji, or at least ask how I'm doing? He has no idea I am in LA. I haven't told him so how could he? But the fact that we've spent almost a week without even talking doesn't seem to have fazed him that much.

I call him and it rings for so long that I assume it'll go voicemail. Giving up, I lower the phone to press *end* when I hear Ethan's voice, "Liv, what's going on?" Not even a "hello."

Bringing the phone back to my ear, I stumble over my words. "Hi, nothing. I'm fine." I pause, gathering my composure, then, "I'm in LA."

"LA? What on earth are you doing there?"

"Visiting Bex," I respond without feeling the need for further elaboration.

"Who?"

"Bex. Rebecca. You know, my best friend." I try to remain calm, but inside I feel like screaming.

"Oh right, yes, of course. Bex." Ethan says her name as if he's never heard it before. "Liv, listen, darling. Don't you think that's rather impulsive. Going to LA. What happened to Provence? You've put me in a bit of a pickle here with Alan. I'd already told him that you'd be calling Clarissa for an impromptu getaway. Shame that our reservation went to waste."

Pickle off, I think.

"I always take out travel insurance. Don't worry, we didn't lose any money canceling. And Clarissa is a big girl. She can take care of herself. I'm sure she spent all weekend at Selfridge's anyway. How's Dubai going?" Not that I'm particularly interested.

"It's going. I've got to be in Zurich next week. At least the weather will be tolerable there," he says. We haven't spoken in a week and we're already talking about the weather?

"Oh, well, I guess I'll see you soon even if for a day. My flight lands on Sunday morning. Why don't we do lunch at The Wolseley? I think we should make some time to talk." I put myself out on a limb.

"Yes, let's do that. Nice idea, darling."

"Okay, well, see you around then," I say half-heartedly. It wasn't meant to be the end of our conversation, but Ethan responds with a "Bye, darling" and that's that.

I'm staring at the phone again. Was that conversation even real? Bex is right. I can't keep hiding. But that's all I want to do right now. Hide. Not call Ethan back, not even go back "home."

As if to rub salt in the wound, I open the text from Clarissa.

Sweets! Where are you? Did you go to France? Alan said something about a girl's getaway.

Call me! Xx

Knowing Clarissa deserves a response, no matter how belated, I type in: *Hi babes, ended up in LA, crazy I know! See you soon. Drinks this week?*

I throw in a heart, flowers, and a martini glass emoji, hating myself as I do it.

I give in and open Instagram and go to Clarissa's account. An over-filtered, ultra-bright photo is the most recent one posted. A selfie of her and two friends with drinks in hands. #boysaway-girlsplay #prosecco #lovemygirls #missyoualan. Aren't we too old for this? Alan isn't even on Instagram, but it's like Clarissa has to call him out to remind herself that they're married. And then on autopilot, I do exactly what I know I shouldn't do. Francois. I scan through his page like the Terminator, looking at every image, every hashtag, like a forensic scientist. Of course, there are lots of posts from the last few days. It's all part of building his image, his brand. He knows exactly what he's doing. All these photos of young things and late-night party posts make him seem cool, relevant. I was a thirty-nine-year-old blip on the radar for him. I'd be very out of place in this photo lineup.

I toss the phone out of my hand, a rotten appendage that I'm finally free of. I curl up into more of a ball and almost fall asleep. But then I reach out for my phone. I want to pretend everything's okay, just for a little bit longer.

"Hi, Mommy, it's me. How are you?" I say in an upbeat voice.

I hadn't even told my mom and dad that I was over on this side of the ocean. Guilt gently gnaws at me as I explain that no, it wasn't the middle of the night in London, that I'm in LA.

"Everything's fine, Mom. I'm here on a surprise trip to see Bex. How are you and Dad?"

"Oh, we're fine, honey. Daddy's been working out in the yard today. Putting up wire around the tomato plants. Although you and I both know it's not going to stop those damn squirrels. The neighbors complained to the cops about him using the BB gun on them."

In my dad's world, tomato-eating squirrels are more of a suburban menace than the opioid crisis.

"What are you and Bex up to? I sure do miss that girl. Please give her a big hug from me. Is she still single? I just don't understand it..." My mom's voice tails off in genuine confusion.

"It's complicated, Mom. She's doing fine. We're having a great time."

"I'm so glad you're not out there having to date. It just seems so confusing these days. Dangerous too! All these horror stories of online dating and those app thingy's. I saw the most awful story on *60 Minutes* of some poor girl who was almost killed on a date. Thank God you have Ethan. How is he, by the way?"

"He's fine. He's in Dubai on a trip."

"Dubai? My goodness. Seems he's always on the road, but I guess that's the price to pay for being such a successful lawyer." I can hear the pride in her voice. For her generation, being married to a lawyer is *almost* as good as a doctor. "I hope you two can make it back home for Christmas."

My heart twists. Ethan hates going to my parents' house. He always wants to stay at a hotel, which my parents would take as a huge insult. The house is small and could probably be admitted to the Smithsonian as a time capsule from 1974, but my mom is still house proud. She keeps the place tidy and does her best. We haven't been back for Christmas in four years. And I almost got a stomach ulcer from the stress of Ethan complaining behind their backs at every turn.

"I hope so, too, Mom. I gotta go. Give my love to Dad. And tell him to be nice to the squirrels."

"I love you, my little Lou Lou. Be good."

"Bye, Mom. Love you, too."

I'd been mindlessly picking at a scratch on my arm throughout the conversation, or rather nervously, once she started asking about Ethan. Looking at my nails, I realize it's leftover mud from Sunny Dale. I'd been in so much of a post-spa daze that I hadn't properly washed it all off when it was time to leave.

I tiptoe out of the bedroom. A light glimmers from under Bex's closed door as I head to the bathroom. I guess she's on her laptop. The pipes squeak as I turn on the hot water and watch it fill the tub. I know it's crazy to be taking a bath after a day at the spa but I don't care. At least there are no drought restrictions in place. Nightly baths have become a ritual for me back in London. The damp cold still sticks with me, even after all the years over there, and a hot bath is the only remedy. Right now, it's not the London cold that's chilling my bones but the icy feeling from my call with Ethan, from the fake-nice text to Clarissa and from lying to my Mom that everything's fine. I shiver as I step into the tub and crouch down into the warm water. I lean back to rest my head on the cool ceramic of the gleaming white tub and let my body sink into its depths.

I gently scoop water over my arms and the leftover mud swirls away to join a trail of blood. A faint ribbon of red, dissolving in the hot bath water. My period. At least it didn't come earlier today at the spa, but I'm not exactly relishing the reality of a twelve-hour flight on my period. I should be grateful that I'm still having them. I wonder how much longer I'll get to "enjoy" it. It's crazy that I'm worrying about menopause, or God forbid, early menopause. When did my life get so confusing and emotionally turbulent? I'm going through such highs and lows it feels like this should be my first period. Maddie and I could celebrate by getting ice cream together.

My mom's friend Mona was always complaining about her menopausal hot flashes. She lived two doors down from us and would always be popping over for a cup of sugar or milk. Back before mobile phones and the Internet, it seemed there was always someone knocking at the door. Mona would waltz right on in and sit down at the kitchen table. Mom would usually roll her eyes behind Mona's back, but I know she secretly loved the impromptu visits. I didn't know what menopause was; I hadn't even gotten my first period then, but I remember exactly what Mona said. That it was like "being blasted with a hair dryer in the Sahara Desert, worse than turning on a heater in hell."

Well, I think, as I sink up to my neck in the warm water, *just one more thing to look forward to in life*.

Chapter Sixteen

KEEP ON KEEPIN' ON

BEX

I'VE FALLEN DOWN THE RABBIT HOLE OF POPCORN CEILING removal videos on YouTube. There's something hypnotic about watching what was once bumpy and jagged scraped away to something smooth. They make it look so effortless, but I know the truth of the matter—nothing is ever as easy as it seems.

Today has been sobering...or not. I take a sip of my wine, which I retrieved from the kitchen after Liv and I parted ways. I had no idea that Liv was living in a loveless marriage where infidelity was as convenient as a McDonald's drive-thru. I hadn't realized how out of touch with each other Liv and I had become. How hidden the truth can be for everyone. How complacent I really am in my own life.

Lying here in bed, back in my nightgown, staring at the ceiling and sipping my old standby, Trader Joe's rosé, I indulge in the cloud of melancholy that's dampened my spirits. Nothing has changed. Not that I thought it would, but a little glimmer of hope did ignite inside of me when Liv told me she was coming here. A small part of me that thought things would be like they were back in the day when we had no worries and the world was completely open to us. No obstacles, no barriers, no baggage. And, I have to admit to myself, there were moments this past week when I did feel like the old Bex and I loved it. I miss the old me. Fearless, driven, and free. But now I'm back to where I started: stuck. And it seems that Liv is feeling the same way. We're both soaking in a tub of apathy.

I get out of bed to sort through the pile of clothes from when I was trying to figure out an outfit for my millionaire date. God, what a disaster that was. My mouth sours at the thought. I reach for the discarded dress that Liv begged me to wear—a strappy red number that we bought in a consignment store in Buckhead a bazillion years ago. It's Versace, and at the time it was a total score. Now, it's too short, and too tight in all the wrong places. I hold it up to my body and look in the mirror, wishing for that lost feeling of youth and opportunity. Things sure have changed.

When I was in my twenties I felt like I couldn't make a wrong turn, that any mistakes could be easily erased. I didn't even worry about making mistakes. It seemed there would always be time to find my way. Now, as I'm pushing forty, my choices feel permanent, my mistakes don't just affect me but also my daughter, and I don't have time to lose my way on wrong turns. As a result, everything now feels too precarious, too fragile, and so I'm stuck; stuck in the mud of my day-to-day complacency. Of just getting by. Of accepting where I am and not wanting to tip a single domino for fear they all tumble.

I set aside the Versace. *Maybe I should take it by Encore Couture and see what I can get for it*, I think as I thumb through the stack of mail I brought up with me from the kitchen. Nothing but junk and bills. I could certainly use the extra cash this dress might bring. Tossing the mail aside, I pick up my phone and check my email to see that a rush order has come in for a custom-made piece. With a quick glance at my voicemail, I note there are no messages from anyone. It's disappointing and boring. Life is as it was, and I'm hearing the whisper of reality getting louder. Maddie comes home next week, my Etsy shop will continue to get orders, and I'll lie in bed at night alone, watching *Outlander*, lusting after Jamie while wallowing in my non-dating hibernation, until I pick up my phone and start swiping. And the cycle will repeat...

Oh, Liv. I have to give her credit. She tried. She really did. And I did like her "Yes Factor" philosophy. She was right, I have been self-sabotaging, making excuses, and closing myself off. I should try to stick with the "Yes" motto. If someone seeks me out, I'll say yes, but I'm done chasing after love. The apps, the swinger parties, the weird yoga, the Hollywood bars—it's definitely not for me. If I meet someone out in the world and it happens, well, then it happens. Kinda like Devon.

I take this month's edition of *Simple* magazine from the mail pile to use as a coaster for my wineglass and pick up my laptop to see if I can find Devon on the Internet. I type in a variety of options—"Devon Antiques Sierra Madre," "Devon Wood Refinishing," and a handful of other search words that come to mind. This is ridiculous. The search is fruitless and I know it. He just vanished into thin air. Actually, no, *I* vanished into thin air.

I rest my head in my hand. I know I can't keep beating myself up about it, but I can't help replaying how I dashed off without a goodbye. And then I can't help but replay his smile or the way his lips felt next to my ear. Or how comfortable I was in his presence. Or the way my insides zinged when his hand touched my leg. God, I really blew it. Maybe we'll match up on another dating app? Crazier things have happened.

Am I just putting too much stock in the experience? Did I read the situation wrong? Could he be thinking about me like I'm thinking about him? Did he feel the electricity between us that lit me up like the Aurora Borealis? I want to reach my hand down to feel the heat between my thighs, but I'm wallowing in too much regret and it kills the high. But those eyes, that voice.

My phone rings. I can't seem to get through a Devon daydream without interruption! It's Patrick, so I answer instantly. There's no reason why he should be calling me right now.

"Hello?" I pick up with apprehension.

"Hey, B. Sorry to bother you, Maddie said Liv is visiting, so I'm sure you are busy drinking." Ouch. He knows how to push my buttons. "Anyway, Amber and I are leaving in the morning to pick up Maddie from camp since she's dealing with these, uh, female issues. And I was wondering—" Patrick was never comfortable talking about anything that had to do with women's bodies.

"Wait. What?" I interrupt him. "The last time I talked to her, she said she was fine. That everything was handled. I don't understand." I rack my brain trying to figure out exactly what happened between then and now.

"Yes, well, she called and said that she was crampy or something and that she wanted me to pick her up right away. I told her that of course I would, and that I'd bring Amber along to help out with any girl talk she might need." In the background Amber cheerily adds something that sounds like "happy to help!"

"Patrick, firstly, I've already talked to her about this and second, you can't go pick her up. It's not the end of the world! I got my first period in gym class during a volleyball game! Nobody's first time is convenient."

"God, B, I don't need all the details." Patrick really can't even handle talking about something that happens to every woman. I smirk to myself and shake my head. Typical. "Anyway," he continues, "I'm not leaving my daughter up there when she's alone and upset. Amber can take care of her. Make her tea or something."

"Look, I already told her specifically that I was *not* coming to get her. She's mature enough to handle this on her own. Maddie's playing both sides here and you're falling for it. Why are you always saying yes when I say no, giving Maddie everything she wants when she wants it?"

"No, I do not do that. That is completely untrue. I don't." His voice fades because he can't think of an example to back up his claim.

"Exactly! When are you going to realize that you bending

over backward for her isn't doing her any favors in the long run? I mean, going to rescue her from camp is not going to suddenly make you Father of the Year. You'd have to do a lot more to win that award. Like act like an actual father and spend some quality time with Maddie instead of globetrotting with wife number two."

And boom, here we go. Patrick's gotten to me and I've gone too far by getting mean and petty. But, I'm sick of him catering to Maddie's every whim and in the process undermining my role as a parent.

I take a deep breath to calm my frazzled nerves. "Listen, I know you love Maddie and want to do what's best for her. But trust me, she can handle this. I know she can."

There's silence on the other end of the line as Patrick takes in my words. When he mumbles, "I guess you're right," I hear the reluctant defeat in his voice. "It's just that she said that she needs me and I don't want to let her down. Again."

His "again" softens my heart. He isn't oblivious to his short-comings after all.

"You know what?" I relent, "Why don't you and Amber pick Maddie up from camp at the end of the session. Y'all can make a thing of it. Plus, you'll be there for the awards ceremony and all that. I'm sure she'd love for you to be there." I should give Patrick the room to be a better dad.

"Sure, that'd be great. Thanks, B." He sounds tired and I can picture him sitting down on the couch with a scotch, swirling the glass around like he always does when he's stressed.

"I'll email you all the info. Have a good night." As we exchange goodbye's I feel my mood return to equilibrium. That talk with Patrick took me from zero to sixty almost instantly, and it's a relief not to be on that roller coaster with him on a daily basis anymore. I shake my head thinking about the constant griping we both did at the end of our marriage.

Deep breath, Bex. I put the conversation behind me and move forward. My thoughts turn to Liv in the bedroom across the hall and I wonder how she will move forward after she leaves here. Is she squandering her happiness for a rich husband and a life that gives her just enough to get by emotionally? As much as I hate it, I can't blame her. We all do it to some extent. I know I did. When does compromise cross the threshold into full abandonment of self? When do the scales tip so far that you're swimming in a false sense of security that's so strong that you don't even know when you start to drown?

I don't know what she's going to do. I don't know what *I* am going to do either. What I do know is that we just have to keep on keepin' on. One foot in front of the other.

Liv's visit, the events of the past few days, dealing with Maddie and Patrick—trying to understand all of it is impossible. Is this the life I thought I'd lead? It's not even close and my complacency is squandering any opportunity to truly live a full life. And what makes my situation doubly tragic is that I'm showing my daughter that this is okay. That getting by and just accepting what is served to you on the platter of life is "just fine." Jesus, my biggest fear in life used to be that I'd be ordinary and, well, just look at me now.

Thank God Liv came to LA to remind me who I am. That I am a "yes" person after all. That new experiences and adventures are in my grasp, and that I deserve them. I've spent far too long shutting myself away in the safety of my little familiar world.

When Liv leaves, I'm making a resolution to stay open. To stay in the "Yes." But, until then, I still have another episode of *Outlander* to watch...

Chapter Seventeen

EBBS AND FLOWS

LIV

A RUSH OF SEA AIR HITS ME AND FILLS MY LUNGS. IT'S ALMOST too much to bear. I gulp it in and lean over the railing to look down at the cliffs and out onto the beach. Santa Monica will always be the same. The concrete swathe of sidewalk snakes its way down south to Venice, dotted with rollerbladers, morning joggers, and happy tourists on bikes. A confetti sprinkling of neon Lycra and tracksuits. The faded blue lifeguard towers in the distance are like old friends. It's a view I've seen so many times on TV and movie screens, but also one that I used to see regularly when I lived here. The blending of all these images in my consciousness makes the place seem like a familiar dream. I look toward the pier and can see it's just waking up. I am, too.

The drive over from Bex's house was sleepy and slow. I haven't even had coffee yet. Bex had to stay at home to deal with a rush order—"Etsy 911" she'd said—so she couldn't join me. I'd woken up almost as if possessed: I needed to see the ocean. I'd been here almost a week with no view of the beach. I was yearning to walk back into this familiar dream. To see the ocean disappear into the horizon. To be on the edge of everything.

I head toward the rickety wooden stairs that lead down to the sand. When Ethan and I were dating, this walk was one of our rituals when he would fly out to visit me. At the time he was based in New York and I was out here in LA. I remember the feeling of anticipation, waiting for that moment when I'd recognize him in the crowd of weary passengers exiting into the baggage terminal at the airport. It was an instant injection of buzzy adrenaline, anticipation, and desire. Where did those feelings go? We've sent a man to the moon, but we can't bottle that particular feeling. If that feeling were bottled and sold, would I even want to feel those feelings again for Ethan? Or enjoy that rush with someone new?

Ethan always liked to joke about LA residents and their penchant for hiking and fitness. *Where do they think they're going with their rucksacks and water packs? This isn't the Serengeti.* Or *What's so wrong with a gentle pace. Look at this chap taking two stairs at a time. He'll need a hip replacement by the age of thirty.* I've now realized those snide remarks are Ethan's regular mode; but at the time, with his accent still a new thrill for me, I thought he was being witty and sarcastic. I cringe thinking about how I'd laugh and play up to his clichéd views. Looking back, we were both playing roles.

Lost in my thoughts, I've walked too far and circle back to find the entrance to the stairs. This is the place, I just know it. But I'm confused. I guess Santa Monica *isn't* always the same. The railing is uninterrupted, there's no break for an entrance to the stairs which we'd wandered down so many times.

I really didn't want to pull out my phone, but I need to look for directions. What the hell happened to those stairs? I give myself a police pat down. Shit, I left my phone in the car. I turn around in circles and give up. Things change. The stairs are gone. That feeling is gone. In resignation, I rest my head on the railing, arms crossed over it for support.

"Hey, you okay?" a man asks me.

"I'm fine." I don't even look up. I don't want to deal with anyone. And this guy's probably some creep like most of the guys Bex and I have been dealing with all week.

"Okay, just checking I don't need to call the paramedics."
Then in a louder voice he says, "Whoa, girl, no, sit!"

I jerk upright, mild emotional breakdown over and ready for
ninja mode, or at least, screaming mode. A swift kick to the balls
and I'll jog right on away from this guy. But I already feel a
knock to the chest and I stumble down onto the dusty footpath.

"Derby, down!" The man pulls a shaggy dog off me and begins
to apologize profusely.

Stunned, I wipe the dirt off me and look up to see a tall guy
with a thick head of wavy blond hair holding the leash to a
caramel-colored dog that's straining to break free.

"Oh my God, Jesus, you scared me. I was about to kick you
in the balls." I'm still a little shaken up but mostly giddy with
relief that I haven't been attacked by a weirdo, just by an overen-
thusiastic, oversized puppy.

The man gives a hearty laugh, his face crinkles into a pleasing
fan of lines around his deep blue eyes. Under the bright light of
the sun, I get the full experience of his commanding presence. I
don't know what's come over me, but I want to run my hands
through his thick, wavy hair. Maybe it's the relief of not being
attacked by some crazy person. But no, it's *that* feeling. The
billion dollar they-can-send-a-man-to-the-moon-but-they-can't-
bottle-that-feeling feeling.

He extends his hand to help me up off the ground. I grasp
onto it hard, and in a second I don't want to end, he pulls me up
to standing. His hand feels warm and strong. He then proceeds
to shake hands as if we just met, and I haven't just been on the
ground, still covered in grime from the footpath.

"I'm Adam. And this is Derby. She's sorry for being impolite.
She just gets a little crazy the closer we get to the beach."

"I'm Liv. Nice to meet you. And nice to meet you, too,
Derby." Our hands are still clasped together. I gently pull away to
hold my hand out to Derby who sniffs it cautiously then leans in
for a cuddle.

"I know this is a strange question because it is right there." I point toward the sand below. "But how *do* you get to the beach? I was looking for the stairs and I swear they used to be here."

"They did. But the city tore them down. Too old and dangerous. I'm heading to the ones off Adelaide. They're this way if you want to come along." He doesn't need to point the way because every inch of Derby is veering in that direction.

It'd be kind of strange to just follow behind him, both of us going to the same place, so I walk alongside him, with Derby gently galloping beside us. She seems to have calmed down now that she's headed in her desired direction. Adam deftly maneuvers around me so that he's on the side of traffic as we walk along the footpath. My grandmother always said a gentleman walked on the side of traffic. Maybe people think that's old-fashioned. Yes, a woman is perfectly capable of walking next to traffic. It's not necessarily a male/female thing, it's that Adam is aware of the tradition and follows it. He cares about being respectful, and he isn't afraid to show it.

I turn to look at him and as our eyes lock, we both smile.

"I love how everyone is so healthy in this town. Always going hiking and jogging," Adam says without a hint of sarcasm.

I marvel at the strange but amazing world we live in. This man couldn't be any more different from Ethan if he tried.

"It's great. I used to live here, but I can't exactly say I was going hiking and jogging. And now, forget it." I'm feeling unusually talkative.

"My brother lives here and I wonder half the time how he holds down a job. It seems like every other day he's doing or planning his next outdoor adventure. He wanted to have his bachelor party at Joshua Tree, but his friends wouldn't have it. So, it's Vegas, of course." Adam laughs.

"Well, you could always hike through the desert to the bachelor party."

"I just want to get through it all and then on to the wedding with no drama. Plus, I'm still kind of jet-lagged. So I need to get on top of things."

"Jet-lagged? So you don't live in LA then?"

"No, I live in Hamburg. I've been living there for almost four years now. I oversee transport and logistics for a shipping company. But I grew up in Houston. My brother James made a beeline for LA right after college, and now that he's getting married, looks like he'll stay here."

"Hamburg. Well, that's a long way from Houston, and LA. I'm based in London."

"Really? How long you been there?" he asks with interest, slipping into a Texan accent I hadn't heard previously.

"It's been a while," I answer vaguely, not wanting to get into my backstory. I just want to enjoy this walk, the freedom of the ocean. "So, a bachelor party?" I change the subject.

"Yup, big brother here had to come over to make sure things don't get out of hand. So far so good, I think. The wedding is this Sunday in Santa Barbara." His eyes glance at my left hand. I hadn't put my wedding ring back on after taking it off for the day at Sunny Dale. And considering London's gray skies, there wasn't a telltale tan line. "Not a believer?" he says with a sly smile.

"Well..." I hesitate, not wanting to lie to him but not wanting to tell him the truth either.

"Don't worry, me neither. At least not for the moment. Thankfully, my baby brother's marriage can take my mom's mind off my divorce. It's already bad enough in her books that she's not a grandmother yet."

"I'm sorry," I say with real concern. I've only met him, but I feel so comfortable with him. I forgot how open and easygoing American guys can be. It just feels natural. Whereas with Ethan, sometimes I wonder if he's ever really himself. Do I even know who he is anymore? Did I ever?

Our pace slows to a stop and with a resigned shrug Adam says, "You know how you *know* you're not doing what you should be doing. Like you're in one of those dreams where you want to wake up but you can't move, no matter how hard you try, no matter how much you struggle?" He seems to be looking right into the center of my soul.

"Yes." I'm staring back into his eyes and feel a warm glow deep inside me.

"That was my marriage. That was every step of my twenties, thirties, hell, half of my forties. I don't know what happened. One day I finally *moved*. I finally woke up. Have you ever had one of those dreams?"

I let out a loud sigh that's almost a laugh, and then before I know it my eyes are welling up and I feel like I'm about to start bawling. I want to crawl up into Adam's arms. I want to feel safe and loved and wanted. I want to feel awake. *Alive.*

I hastily wipe away the tears that are now falling. "Welcome to my life."

Adam brushes a tear away with his thumb. I imagine just letting go so I can rest my cheek in the palm of his strong hand.

"You'll wake up. Everybody's got their alarm clock. You just have to make sure you hear it, make sure you recognize the sound of it." As he says this, we're drawing closer together like two connecting ends of a magnet. Our lips are almost touching.

But Derby lets out a loud flurry of barks that jolts Adam and me out of our moment, then she breaks into a sprint worthy of winning her namesake.

"Derby! Stop!" Adam runs to get her. I follow breathlessly, the sound of my heartbeat pulsing in my ears. I feel electrified with feeling, synapses bursting, a whole whirlwind of intricate physical and mental miracles happening in my body. I yell out a whoop of energy. Up ahead Adam has captured Derby and they're both waiting for me.

I finally reach them, completely winded. Laughing as I try to recover my breath.

"Here we are! You ready for this?" Adam looks at me as he strains to hold on to Derby's leash.

We've reached the top of the vertiginous stairs, one long line down to the beach. Adam looks around sneakily. "I know I shouldn't do this, but what the hell. She loves it too much." He unhooks Derby's leash—after all that chasing, he's now setting her free—and she makes a break for it, a bolt of fluffy fur gleefully racing toward the beach. "She'll wait at the bottom of the stairs. When James breaks the rules and lets her go, he gives her her favorite treats, so she won't budge until she gets her chicken."

He takes one step, then turns to look back at me, extends his hand. "Come on." His energy and enthusiasm are contagious.

The stairs are indeed sturdier than the old ones Ethan and I would use. My legs are moving fast, an aerobic dance as I tap my way downward. Adam is doing a kind of half jog. His tall body, lithe and muscled, moves with ease down the stairs.

He even takes some two at a time.

After giving Derby a handful of dried chicken, Adam runs down to the water's edge with Derby sprinting in front of him. Having reached the wet sand, he turns toward my direction. His silhouette framed by the crashing waves behind him. A man, the ocean. Maybe it's being winded from the cascading flight of stairs, but I feel breathless at the sight. He beckons to me and I run/walk to meet him; the sand pouring into my tennis shoes.

"Let's go in," Adam says. And I know he's talking to me this time because Derby's already wading in, her shaggy mane soggily draped around her.

"In the water? But I don't have my bathing suit on."

"Me neither." Adam peels off his T-shirt to reveal a pale midsection, padded from a little too much German beer drinking, but still pleasingly solid and sculpted.

"I don't know..." I try to remember what underwear I put on today, if it has holes. I know for sure I didn't coordinate bra and panties, let alone sexy lingerie bra and panties. Today's a Hanes day, and hopefully a Hanes day without any holes. Either way, not something I want to publicize.

"It'll be fine. There's hardly anyone here."

"I'm okay. I'll stand guard. Like Hasselhoff." I cringe.

Why can't I just let go? What's holding me back from racing into the water with him? I feel so self-conscious all of a sudden, butterfly wings beating fast in my stomach. I'm sure he can hear my heart racing. A vision of Francois and me quickly enters my head. It's one thing to throw away inhibitions when tipsy in an anonymous hotel room. But this, with Adam, this connection and energy. I don't remember the last time I felt it.

"At least get your feet wet." He points to my still shoed feet.

Realizing that I'm acting like a nun, I untie my shoes. But what about my toenails, *and my lack of toenail*, I think to myself. My pedicure is practically all worn off after the day of soaking, sunning, and scrubbing at Sunny Dale. *Say yes*, I hear a voice say in my head. It's Bex's voice. Strange to hear my mantra in her voice, giving me my own advice. It's a lot harder to actually do. I make a mental note to apologize to Bex for how much I've pushed her throughout this week.

Screw it. I kick off my shoes, but then try to burrow my toes into the sand.

Adam doesn't even notice.

"Last chance!" He pulls off his jeans then turns to dash into the surf. I assess his navy blue, cotton boxer briefs as he body-surfs into a coming wave. Okay, so he's not Marky Mark Calvin Klein era, but he still looks damn good for mid-forties. Putting aside superficial physicality, it's his confidence that is the most attractive. The comfortable and easy quality of a man at peace with himself.

"It's beautiful," he yells out. "Like you!"

The sound of the waves almost obscures that last part. But I heard it.

I walk in, and the cool water envelops my feet. I wiggle my feet and scoop up a bit of wet sand with my toes. It feels good. It feels free. A wave sneaks up and splashes over my knees, almost wetting my shorts. I squeal and jump back onto the dry sand.

Adam's making his way out of the water and stands in my fading footprints.

"Did you hear me?" He holds out his hands.

I can't speak. I'm too scared, too confused and too hopeful because, yes, I did hear him.

I walk over to him. "I think so." I feel the water rise back over my feet, not giving a damn if a wave gets me.

"Look what I found. Hold out your hand."

He places a small shell into the palm of my hand. It looks like an elongated miniature conch shell.

"It's perfect." I hold up the shell to take a closer look.

"Maybe you'll hear something if you put it by your ear. The ocean. A sound. To help wake you up," he says, alluding to what he told me at the top of the stairs.

I close my hand around the shell and look up at him. "Thank you."

"I want to see you again." Adam holds my face with his wet hands. I catch a scent of the salty ocean water mixed with the hints of his aftershave. I know this is usually where I should close my eyes, the picture perfect movie moment. But my eyes are open and mesmerized by his. "Do you want to see me again, Liv?"

"Hey, I'm back. I'm going to go pack!" I call out to Bex as I hastily make my way up the stairs to my room.

"Did you have fun? What time does your flight leave tomorrow?" Bex yells up to me.

"Three thirty-five. Yeah, it was good to see the water."

How could I even begin to tell Bex about meeting Adam? I'm still trying to process it myself. I'm not even sure it was real.

I scan the room; just barely a full week here and I've

managed to make a mess, in more ways than one. I'm going to miss those lace curtains and the sunshine. I'm going to miss Bex. I sit down on the bed with a thud and pull out my phone to see if I have any messages. The butterfly wings stop beating as I see who I have a missed call and voicemail from.

"Hi darling, I've got to fly direct from Dubai to Zurich because of a client dinner on Saturday night so I'm afraid I won't be able to come back to London to see you on Sunday for lunch. Sorry, darling."

And that was that. A voice recording. Digital bits and bytes of a husband. Not even a tape whirring around in an old answering machine, so at least there'd be some physical manifestation of him. In fact, he sounds positively upbeat, and certainly not sorry.

He's my ghost husband, I think to myself. What am I doing? I flounce back on the bed, staring up at the ceiling. Who has a client dinner on a Saturday night? And why was I still bothering to ask myself these questions? I know the answers. And now Bex does too. No more hiding from it. My mind wanders back to the encounter with Adam.

I hear the door open a crack.

"Don't go," Bex says. "Look at all this stuff, half your closet is already here anyway."

"Forget packing. Let's go hang out in the backyard. I want to soak up the last of this LA sunshine." Remembering the feeling of being with Adam, I really *don't* want to pack. I also remember who's in traffic on his way over here and smile.

"What? You're acting strange. Look at that grin on your face? What's going on?" Bex says.

"Nothing. Just all that ocean air. It's purifying!" I hop off the bed and head downstairs.

Back under the canopy of Bex's trees, I feel right at home. The swaying fronds of palm trees against the setting sun are a peaceful farewell on my last night in LA. Liv and I banter with casual and easy chitchat, choosing not to rehash the millions of emotional miles we've each traveled this past week together. It's like we're back in our teenage bedrooms, a constant chatter between us.

"Oh my God, remember that time in seventh grade you stole your mom's credit card number to buy Girl Scout Cookies?" I pour Bex another glass of wine. Why quit now?

"Ha! Yes! There was no way I was going to let Katie Greenwood be the top seller of Troop 903 again," Bex says, still sounding ruthless.

"Thirty boxes of thin mints. And practically five crates of Samoas. You know, looking back on it, your parents were actually pretty cool about it."

"My mom was pissed but my dad thought it was great. I think it took us at least two years to get through them. Good thing they hardly expire." Bex laughs at the memory.

"Katie Greenwood. I wonder what happened to her." Katie Greenwood was the goody two-shoes of our class. As an adolescent I couldn't unravel my feelings about her—a mixture of jealousy, hatred, and admiration that tattooed her in my memory.

"Please, like you've never Facebook stalked her before? I'll tell you what happened to her." Bex gears up and I can tell this is going to be good. "She married Jeff Henderson, remember him, quarterback?"

"Of course, I remember Jeff Henderson. Who doesn't? Most Handsome *and* Valedictorian."

"So she and Jeff married right after college. Had four kids together."

"Four kids? Jeez!"

"And then he left her." Bex is solemn. "For Alison."

"What!" I spit out a mouthful of wine.

"Last thing I heard from my mom was that Katie moved back home with her parents so they could help with the kids."

"I thought Katie Greenwood would be the queen of a real estate agency. Glamour photo on a For Sale sign in front of McMansions." I'm genuinely baffled. "Seriously, in my mind, all these years, Katie Greenwood has been living the perfect high-income suburban life, two point five kids, marble countertops, jacuzzi bathtub, hot *and* smart husband."

Bex chuckles wryly. "Nope, she got jilted by a husband who ran away with her sister. So the aunt of her four kids is now also their stepmom."

"Holy shit. So nobody's got the perfect life then."

"Liv, you gotta know by now that *nobody's* life is perfect."

We both turn as we hear a car door slam in the driveway. Craning her neck, Bex tries unsuccessfully to get a view from the low-slung seat of the lounge chair.

"If that's my neighbor Opal, don't talk about real estate, cross-stitching, or African Parrots, she will go on and on," Bex commands in a hushed voice.

Through the open backdoor, we hear the front doorbell ring.

Bex looks at me. I do my best to act natural.

"That's weird, Opal never rings the doorbell." Bex hops up and makes a dash inside. I'm hot on her heels because there's no way I want to miss what's coming next.

Right as her fingers touch the handle to open the front door, I almost reach out to stop her. To ask her not to be mad at me for doing this one last thing. For making a bet that I hope to God is the right one.

She opens the door and seems to freeze. Her face lights up, then I think she might start crying.

"Devon?" Her cheeks are flushing.

He smiles. That smile.

I look at Bex and I know I played my hand right.

"So, where do you think you'll hang it?" Devon unwraps the brown paper and bubble wrap from the Eastlake mirror.

"Over there." Bex points decisively to an empty spot in her foyer. Devon follows with the mirror and stands beside Bex. He places the mirror on the wall.

"You're going to need some new fastenings to really hold it up properly. But it looks good here." He nods, commending Bex's design instincts.

I watch from across the room and see Bex and Devon's reflection, standing shoulder to shoulder in the mirror. Like a family photo that's been on the wall for years.

Chapter Eighteen

HELLO. BUH BYE

BEX

PEEKING THROUGH THE LIVING ROOM CURTAINS, LIV AND I wait until we hear Devon's truck door slam and the engine purr to life before I turn toward her and lose my mind. In pure excitement.

"Oh. My. God!" I scream and jump up and down like a high school cheerleader whose boyfriend just scored the winning touchdown at the homecoming game. I nearly knock over my grandmother's vase on the side table from the flailing.

"I take it you're not mad?" Liv says with a hopeful smile on her lips.

"Mad? Are you kidding! No! I'm thrilled, you minx! I don't know how you did it, but you did it!" My voice is boiling over with energy and I feel like I'm floating two feet above the floor.

"Well, then." Liv joins me in jumping up and down. Our hands clasped, our faces red, and our mouths open in wide smiles, reminding me of the day my eighth grade crush called me to ask me to go strawberry picking with him. Liv and I screamed like two cats in a bag.

"Bex?" A male voice. Devon's voice. I stop in my tracks with my back toward the door.

I look at Liv, who is facing the front door and say as quietly as I can, "Don't tell me..." She just nods in silent assent. *Shit!* I slowly turn around and attempt to get my breathing back to normal. I open the door.

"Sorry, I left my jacket on the back of the couch. I knocked a couple of times, but I guess you didn't hear me."

I glance over my shoulder, and sure enough, there is his denim jacket in plain sight. I'm mortified that he overheard me acting like a girl gone wild. I wipe off my damp brow with the back of my sleeve.

Then with a grin he says, "I'm excited too." With that, he takes his jacket from Liv's outstretched arm and starts to walk away. "I'll talk to you soon!"

This time, Liv and I both stand at the front door as he heads to his truck and backs out of the driveway. No hiding behind the curtains this time. But standing like the women we are in full sight, waving and smiling, not ashamed of our excitement but proud of it.

Lying in bed, energized yet relaxed, I close out Amazon after making sure that the scraper I just bought is being shipped to the correct address. Popcorn ceiling, be gone! It's time I made some changes around here. Out with the old, in with the new.

I then place my thumb over the Tinder icon on my screen until it quivers and the *x* appears. I proceed to delete it and every other dating app from my phone. I am so done with this millennial style of dating. I'm a single woman, living in a twenty-something dating world, but that doesn't mean I have to play by these new rules.

"Buh bye, Tinder," I mutter. I'm feeling confident about

Devon and if I'm wrong, so what? I'll just go out on my own if I feel like it, order myself a Pappy like the *adult* I am and see what happens. Maybe that Laker will make an encore appearance!

Content with my choice to delete the dating apps, I drop my phone onto my comforter and listen to Liv knock around in her room on the opposite side of the landing. I'm tempted to get up and go help her, but the need to just lie in bed and savor the surprise of today is too much. Liv really knocked it out of the park.

As I reach to turn out the bedside lamp, my phone rings. I purse my lips in annoyance, assuming it's Patrick, but when I look at my phone, I see it's Devon. *Devon!* The fact that he's calling and not texting is such a shock! So atypical of every man I've interacted with in years, that I'm hesitant to answer. A phone call? How odd. How refreshing! *Here we go,* I think to myself. Time to say yes to new beginnings. I turn off the light, pick up the phone and simply say, "Hello."

Chapter Nineteen

CRUISING ALTITUDE

LIV

"YOU GOT EVERYTHING?" BEX SAYS IN HER MOM VOICE AS WE pull out of the driveway for the airport. "Passport, keys, phone, money."

"You make it sound like you really don't want me to leave anything behind."

Bex slows to a stop at the curb and turns to look at me. "Liv, you know you can stay here anytime. I mean, you can come live here if you want to."

"We're too young to be the *Golden Girls*. But I'll keep it in mind," I joke away Bex's sincerity. I hate goodbyes and I can't believe it's already time for me to go back home. *Home...*

Flashes of LA blur into one as we make our way to the airport.

"Hey, can we stop at the drug store? I want to pick up some eyeliner," I say.

"Eyeliner?"

"Yeah, CoverGirl. I always stock up when I'm on this side of the pond, but I forgot until now. It won't take long."

"CoverGirl? Don't you have all kinds of fancy French brands over there in London?"

"Have you tried Liquiline Blast?"

"I have not. But, let's wait until we get closer to LAX. There's a bigger CVS over there on La Cienega."

After about fifteen minutes of silent driving, we pull into a parking lot.

"You coming?" I hold my door open about to jump out.

"Nah, I'll stay here." Bex seems slightly distracted, but happily so. I know she's daydreaming about Devon.

"Okay, be back in five." I dash into the CVS and make a beeline for the cosmetics section.

Silver Spark, Black Fire, Green Glow—who wears neon green eyeliner?

Where the hell is Brown Blaze? I rifle through the hanging cardboard and plastic enrobed eye pencils and mascaras, knocking a few down in my haste to find what is truly the perfect shade of dark espresso brown.

I take a quick walk around to see if maybe there's an end aisle display of CoverGirl. Nope. I walk back to the original display area and kneel on the floor, scrounging around to see if any brown pencils might have fallen underneath the shelves. This eyeliner has suddenly become the one thing that will make my life perfect. I have to find it before I get on the plane.

My head is pressing against the cold industrial linoleum floor, in fact, I'm almost lying down flat on the ground trying my best to make my arm longer, which is now wedged under the narrow gap of the display shelf.

"Liv! What are you doing?"

I look up, ungainly, get on all fours, and then stand up. Bex is staring at me in a mixture of bemusement and concern.

"How far away is the next CVS?" I swat away dust bunnies that have floated on to my hair and clothes like magnetic dust.

"Um, I don't know, like ten to fifteen minutes."

"Let's go. They don't have my color here." I turn to the eyeliners once again and start taking them all off the shelf, in one last ditch effort that a brown one might be hiding in the back.

Bex takes the eyeliners out of my hand and puts them back on the shelf.

"We don't have time. It's in the other direction. Away from the airport. You need to be at check-in, like now."

"There's time."

"I can just mail you a few, for God's sake. Who misses their flight over eyeliner?"

I turn to Bex, deadly serious. "No, you can't just mail some to me. Customs are a nightmare. They'll hold on to it and make me pay tax. I probably won't even get a notice and the eyeliners will all rot in a warehouse out in the boonies!"

"Liv, get a grip. It's a six-dollar eyeliner."

I know what she's saying is true. In the back of my mind, I can see that I'm behaving irrationally, but I'm out of body at this point, like watching myself from afar. A knot tightens in my stomach. A fight-or-flight sensation. A feeling that I don't want to take flight, but I'm not yet able to fight. Adrenaline gushes through me and I feel like I'm going to faint.

"I just. I just need—" I burst into tears, my head in my hands. If I press hard enough into my face, maybe I can make these tears stop. My wrinkles and crying grimace feel like they'll be etched in stone. A midlife makeover of despair and cliché crisis. I don't want to leave. I don't want to stay. I just want to fall down, right here, in aisle five and disappear.

Gasping for air and almost hyperventilating, I lean into Bex and hold on to her for dear life. My tears, snot, and saliva make a damp patch on her shoulder. Seeing it makes me think about Bex as a mom. Maddie on her shoulder, baby burps, and changing diapers. Love, safety, completeness. A deep well of sadness bursts inside. It's not about not having a baby. I can deal with that, and I'm pretty sure I've come to terms with it. It's that I don't have love. That I want it. How am I supposed to go back to the sham of my marriage?

"I don't know what I'm doing," I whisper in a staccato of crying gasps, my head on Bex's shoulder.

"It's okay." Bex smooths my hair. "It's okay. None of us do."

The valium Bex gave me has finally started to kick in. I recline my airplane seat and pull out the remote control that's wired to the armrest. Ugh, this thing must be covered in germs. I cringe and press the greasy buttons to switch on the in-flight entertainment, looking for something to watch. *Dirty Dancing* in the Classics section alongside *Casablanca* and *Some Like It Hot*. Really? Sure, it's a classic, but a *classic*-classic, as in black-and-white classic? When did my favorite childhood movie reach this category? And where is Patrick Swayze now? Dancing in stardust.

I put the controller back and fidget in my seat, doing my best to adjust the cheap Styrofoamy pillow around my shoulder to settle in for what I hope will be a long sleep. I say goodbye to the Pacific ocean as we head east and the blue fades away, the same ocean that Adam was swimming in. Knowing that in a few hours the plane will be crossing a different ocean. A big expanse of nothingness, of deep memories, yearnings, and unfulfilled needs. Imaginings of a future, missing something familiar that you haven't even met yet.

Where does Ethan even fit into that?

At cruising altitude, the white noise and dimmed lights of the cabin lull me into a meditative state. I just want to sleep in this suspended animation, between lives, between my past and present. I close my eyes and it feels like I'm falling.

I remember when Bex and I were kids at the pool, we'd hang on to the edge at the back end of the diving area, away from the boards so we could watch people jump. The sixteen foot depth of chlorinated blue beneath us seemed endless, as deep as the ocean. We'd watch the older kids drop from the high dive. Some would fearlessly walk to the edge, bounce up and down a little before taking the plunge. Some held their nose with one hand, then did a kind of one legged jump, curling their knees up as they fell toward the water. A few would attempt a dive, and often someone would land with the wet slap of a belly flop. But it didn't matter, we watched all of them in awe. They'd climb up that ladder, leave the safety bars behind them as they'd walk to the edge and jump, belly flop or not.

One humid August day, toward the end of what seemed an eternal stretch of summer, Bex said, "Let's do it. Let's jump off the high dive."

I was shivering even though the water was warm, struck with paralysis at the thought of such a challenge. I couldn't say anything, could only hold on to the ledge with one hand and look up at the diving board, trembling and shaking my head no. It had never seemed higher. I still regret that moment and wonder if my life would be different if I'd said yes. The memory of Bex high above the pool. She seemed like she could float up and fly away. I watched from below as she jumped, and I'll always remember the electric energy of her head bursting up above the water after she'd plunged to its depths. She swam toward me in a fast doggy paddle, smiling and shouting out to me that I had to try it for myself.

But I didn't. I just couldn't.

I don't want to be paralyzed anymore by fear. I want to climb the ladder, walk to the edge and jump. What am I so afraid of? Hitting the bottom? Not being able to swim on my own. Giving up? That's what I'd felt like on the floor at CVS, just me and the dust bunnies.

Bex had taken the plunge. She made the decision all the way back then when we were little, consciously or not. To jump from the high dive. To divorce Patrick. None of it was easy. But she did it. She did *something*.

So what if Bex has been living like a nun for a while. Who has the time to date regularly? After this week, the idea of dating sends chills down my spine. Besides, Bex is too busy being a mom to worry about being someone's girlfriend.

This whole trip, this whole project of mine to get Bex out there, I know now it's been about me. I'd been so eagerly pushing her to jump—to "say yes"—when all along, it's what I've been wanting to do myself. I want to jump off that high dive.

Do I try to make it work with Ethan? After everything that's happened, how could I? We'd definitely need to stick with seeing a counselor, at least once a week if not more. I can't solve this on my own. But I can just imagine how that would all go. Exactly how it has been the few sessions we've been to. He'd probably just say that I'm bored, that I'm having some kind of midlife crisis. That I should get involved in a charity, or that things would be different if I had a baby to keep me busy.

I don't even think he'll bother with working on our relationship. He already said that he didn't think we should keep going to counseling. I have this feeling in the pit of my stomach that he's daring me to leave him. So he'll be free to trade me in for a newer model, someone to be the mother of his future children. I know he secretly blames me for not being able to give him all the props and accessories he needs to be the perfect partner at Treadwell & Sloane: wife, a towheaded toddler, a second baby on the way.

But something had attracted us together in the first place. Our curiosity, our hunger to explore the world. Sharing our ambitions and wanting to succeed in life. We used to talk for hours about our goals, our dreams. I miss that. Maybe I'm being too cynical. Maybe we could actually work it out. After all, we'd made it this far, even if it wasn't perfect. We could have a second wind in our relationship—maybe our forties and fifties could be a new beginning, a new adventure, a new romance together. But he hit on Bex. Drunkenly, but still...who does that?

What was it that Adam had said at the beach? That his

marriage was like being in one of those dreams where you can't wake up but you want to.

Adam...I smile to myself, my eyelids heavy. My muscles relax and I fall deeper into the airplane seat. I reach into the pocket of my jacket to touch the shell he gave me, still gritty with sand. God, it would feel so good to fall asleep in his arms.

Chapter Twenty

TREASURE FOUND

BEX

THE CAR FEELS EMPTY WITHOUT LIV IN THE PASSENGER SEAT beside me. The radio is off and my phone is plugged into the car charger. I take a deep breath and loudly exhale just to push away the silence. It's back to reality. But with a twist. Because I have a date with Devon tonight. I smile to myself as I crack the driver's side window to let in the outside world.

Liv's "Yes Factor" mission was a whirlwind, but I have to hand it to her, she really pulled through in the end. I've always dreamed of Ed McMahon from *Publishers Clearing House* showing up at my door with an oversized cardboard check, but the unanticipated arrival of Devon was even better than a million dollars. Liv truly redeemed herself after all the dating blunders of this past week. I guess that horrible night at Glamour & State had the best payoff! Liv hacking my dating apps, the infantile guys, and the fight I had with her as a result; it all happened for a reason. I still can't believe she ran into Chloe. Thank God for Liv and Chloe breaking the rules.

I just hope I was able to help Liv even a fraction of how much she's helped me. The fact that I didn't know the truth of her marriage says a lot about how much our relationship needed a pick-me-up. I know that Liv is one to shield and divert, but I see now that being a good friend means pushing past comfort zones, just like she did for me. Liv has always projected the "everything is great!" face to the world when inside she's crumbling. She's going home to a big mess of problems and questions, and she is going to have to make some decisions. I hope, for the sake of her happiness, that she does.

⸻ • ⸻

I should have picked up a new mascara when I was in the CVS with Liv. But seeing her scrounging around on the dusty floor, looking like a dandelion puff ball, really threw me for a loop. Now, as I comb through my clumpy lashes in preparation for another date, my nerves (and hand) are so jangly I've smeared mascara all over my lids. Deep breath. I haven't had a *real* date in four years. Like, a man-picks-you-up-from-your-house-and-takes-you-somewhere kind of date.

Devon and I have been texting all day since our phone call yesterday evening. Just playful banter with an occasional sexy tone. He seems as excited as I am about this date and said he has something magical planned. I asked him to at least give me some indication of dress code. With my luck I'd be in jeans and a T-shirt and he'd have a reservation at Prado or something equally fancy. Or, I'd wear heels and we'd end up at Disneyland—he did say magical, after all! Thankfully, he told me to dress "cozy casual." Just my speed.

At exactly 5:58 p.m., I hear Devon's truck pull into my driveway. Appreciating his punctuality because my nerves can't handle waiting around any longer, I slip on my silver Birkenstocks (thank you, eBay), take a final look in my new Eastlake mirror (thank you, Liv), brush back a few flyaway hairs, and give my ponytail a final scrunch and fluff.

Buzzing with jitters, I answer the door before Devon even has a chance to knock. "Hi," I say, breathy with anticipation, my eyes drinking him up.

"Hi." His voice is deep and intense with a barely concealed expectancy. "You look beautiful. You ready?"

Smiling ear to ear, I grab my purse off the art deco hat tree by the door, sling it over my shoulder and nod, stepping out onto the front stoop. Devon gently takes my hand as we walk toward his truck. I feel giddy from his touch and the warm night air. *This* is the date I've been waiting for. All is right with the world.

"Bex!" A screech like a velociraptor attacks my ears and the serenity of the moment evaporates.

"Keep going," I mutter, keeping my head down and picking up the pace as I walk down the driveway. I feel like I'm in an airplane that's going down, shocked by the sudden change in altitude.

"Bex!" My neighbor Opal squawks for the second time, waving her hands like air traffic control. Why today, of all days?

Devon, being the gentleman that he is, stops and turns to smile at Opal.

He has no idea that this date is about to crash land! She may look old, sweet, and innocent, but she's nosy as all get out. Yes, she can spot a thief a mile away—there hasn't been a robbery on our street for years—but it'd be nice if she could take a break from neighborhood watch so I can have some privacy and enjoy my first real date in a century! But, not wanting Devon to think I'm rude, she does sign for my UPS packages after all, I introduce them in a hurried tone. "Opal, this is Devon. Devon, this is my neighbor Opal."

Devon's friendly nature manages to turn Opal's frown into a straight line, which is as close to a smile as you can get out of Opal. "So nice to meet you," he says.

Opal gives him a once-over devoid of all subtlety and then

concludes her inspection with a quick approving nod. Crossing her birdlike arms, she turns to me. "Bex, honey, you need to wear a sweater. Once the sun goes down, it'll get chilly."

Oh my God, it's like I'm seventeen again!

"Thanks for your concern, Opal, but I'll be just fine. I have on long sleeves and it's a nice night." I pull Devon by the hand in the direction of the truck.

"Well, don't stay out too late!" she screeches at my back. "Come see me when you get home. I want to know how it goes. I'll just be up watching *House Hunters*!"

"Bye, Opal." I wave and hop up into the passenger seat while Devon holds the car door open for me.

<hr />

We drive north on the PCH, my hand still in Devon's, and I can't help but laugh out loud.

"*House Hunters*? Please! She'll be up spying through the curtains, that's what she'll be doing! Alphabet soup."

"Alphabet soup?" Devon says.

"She's LAPD, CIA, and FBI all in one!" I say, as I've said dozens of times before to my friends and to Maddie, who'd be rolling her eyes, but never before to Devon. It's a thrill to talk to someone who hasn't heard all of my stories yet; an attentive audience of one who will laugh at my tired jokes and anecdotes because he's never heard them before. I shimmer with the hope that this newness brings, that makes me feel witty and fresh.

It *is* like I'm seventeen again. I'm reminded of my first date with Steve Tyrrell, my high school boyfriend, when he came to pick me up in his burnt-orange Chevy. God, what a beater that thing was! It was a miracle we'd even backed out of my parents' driveway. Once on the open road, we rolled down the windows and drove for miles, scream-singing Tom Petty songs and feeling like we were flying as the truck kicked up dust on the country roads. We parked behind the abandoned barn on the Schill's property and made out to a symphony of cicadas. Steve got me home five minutes before my midnight curfew because he didn't want to give my parents any excuse to keep me from seeing him again.

The tragedy of youth is not knowing how good you have it. How simple it all is, before the rush of life and work, kids, and making ends meet. Yet, as I sit next to Devon, so many years after that first date in high school, and the hard road I've traveled since, I appreciate how good *this* actually is. How even though my life is complicated, this moment still feels simple and right. I look at Devon's left hand on the wheel, and his right hand in mine, his gaze focused on the road, relaxed and serene. I think to myself, *I want this feeling forever. I want him forever.*

I'm no psychic and the fact is, I'm not even Devon's girlfriend yet. But I don't care. Sometimes you just have a feeling you can't deny. The thought doesn't even scare me. It might scare him if I said it out loud, so I won't. I'll keep it secret in my heart, for now, and just enjoy the ride.

Hours later, lounging on a large quilt on a Malibu bluff overlooking the sparkling ocean, Devon wraps his arms around me as we watch the sun sink below the blue horizon. A short hike and an incredible picnic dinner beats any high-end LA restaurant.

Devon has definitely wowed me with this date. I flipped through so many scenarios in my mind of what it would be like and never thought of this one. It has all been an adventure—the picturesque walk through the tall reedy grass, the seamless conversation, the cold crisp bottle of wine—Devon did not disappoint. I couldn't have imagined a better first date.

"So, Bex, what's your dream trip? Where do you want to go to the most in the entire world?" Devon whispers into my ear.

I sink into him, my mind racing through all the places I've

wanted to go. I've always dreamed of going to Bali and staying in one of those glass bottom huts over the water, watching the ocean life swim below. I've wanted to go to Greenland, I have no idea why or what's there, but it seems like a strange place and I want to see it. I want to go to Austria and run through the mountains singing "The Hills are Alive!" The world is so big and there is just so much to see and do. I haven't done any of those things. Mostly because I don't have the money or the time, but also because I wouldn't want to do it alone.

"Machu Picchu. I want to do that four-day trek and on the final day at sunrise step into that magical space between heaven and earth," I say, the wanderlust hanging heavy in my voice.

Devon sits up. "Let's do it!" I raise my eyebrow skeptically. "What? Let's do it!" he continues. "There's about a month of summer left, let's take Maddie and Chloe and hike thru Peru!" I start laughing, equally astonished and excited by the idea. Devon's laughing too. "I know I sound insane. I mean, we just met..." His laughter trails off and he's suddenly quiet as he looks me directly in the eye. "We've just met, but I have this feeling..." He doesn't finish his sentence but I nod slowly. I know the feeling.

I want to call Liv right now and scream again, *You did it! You did it!* Thank God she knows me better than I know myself.

"I know what you mean." I lean forward ever so slightly, spellbound by his magnetism. His eyes haven't strayed from mine and his hand moves gently to the back of my neck like the brush of a feather. I melt into the moment, the intensity of it sinking into my bones and muscles. There is stillness. There is my heartbeat. And there is Devon.

Meeting him halfway, our lips only just touching...we breathe. Then magic. Just like he promised.

"Do you want to come in?" I say to Devon, stealing a quick glance over to Opal's house, making sure she isn't about to pounce.

Devon seems a little nervous. "Are you sure? I don't want to overstay my welcome, but I don't really want the night to end either."

He stuffs his hands into his back pockets, which makes his chest look even broader in his long-sleeved tee. I can practically see the air sizzle between us, charged full of nerves and anticipation. There's no reason to rush a good thing, but then again, I've been living in a romance desert, so I'm ready for a downpour.

Sitting on the couch with our hands wrapped around my no-stem wineglasses, our banter has carried us into the night. My beloved Ingraham mantle clock reads 10:36 p.m. and even after an action-packed week with Liv, there is not a bone in my body that is tired. Although, the bedroom doesn't exactly sound like a bad idea.

Devon is recounting the last Christmas he spent with his extended family in New Orleans. "Yeah, so then, it's time for dessert. The much-awaited chocolate pie that my mom has made *from scratch* every year since the day I was born, and her mother made *from scratch* every year before that. It's an incredible pie, and she makes three just so everybody can have two slices."

"Sounds delicious!"

"So, Mom starts slicing the pie and passing the plates around, and one by one we each dig into our pie. And you see everyone kinda grimace and look at each other like—" Devon makes his eyes go wide with a WTF expression.

"Oh God! What? What happened?" I'm already half laughing because I know this is going to end badly.

"There was a layer of wax paper between the filling and the pie crust, and the crust was completely raw. We totally busted her for store-bought crusts! All these years *'from scratch,' busted!* She was mortified but insisted we eat the filling like a chocolate pudding." He is laughing and shaking his head in remembrance and I'm grinning at him, loving everything about this man and this moment. "My family will never let her live that one down!"

Devon pauses, and then his eyes meet mine. The room stills in a moment of reverence as he puts down his wineglass. My own glass had been drained and set aside during his story so my empty hands fidget as I nervously rub the dry skin of my cuticles, trying to calm my reawakened nerves.

We're facing each other on the couch and the room seems to spin away. I know what's coming and I feel like I might burst. I'm torn between wanting to rush things, to feel him now but also wanting everything to slow down, for this moment to be frozen in time so I can savor the delicious anticipation.

Devon reaches out his strong hand to trail his fingers alongside my face, and my lips part with lust as I lean into his hand. He tilts his head forward to graze his lips across my neck, gently inhaling me. His lips are so light that I'm silently begging for him to devour me, but at the same time I want to see how our rhythm builds naturally. I moan as his lips continue their journey across my neck, up behind my ear. He inhales the scent of me and rustles my hair as he takes my hair out of the confines of a ponytail. God, this feels so good. I could do just this for hours but the pressure building inside me is too powerful. My breath shortens in anticipation as his lips come closer to mine again. We kissed on the cliff earlier tonight, but that felt tame and sweet, a tentative first touch, a testing of the fire. Now that we're alone in the privacy of my home, I want to go further. I want our spark to build into flames. I've never wanted anyone this badly and my body is lighting up with need.

I slowly stretch out my legs and lean back onto the couch, my mouth drawing him down with me. The energy of his body on mine. I wrap one leg around him, yearning to bring my hips closer to his, wanting to feel if he's as turned on as I am. I'm pulsing with need and close my eyes as our kiss deepens, his tongue in an adagio with mine. I want this dance to go further and my couch, which is feeling smaller by the minute, is not the stage for our performance. As I adjust my legs and wrap my arms tighter around him, Devon ungracefully falls off the couch, just barely missing the coffee table. I laugh then shriek when I realize he's grabbed on to my shirt and is pulling me down on top of him.

"Well, looks like Pottery Barn lied. This couch isn't big enough for two people!" I laugh out. "Come on." I awkwardly get back on my feet. I reach out my hand, and leaning back, use all my strength to pull him up to a standing position. I lose my breath again, feeling small beside his towering magnificence. I step into his body, pressing my breasts to his chest and look up at his lips before meeting his glowing dark eyes. I'm exploding with a potent combination of nerves and lust as I grab on to the waistband of his jeans. "Let's go upstairs," I whisper.

He agrees, not with words, but with his hands, his breath, his lips crushing mine.

———————————•◦•———————————

Okay, Bex. He is amazing; you are ready for this and it's gonna be incredible. I left Devon panting on my bed, fully clothed, excusing myself to the bathroom for a quick pep talk, and pee. It's not that I don't want to do this, God, I *really* want to do this, but I need a moment to check in with myself, and to check that I still have some condoms stashed away in that small Estee Lauder makeup bag I got as a free gift from Macy's years ago. Yes! They're still there, and they're not expired. Thank goodness this is happening now and not in two months!

There was a time in my life when I thought sex on the first date was slutty. Overall, reckless and wild. But I'm my own woman, damn it, and I haven't had sex in years. *Years!* I'm old enough to decide who I want to have sex with and when. I may have acted somewhat impulsively with Mr. Oscar Mayer Felon a few days ago, but even then, I knew what I was getting into and I knew my limits. But this is different. Devon feels like something real. This is not a dating experiment. This is not a "Just Say Yes" moment that I'm talking myself into. I'm checking in with my heart about this and my heart, and my lady bits, want Devon with a red-hot burning need.

I take a small swish of Listerine, pull off my top and adjust my modest Victoria's Secret bra for maximum cleavage before I turn off the bathroom light and open the door. There's a glow from the full moon and the streetlights, so I don't need to turn on my bedside lamp. Devon is sitting on the edge of my bed, a powerful silhouette focused on me.

"Takeoffyourshirt," I whisper to him seductively, streaming the words together in a sexy command.

"What?" he sounds a bit affronted and doesn't make a move.

I say it louder this time while trying to keep the sexiness in my voice, "Takeoffyourshirt." I'm loving this bossy side of me! I feel like a dominating sex kitten and slink over to him. I read a scene like this in a romance novel once and thought it was so hot. But it is kind of hard to sexy-whisper loud enough for someone to hear it across the room.

"Bex, I don't know what you're talking about. Why would you say that?" Devon's face is scrunched up in confusion. The guy in the romance novel definitely didn't respond like that.

I stop in my tracks, suddenly feeling nervous and embarrassed about the situation. I give him a puzzled look. "Why would I say what?"

"Why would you say 'dick, you're assured'? I thought things were going well, but this is kind of strange." He moves to stand up. "Maybe I should just go."

"No! Wait, don't go! I was saying 'take off your shirt.'" I enunciate every syllable, this time in a loud and clear voice, the opposite of my sexy-whisper. "You know, trying to have you do a sexy strip thing? Trying to be a seductive, sexy woman in charge? I don't know." I cross my arms over my cleavage, trying to shield myself from the embarrassment. "Like, trying to...act like...I know what I'm doing."

Devon breaks out into a full-on belly laugh. He can hardly keep himself upright, he's laughing so hard. I sink even further into my shame. "I feel stupid. I'm sorry."

He pulls himself together and reaches for my hand, pulling me between his thighs. "Bex, it's okay. Don't apologize. I'm flattered by what you were trying to do, but I think the point is, you don't have to try. You don't need to *act* sexy because you *are* sexy."

I close my eyes and bite the inside of my cheek, wondering how the hell he could think I'm sexy after all this. I feel like an awkward teenager who's never even kissed someone. "Bex, it's okay. Everything you are is enough. Let's just relax and do what comes naturally and give each other some grace. It's been a long time for the both of us." With that, I feel his strong arms embrace me as he lies back on the bed and pulls me on top of him. We instantly bump heads, and this time *I* burst out laughing.

"Weren't you just saying something about 'grace'?" I tease, and he laughs good-naturedly. I rub my forehead and roll to the side, reveling at the sight of his smile in the moonlight. There is a pause. And the proverbial "reset button" is pressed.

Devon kisses me deeply, then slowly peels his shirt off. My

white sheets makes his skin stand out in a beautiful contrast. His kiss feels warm and magnetic—I can't get enough.

After a passionate make-out session, our clothing eventually disappears and we lose ourselves in each other.

"Bex, you are a treasure."

———————◆•◀———————

Devon had to get up early and head home, but not before he ravished me again, for the third time, I should add. It may have been over four years since I've had a roll in the hay, but I have a feeling that Devon and I will make up for that lost time pretty quickly.

After he left, I didn't shower right away, wanting his smell to linger on my skin for a little while longer. I get chills just thinking of his body next to mine, and the memory of his touch makes me weak with desire. And now, I'm having trouble focusing on the matter at hand, which is making my morning coffee. I'm floating around the kitchen in a groggy, gleeful post magic glow, relishing the memory of Devon all over me.

As the coffee machine brews a steaming gurgle of coffee, I reach for my phone to text Liv. I know she's probably landed in London by now, and I'm dying to share my news with her.

Hope ur flight was good! My flight was prob better! Devon sent me into orbit. I haven't landed yet! Call me! Must give BIG report! Hahaha!

Love you

Miss you already

Thank you for being a friend. You always show up right when I need you.

HIGH DIVE

LIV

THE CRASH OF THE SERVICE TROLLEY INTO THE BACK OF MY seat jolts me awake. I blink into the bright light of morning, looking around at my fellow passengers who are placidly hunched over their tray tables, eating cold, chewy croissants, and sipping glowing orange juice. There's no way I could have slept the whole flight. I have a new respect for the '50s housewife drug of choice and wonder how hard it'll be to get a valium prescription in London.

I try to get the attention of a flight attendant so I can have a cup of coffee, but she's already sweeping through the cabin, dumping half-eaten breakfasts into the trash and hurriedly preparing for landing.

I peer out the window as we start the descent in to Heathrow, leaning forward to see beyond my window seat neighbor who's reading the inflight magazine, every passenger's last ditch effort to stay occupied before giving up and catatonically staring at the seat in front.

She puts the magazine down in her lap and pushes the window screen up all the way.

"There, now you can see what a beautiful English morning we're coming home to," she says with gentle sarcasm in a Queen

Mother accent. "Are you looking forward to seeing Adam?" She gives me a little wink.

"Adam?"

"You were saying his name in your sleep. Sounds like somebody's going to have quite the reunion today."

"Oh, uh...Yes." I'm at a total loss for words. I've been valium-high-altitude-sleep-talking about Adam! Maybe she didn't hear me right.

As we taxi to the gate, the captain's reassuring voice booms, "Welcome to London, folks. As you can see, we've got light rain. Temperature of about sixty degrees Fahrenheit, fifteen degrees Celsius. You may now use your mobile devices."

Against a symphony of seat belts unsnapping, and chiming devices, I check my phone. A string of messages from Bex pops up, starting with:

Hope ur flight was good! My flight was prob better! Devon sent me into orbit.

Good on you, Bex. I smile and give a silent high five across the ocean. Then I stand up to get my carry-on bag from the overhead bin and join the shuffling line of passengers waiting to leave the plane, each one on their own journey—to rush for a connecting flight, to look for a chauffeur holding a sign with their name on it, or to be met by a partner, maybe even with flowers. And my journey...? I'm bouncing up and down on the high dive, getting ready to jump.

AUTHORS NOTE

Thank you so much for reading The Yes Factor! *If you want to hear what happens next with Liv, drop us a note on our social media. We'd love to hear from you!*

https://www.facebook.com/ByErinAndEmma

https://www.instagram.com/ByErinAndEmma/

ABOUT THE AUTHORS

Erin Spencer and Emma Sable are two Southern girls who met in L.A. at a mutual friend's engagement party. They bonded over their shared love of fried shrimp, queso and The Golden Girls. After a girls' night out in Hollywood to celebrate Emma's birthday, the two were inspired to begin writing *The Yes Factor*, their first novel together.

To celebrate finishing the novel, Erin and Emma travelled to the Amalfi coast where they enjoyed a week of sunshine, pasta and Pinot Grigio. And where a few notes might have been scribbled for their next book!

Erin lives in L.A. and Emma now lives in London.